MURDER MOST FESTIVE

ADA MONCRIEFF

Poisoned Pen
PRESS

Published by Poisoned Pen Press, an imprint of Sourcebooks
P.O. Box 4410, Naperville, Illinois 60567-4410
(630) 961-3900
sourcebooks.com

Originally published as *Murder Most Festive* in 2020 in the United Kingdom
by Vintage, an imprint of Penguin Random House UK. This edition
issued based on the paperback edition published in 2020 in the United
Kingdom by Vintage, an imprint of Penguin Random House UK.

Library of Congress Cataloging-in-Publication Data

Names: Moncrieff, Ada, author.
Title: Murder most festive / Ada Moncrieff.
Description: Naperville, Illinois : Poisoned Pen Press, [2021]
Identifiers: LCCN 2021014772 (print) | LCCN 2021014773
   (ebook) | (trade paperback) | (epub)
Subjects: LCSH: Christmas stories. | GSAFD: Mystery fiction.
Classification: LCC PR6113.O533 M87 2021 (print) | LCC PR6113.O533
   (ebook) | DDC 823/.92--dc23
LC record available at https://lccn.loc.gov/2021014772
LC ebook record available at https://lccn.loc.gov/2021014773

Printed and bound in the United States of America.
KP 10 9 8 7 6 5 4 3 2 1

1

Christmas Eve had arrived in Little Bourton accompanied by a liberal scattering of snow, and Westbury Manor, its imposing turrets newly sprinkled in white, was preparing itself for imminent festivities.

It may be argued that the true toil of these preparations was to be found belowstairs: in the pressures of obeying the orders issued by the indefatigable housekeeper, or in the meticulous plucking of not one but three turkeys—one would not suffice, for this year Lady Westbury had, in one of her endearing whims, chosen to open the family circle to a select handful of additional guests—or in ensuring that the fresh kidneys and bacon to be served for the guests' breakfast were not confused with the day-old kidneys and bacon to be served for Bruno's dinner. The Westburys' skittish and demanding Labrador was notoriously fussy about his meals.

Indeed, one may sympathize with such an argument. But to

locate the true toil of Christmas preparations, we must convey ourselves upstairs, pausing perhaps to admire the grandfather clock rumored to have been carved from an oak tree under which Lord Byron himself had once lain (decency dictates that we refrain from further speculation), and into the library, where a scene of true Christmas toil was unfolding at precisely five-and-twenty minutes to five.

"Must you be quite so incessantly unbearable? I'm sure this performance impresses that band of merry idiots at the club, but—" Lydia Westbury was cut short by the smash of a whisky glass, mercifully not a crystal one, and the uproarious hooting that accompanied it.

"Oh, do excuse me, sister dearest. I always did have rotten luck with my grip. Caused no end of bother to the cricket chaps. I just thought I ought to do something to stop your whingeing. It really is most tiresome." Draped in a leather armchair, his velvet dressing gown carelessly cascading off one shoulder and his slippers discarded somewhere near the philosophy section, Stephen Westbury smirked and, putting the decanter to his mouth, drained what remained of the whisky.

Lydia glared at him, lounging so indolently before her. Each visit from her younger brother saw her aghast anew at his unrepentant arrogance. As children, it had been galling enough. Governess after governess indulged him, taking as gospel his account of disagreements in which he had cruelly bruised Lydia with his words, their brother, Edward, with his fists. Stephen had floated through childhood impervious to unfairness; his siblings, on the other hand, had been constantly oppressed by it. The advantages and opportunities lavished upon him had been manifold, and Lydia's resentment only continued to calcify as they entered adulthood.

The years had taught her to cultivate a studied indifference to his actions. She bit her tongue when he brought his insufferable cronies home for the weekend and ignored them as they indulged in hunting by day, drinking by night. She never kicked up a fuss when one of the clowns "accidentally" blundered into her bedroom at night, necessitating a firm and swift push back *out* again. This year, however, she was in no mood to countenance his behavior.

"The least you could've done was come to the service this morning. Oh wait, of course, I forget myself—you're Stephen Westbury, big man of the City, motoring down from Chelsea to grace us all. There's no earthly reason you would consider anyone else's feelings, especially not at Christmas. How utterly silly of me."

Stephen dangled his leg over the arm of the chair and ostentatiously yawned, a gesture designed when he was thirteen to provoke her, and faultlessly finessed since then.

"Well, it appears to me that I'm rather deserving of a little entertainment at Christmas." Stephen carelessly drove his hand through hair that had always given him a decidedly cherubic demeanor—an illusion that had seen him disentangle himself from innumerable scrapes during his school career and beyond.

"Money doesn't make itself. I work like a beast at the bank, and I shall jolly well take my fun when and where I can. Yes, fun, Lydia, a concept alien to you and our dear little brother. So do excuse my enjoying myself while little Edward scurries around the gutter being a holier-than-thou do-gooder telling us all how awful we are because we don't live in squalor. And while you maintain your profoundly pathetic commitment to being an old maid rattling around this blasted house—which won't ever actually be yours. Yes, do accept my apologies."

Snarling and indignant, her hazel eyes flashing, Lydia spat, "You're an ass, Stephen, a pompous ass, and when you inherit this house, I hope it crumbles around you!"

"Well, well, well, is that kind of language really called for, darling?" Lord Westbury placed a rather trembling hand on his daughter's shoulder. Lydia, consumed by indignation in the face of Stephen's goading, had failed to notice her mother and father entering the library behind her. Stephen, ever vigilant to the presence of his parents and therefore eternally well-placed to manipulate a situation to his advantage, had been gleefully aware of Lord and Lady Westbury witnessing his sister's outburst.

Lady Westbury glided over to her son and kissed his forehead lightly. Still a striking woman, her understated charisma and attractive composure had earned her ardent fans ever since she was a debutante and invitations to her soirées were, to this day, highly coveted.

Turning to her daughter she purred, "Darling, I really think you ought to exercise a little more delicacy. It is rather unbecoming to hear such ugly words issued from so pretty a mouth."

"Oh Mother, it's 1938, not 1838. Shockingly, it's believed in certain quarters that women might—just might—be able to curse without spontaneously combusting. And in any case, I'm not one of those prim little moppets you seem intent on convincing everyone that I am," Lydia retorted, pacing to the window in a bid to avoid the smug face of her brother. "I shan't need smelling salts for uttering the word 'ass,' any more than I shall swoon should any gentleman dare to address me."

"Damned shocking business if any gentleman bothered to address you anymore, eh, sis? You've scared 'em all off, haven't you?" Stephen stretched and winked at his father.

"Now, now, Stephen, let's have none of that." Lord Westbury's somewhat half-hearted reprimand was accompanied by a suppressed smile. Lydia had always been a mystery to her father. Three proposals she had received, and three proposals she had declined—in increasingly impatient terms. Lord Westbury had countless questions regarding his only daughter's predicament— thirty-two and unmarried—but, having witnessed the short shrift with which she treated most enquiries on the matter, he knew he would never dare pose them. Stephen, on the other hand: three years younger than Lord Westbury's riddle of a daughter, a chap one knew the measure of, a solid chap who would undoubtedly take the Westbury name to ever greater heights.

As for his youngest child, Edward…well, the less said about him the better. Running around with all this newspaper business by day, spending his weekends serving up slop for the down-and-outs at the Charitable House Run by Gullible Do-Gooders for the Benefit of Scrounging Swindlers. He was living goodness knew where in London, turning his nose up at his allowance. Lord Westbury knew he mustn't dwell on Edward; that way frustration lay. Where was Edward, in any case? he wondered. No doubt still upstairs scribbling some article about those squalid people he insisted had been doomed to destitution through no fault of their own.

"My boy, I think it's high time you clambered out of your rather sinister attire and readied yourself for our guests." Lord Westbury cheerfully addressed Stephen while stepping rather unsteadily toward the bell on the table. "And let's have this glass cleared up, shall we? Only cheap old stuff anyway—saving the crystal for your mother's special guest tonight."

The tinkling of the service bell was met by a creaking of the door, much to Lord Westbury's bewilderment—these downstairs folk, speedier and stealthier by the day, barely even time for the bell to have rung. Were it one of the downstairs folk, however, Stephen would swiftly have ejected himself from the room for fear of boredom. But his spiteful mirth had found another subject to poke. "What is it that the French say? *Cherchez le* frightful bore droning on about 'social injustice' and the frightful bore droning on about 'social injustice' shall appear?"

Skulking into the library, the youngest Westbury glared at his brother, used to such prodding. He shuffled over to Lydia, now glowering at the other three members of his family. Although only fifteen months apart in age, the temperaments of the Westbury brothers had always presented a striking contrast. Throughout their childhood, Stephen's spiteful gaiety had been matched by Edward's thoughtful intensity, and the two brothers had followed endlessly diverging paths as they entered adulthood—Stephen tumbling recklessly into it, Edward progressing rather more warily. Both had traveled from London for the festive period, the elder in a fog of brandy and cigars, the younger in a cloud of anxiety about events in Europe, events that his family willfully ignored.

"Come to tick us off again about enjoying what we've earned, rather than throwing it into the gutter so those pitiful specimens you consort with can waste it down at the dogs?" Stephen sneered. "Or are we to expect another splash in that rag you write for? Ought we to ask our solicitor round again?"

Lydia clenched her jaw. "Don't listen to him, Eddy—he's being even more of an ass than usual."

Before Lady Westbury could protest about the repeated use of such vulgarity, there was a knock at the library door. The new footman, a local lad, whose pride in his new role was reflected—very literally—in his gleaming shoes, cleared his throat before enunciating, "Milud and milady, a Mr. Campbell-Scott has arrived."

"Oh! Very good, Jim. We shall be with him momentarily. Show him to the drawing room." Lord Westbury clapped his hands together at the prospect of seeing his old friend after an absence of... How long *had* it been?

Never known for his sprightliness, Edward visibly soured further. Lydia's pleading with him earlier that day—"just be civil, nothing more, nothing less, we can all gain something from it"— had ended in a terse exchange, during which Edward had made it very clear that David Campbell-Scott's inclusion in this year's dinner was a most unwelcome one.

"Well, in that case, I'd best get myself dressed and hear what the old chap's been up to all these years moldering about abroad," Stephen said, unpeeling himself from the armchair at a leisurely pace as Lady Westbury surreptitiously offered her arm to steady her husband.

Lydia rolled her eyes. "I daresay that David's achieved more when 'moldering about' than you have in all your City shenanigans. I shouldn't wonder that you might learn something from him if you actually cared to listen."

Stephen, adept at formulating a barb and waiting until his parents had left a room before deploying it, turned to his sister. "Oh yes, we must all listen to the esteemed David Campbell-Scott. Mustn't say a word against old moneybags. After all, as his dearest darling goddaughter, those moneybags'll be yours once the old sod pops his clogs."

2

As the allegedly Byronic grandfather clock languidly struck five (for how else would a Byronic clock strike?), a man of imposing stature stood in the drawing room, dazzled by the famed Westbury Christmas tree. The tree was seven feet of unabashed festive extravagance, festooned with baubles, strewn with tinsel; and nestled beneath its copious canopy were many immaculately wrapped gifts. For David Campbell-Scott, this trip was something of a novelty. In fact, this entire English winter was something of a novelty, it being the first he had experienced since upping sticks and taking himself to Malaya eight years ago in pursuit of fame and fortune. Though fame had evaded him, fortune had become one of his closest acquaintances. And now here he was in Little Bourton, having gladly accepted the invitation to join his old school chum for the festivities.

"Flighty! Old bean!" Lord Westbury bellowed (as much as

his voice would permit a bellow) and strode (as much as his legs would permit a stride) over to Campbell-Scott. So entrenched was the nickname "Flighty" that neither man could recall its precise origins; they were sure it had something to do with their old Latin master, but then again it was equally possible that its provenance lay in that incident with the goose. No matter, it had stuck.

A spectator in possession of an astute eye (in fact, even an eye whose acuity was diminished by the generous measures of sherry now being sloshed into glasses by Lord Westbury) might notice a contrast presented by the two men. Indeed, on learning that they had been born just a month apart, such an eye might widen in surprise. David Campbell-Scott's entire bearing radiated the easy confidence of one who is intimately acquainted with vitality, prosperity, and power. Our spectator would be forgiven for concluding that the frail, stooping figure beside him was perhaps an aging uncle or a doting benefactor. Lord Westbury's sherry sloshing and pipe smoking had caught up with him, as had time's winged chariot.

While our astute-eyed spectator might frown in concern at the evident ill health of Lord Westbury, his wife watched him contentedly as he greeted his friend. David was, as she had identified many years earlier, a man of irreproachable character and admirable ambition. The Great War had seen him prove his valor in the field, while the subsequent years had demonstrated his clear-sighted view of the world, which had rewarded him in his Malayan ventures. How they had laughed when he had announced his intention to blaze a trail in the rubber production business. But look at him now. The only potential blot in his copybook was that rather unfortunate incident with Edward. But, as Lady Westbury was all too aware, her youngest son was a sensitive type, and his refusal to discuss said unfortunate incident made it difficult to place any blame with David.

Lord Westbury and Campbell-Scott were guffawing at some joke or another when Lydia joined them, embracing her godfather with an ease that Lady Westbury rarely witnessed in her daughter.

"Now, David, you must forgive us—we shall be bombarding you incessantly with questions about your adventures! How parochial Little Bourton must seem to you—how parochial *we* must seem to you now!" Lydia beamed.

Campbell-Scott chuckled in his kindly manner, reassuring Lydia that yes, indeed, he would brace himself for the interrogation. Just as he was inquiring as to the rest of the guest list, the newly employed footman made his presence known at the door again. Another gentleman was on the doorstep, but, ahem, his name hadn't been caught.

At this, a figure of almost parodic jollity leaped into view, an improvised white beard hanging from his ears, through which the man treated all to an impromptu yet impressively tuneful rendition of "Good King Wenceslas."

Lydia, whose spirits had been sharply rising ever since Stephen had retreated upstairs to get dressed, was now in a state of elation.

"Hughey! We weren't expecting you 'til tomorrow!" she exclaimed, throwing her arms around the new arrival.

"You know me, Lyds, I like to surprise you," Hugh Gaveston replied. And know him she did, for Lydia and Hugh had been as thick as two particularly pally thieves since long before either of them could remember. His mother had moved in the same circles as Lady Westbury (Hugh had never known quite what that meant but assumed it was something to do with bridge and debs), and he had instantly seen it as his mission to befriend the withdrawn, fiercely intelligent Lydia. Stephen, unaccustomed to being snubbed in favor of his sister, had of course consigned Hugh to the category of galumphing oaf. His unruly, jet-black hair, lanky frame, and predilection for wearing slacks just a tad too short for him (attributes he had carried with him to adulthood) certainly would not dissuade one from attaching such a label to Hugh. But that would be to wildly underestimate him.

Since then, Lydia and Hugh had remained firm friends. Hugh wrote weekly to her when he was up at Cambridge, and she repaid his tales of formals and punting with stories of the short-lived secretarial course she had enrolled on (much to her parents' disapproval). Hugh had consoled Lydia after her premature retirement from typing (something to do with the falling-out between her and that pal of hers, Patricia), while she had endeavored to offer comfort to her friend when he found himself parentless at the age of nineteen—the result of a tragic automobile accident.

The subsequent years had seen Hugh dabble in a series of pastimes befitting a young gentleman in possession of both abundant means and time: oil painting (sabotaged by the inherent ineptitude of his brushstroke); ammonite collecting (abandoned after a nasty incident with a jellyfish in a Lyme Regis cove); and biography writing (jettisoned upon the realization that he found Marcus Aurelius rather boring). Lady Westbury had given him a compendium of detective stories for his fourteenth birthday, and Hugh's boyhood enthusiasm for tales of spectacular sleuthing had led to his being the owner of every single edition of *Mystery Magazine: True Crime Sensations!* Hunting down the rarest titles in the publication's history—the 1927 special on how Scotland Yard foiled the cat burglar of the Cotswolds being a particularly prized copy—was, however, usurped by Hugh's true passion, which he now pursued with fanatical commitment: taxidermy. Zealously devouring any and all literature on the subject, Hugh now spent his hours finessing the needlework required to position a badger's snarl just so and curbing his youthful tendency to overstuff his mammals (the voles of his early twenties resembled nothing so much as corpulent adolescent walruses).

Meanwhile, on the other hand, Lydia's passions had all but been extinguished by her awareness of her precarious position as a husbandless woman of a certain age. Intentional though this husbandlessness was, she was now used to the looks of pity or suspicion conferred upon her—while Hugh, as a bachelor in possession of a staggering inheritance, enjoyed only looks of admiration and envy.

The sherry decanter was circulated by Angela, the plump, rather shy girl who acted as maid; introductions were proffered and Stephen's still-slurring voice was heard from upstairs berating his brother for some misdemeanor or another.

"I was on the point of asking where Stephen and Edward were, but now that question's been cleared up nicely," Hugh said cheerfully. Lydia had rarely known him to be anything other than cheerful when in company. Or when out of company, for that matter. "And who else are we expecting then, eh?"

Lord Westbury made to answer but realized that he couldn't quite pin it down. Who *were* they expecting? Oh, the names were on the tip of his tongue. His wife, who over recent months had grown familiar with his spells of this sort, placed a hand on his arm and tactfully swooped in with an answer.

"A most exclusive assortment of waifs and strays, Hugh, though of course none shall usurp you as Chief Waif and Supreme Stray." Lady Westbury's affection for Hugh was marked by a depth that was evident to all but the most oblivious of witnesses. Ever since that terrible accident, she had taken him under her wing and ensured that he always had a refuge for Christmas. Despite Gaveston Lodge's proximity to Westbury Manor (if Hugh cut across the copse—and he frequently did—he could be reclining there with a cup of tea and a piece of shortbread within fifteen minutes of leaving his own front door), Lady Westbury had always insisted that Hugh stay for at least three nights over the festive period.

"The Ashwells are due any moment now—you know Rosalind and William?—and…well, Freddie…I mean to say Mr. Rampling, has been invited." A deep intake of breath before Lady Westbury unveiled her finale. "Then we're expecting a rather special guest in time for supper too—parliamentary obligations notwithstanding, of course. Anthony de Havilland is joining us this year." The pride in Lady Westbury's eyes was unmistakable: securing de Havilland as a guest was the triumph of the season.

"Yes, we've been warned to be on best behavior in front of Mr. de Havilland," said Lydia. "'His bravery in the war is matched only by his intelligence in the House of Commons,' don't you know." She lightly mimicked the refrain she'd heard her mother bandy around since de Havilland's handwritten (handwritten, no less!) note of acceptance had arrived some months before. Lady Westbury had, to Lydia's ongoing amusement, ceremoniously laid this note on the mantelpiece in the morning room, in pride of place amongst the other cards received from mere civilians. Her daughter's jibe brought a warmth to Lady Westbury's cheeks more noticeable than that prompted by the sherry she was sipping. Perhaps the New Year would lead Lydia to be a little less, well, antagonistic. Perhaps 1939 would lead them all to new beginnings.

"Oh lummy! *The* Anthony de Havilland? Well, I never! Best resurrect my curtsey, eh?" Hugh exclaimed, his woolen beard dangling perilously from one ear.

The door opened once more, and the footman announced the arrival of three more newcomers who, escorted in by the comforting aroma of gammon (a Christmas Eve tradition in the Westbury family), advanced—with varying degrees of elegance—into the room. Our spectator might also fancy that something else accompanied our new players, something that introduced a distinctly discomfiting element into the evening.

3

As every society hostess knows all too well, a triumvirate of arrivals in a drawing room is highly undesirable, for it usually brings with it a conundrum: who should be greeted first? Any random or devised sequence of greetings risks communicating a hierarchy among the guests. And while such a hierarchy does unquestionably exist, to acknowledge it would spell catastrophe. These tricky scenarios demand a delicacy known only to those in possession of the most immaculate breeding and poise.

Fortunately, Lady Westbury's breeding and poise were immaculate. Besides, this particular triumvirate caused her no trouble at all, because one third of this new contingent never did stand on ceremony. In fact, he rather enjoyed trampling upon it at every available opportunity.

Throughout Little Bourton, the name Rampling had once conjured an image of integrity and decency, the family having been a bastion of Sussex society. That era, however, had passed with the death of the long-esteemed Sir Charles Rampling. Here stood his only son Freddie, impeccably dressed, excruciatingly drunk, gaily pulling strands of tinsel from the festive centerpiece before skipping haphazardly around the drawing room to an endless stream of *fa-la-la-la*s. Lord Westbury chuckled and patted Campbell-Scott's arm, explaining, "Young Freddie's liveliness knows no bounds!"

Lydia, standing on the other side of her godfather, muttered, "Nor does his appetite for whisky."

Freddie's presence at the family Christmas was something of a mystery to the Westbury siblings. They all viewed the incumbent of the Highmore estate as a booze-sodden jester destined to drink himself to ruin—a future he was embracing with aplomb. But Lady Westbury had insisted upon inviting him—another hapless waif to add to her collection.

Distracted by the tinsel theatrics, it took several moments for Lady Westbury to turn her attention to the other two guests, transfixed in the doorway.

"My dear Rosie, how divine you look!" Lady Westbury approached her oldest friend, affectionately taking her hands and kissing her lightly on the cheek.

Rosalind Ashwell returned the greeting, complimenting her on the exquisite tree and thanking her for the invitation—which had indeed presented a most welcome surprise. Since her marriage to William Ashwell, Christmas had always been spent, somewhat depressingly, *à deux*.

Lady Westbury, whose patience was seemingly infinite, took

a moment to gather this resource before turning to Rosalind's husband. When she did, her suspicions were confirmed: he was the same staid, unsmiling, standoffish figure he'd always been.

"William," she pronounced. "How good of you to join us."

"Hmm, yes. Was quite the journey, I can tell you. Blasted trains overrun, every Tom, Dick, and Harry and their mother out, people yacking nonstop—when we could have just—"

Before her husband could finish, Rosalind Ashwell, with a diplomacy she had cultivated in her high society days, suggested they indulge in a small sherry now that they had arrived. Privately she thought the journey, though testing, had been bearable owing to the merriment she knew was awaiting her in Little Bourton. If only William would shed some of that stuffiness, then perhaps he would—in a turn of events hitherto unknown to either of the Ashwells—enjoy himself. But no matter: it was this emphasis upon decency and propriety that had attracted her to him in the first place. A reliable, proper, upstanding man. A man who, upon proposing marriage, would commit unwaveringly to his promise.

Once Freddie's larking about subsided, the room hummed with the gentle murmur of polite conversation. How-do-you-dos were exchanged while Freddie slumped in a chair, cradling a second glass of sherry.

Hugh, his makeshift beard discarded, had been listening intently to Campbell-Scott's reflections on the current state of the world (was it really as bad as all that? Hugh wondered) and introduced the Ashwells to his new acquaintance.

"William and Rosalind were friends with my parents as

well, you see. Known me since I was, as they say, knee-high to a grasshopper."

William Ashwell, his face untroubled, as ever, by a smile, firmly shook Campbell-Scott's hand.

Meanwhile, a certain pallor had overcome Rosalind's complexion. A discernible lightness of breath marked her inhalations. Her eyes darted from her husband to Campbell-Scott with remarkable speed.

"Good evening…Mr. Campbell-Scott," she murmured, hardly looking at him.

Campbell-Scott turned from William Ashwell to Rosalind, and Hugh thought he glimpsed…what was it? Doubt? Surprise? Confusion? Before Hugh could reach a conclusion, the scene was cut short by the blusterings of Edward and Stephen as they entered the room.

"Until people like you look around you, things won't ever change—the world's going to hell in a handcart, and all you can do is snuffle around hunting for money like a damned pig," Edward proclaimed.

"Oh, do shut up," came Stephen's affectedly weary reply.

Lydia, mindful of her youngest brother's fraught nature and the sensitivity with which he needed to be handled, immediately approached Edward. He was, however, beyond placation.

"That goes for the lot of you—cossetted and closeted away in your dream worlds, while nightmares are coming true all over England, all over Europe, just you wait—"

Edward's tirade was interrupted by his realization that David Campbell-Scott had already joined the gathering. His stormy face turned to stone and he spat, "As I said, hell in a damned handcart."

Stephen let out his customary hoot as he brandished two newly filled glasses of sherry. "Oh, brother mine, let bygones be bygones, eh? It is Christmas after all." He shoved one glass into Edward's previously clenched fist. Edward snorted in disgust, eyeing Campbell-Scott disdainfully, before swiftly knocking back the sherry.

Lord Westbury, in one of his rare interludes of practicality, suggested, now that all but one guest had arrived, they take the opportunity to refresh themselves before reconvening for dinner "in, let's say, thirty minutes."

4

The drawing room lies empty as we follow our players to their rooms, though to dwell with them for too long would be most unbecoming. One might witness Edward Westbury furiously scrawling in his notebook or Freddie Rampling perched on the edge of his bed clutching his head in his hands. One might overhear William Ashwell's muffled yet unmistakably vexed, perhaps even angry, words; or frown in puzzlement as Hugh Gaveston peers through an eyeglass at a stuffed creature belonging to the *Sciuridae* family.

Instead of indulging in such uncouth observations, let us join our guests once more after they have relocated to the dining room, at precisely half past seven.

"Dear Lord, won't someone make him stop!" Freddie opined, gesturing to the maid to replenish his glass of wine. "I don't give a fig about the unemployed populace of Bethnal Green. I just want to enjoy Christmas!"

Edward seethed, thinking to himself, *another example of privilege blinding itself to the illnesses plaguing society.*

"I think Edward has exceptionally noble intentions, Mr. Rampling," David Campbell-Scott began, "and I do believe that we find ourselves at a moment in history which may well prove decisive in the twentieth century—"

"Pomp and rhetoric!" Edward spat. "Don't presume to patronize me and my 'noble intentions,' Mr. Campbell-Scott. Perhaps we should instead discuss your intentions in plundering Malaya: Is it purely for your own gain, or are you doing it all for the glory of this magnificent so-called *Empire* of ours?"

Freddie rolled his eyes chummily at David and swilled his wine while beckoning for both of their glasses to be refreshed. Freddie was many things, but stingy with alcohol (even when it was not, strictly speaking, *his* alcohol) was not one of them. Besides, if Campbell-Scott was in the warm embrace of wine, then so much the better for Freddie.

Lord and Lady Westbury, from opposite ends of the mahogany table, locked eyes and exchanged exasperated smiles. They were quite used to Edward's crusading performances by now. There was little use in trying to derail him: he would eventually run out of steam. And, moreover, Lady Westbury was consumed with another matter. Namely, the whereabouts of her esteemed MP.

No sooner had the thought crossed Lady Westbury's mind, than Jim—shoes still gleaming—appeared at the door and announced the arrival of a Mr. Anthony de Havilland.

"About bloody time!" Freddie bellowed.

Cheering and raising his hazardously full glass, Stephen added, "Damned if I was going to wait any longer!"

Lady Westbury showed de Havilland to his seat. "Do excuse the boys and their language. One must make allowances for the exuberance of youth."

Stephen winced slightly at the mention of "the boys." Despite Freddie's ostensibly superior social standing—the Rampling lineage was a formidable one—Stephen bridled at any suggestion of his being in league with this perpetually sloshed harlequin. Peacock-like in his pride at his own bad behavior, Stephen couldn't abide Freddie's (to his mind, inferior) version of it. It lacked finesse, sophistication; Rampling reeked of inelegance. While Stephen suffered the fool at Westbury Manor, he would be sure to ignore him at the club in Chelsea they both patronized.

"Oh, I'm quite used to it, Lady Westbury," he assured her. "Back in the trenches I heard far worse. And I do implore you to forgive my lateness. I was detained by parliamentary business. The running of the country, it seems, never stops!"

De Havilland seated himself with the posture of a man accustomed to moving between the wooden backbenches of the House of Commons and the plush armchairs of his club. He surveyed the table around him, scrutinizing each face: Where did weaknesses reside, where were threats dwelling, where could flattery yield rewards? Sozzled young bozo at the end clearly a monied ne'er-do-well; bald curmudgeon brandishing a scowl and a half-full glass; Westbury boys who individually were tiresome, together insufferable; grinning fellow wittering on about lizards (where did Lady Westbury find them?); girl burning with earnestness and intelligence, shame she's the wrong side of thirty; attractive woman whose benign gentility rendered her uninteresting; and back round to Little Lord Squiffy, now muttering to a distinguished-looking older chap. De Havilland's eyes were drawn to Campbell-Scott. Even without donning his spectacles, de Havilland could deduce that evidently here was a man of his own sort. Looked to have been gallivanting abroad, might be worth a brandy with after dinner.

"Ordinarily we would, of course, be standing for such introductions—" Lady Westbury was explaining.

"But ordinarily we're not all damned ravenous!" Stephen interjected.

De Havilland smiled graciously at this interruption. Politics had taught him to smile graciously in most circumstances—to smile until it was time to stop smiling. He was thrilled to attend one of Lady Westbury's renowned functions. Enduring her obnoxious son—or indeed, sons—was a price he was willing to pay.

"I say, de Havilland," Campbell-Scott said, covering his wineglass and thus thwarting Freddie's latest bid to refill it needlessly. "Ever found yourself bounding around in the East? I could've sworn we've met before but can't quite place you."

De Havilland squinted down the table, reaching into his inside pocket for his horn-rimmed spectacles, which conferred upon him the appearance of an elegantly learned scholar.

"The East? No, not me, old chap. Can't say I've ever ventured out there."

"Malaya, specifically—never at all?" Campbell-Scott pressed.

Edward decided to chime in once again. "Oh yes, Malaya,

of course, that was it, wasn't it, *Uncle David*. Malaya was where you made your fortune. Remind me—whatever did happen with that business in Mayfair?"

The younger obnoxious son, de Havilland noted. He also noted the narrowing of Campbell-Scott's eyes at the mention of "that business in Mayfair."

Ignoring Edward, he addressed Campbell-Scott. "Chance would be a fine thing! No, I'm afraid I'm forever enfettered by the shackles of political responsibility here."

Campbell-Scott frowned.

"You might've seen his photo in the papers, though—making waves all over the place with his speeches and whatnot, isn't that right?" Lord Westbury suggested, clapping de Havilland on the shoulder in a display of familiarity not altogether in correlation with his relationship with the MP. "Or, more likely, heard tell about him during the war—we have here a bona fide British hero!"

De Havilland winced perceptibly: a man of humility, Lord Westbury thought approvingly.

"Oh, don't come over all coy now, de Havilland! Hiding one's light under a bushel is no good. And what's more, these young tykes need to know they're in the presence of true English heroism."

Lydia piped up. "Two examples of true English heroism, you mean—don't forget all that David did during the Great War."

Campbell-Scott smiled. "Of course! I hear you're a fighting man. Our paths may have crossed then. Were you at the Somme?"

Was that a falter in de Havilland's gracious smile? A tensing of the shoulders? Before he could answer, his glass emptied its contents onto the linen cloth beneath it.

A fresh glass was sought, a fresh glass was offered, a fresh glass was filled with ruby-red wine as dinner proper was laid before all assembled and the question was forgotten.

Along the table, Lydia could be seen whispering into Edward's ear. Was it Lord Westbury's fancy, or were those two even more conspiratorial than ever this evening? Lady Westbury and Rosalind were bubbling away, exchanging stories of their mutual acquaintances while the only sound emanating from William Ashwell (whose humorless sobriety was particularly oppressive tonight) was his unappealingly loud mastication. Hugh was unveiling the intricacies of taxidermy to de Havilland, and was outlining the challenges of sourcing decent hemp wool in Sussex when they were interrupted by the sound of Campbell-Scott's uncharacteristically raised voice.

"Dammit, man, I said no. Now don't debase yourself any further by begging. Let me be understood plainly. Any money I have is staying exactly where it is—and not financing your sordid lifestyle."

Freddie, usually so inured to social niceties, blanched.

"Please lower your voice—" he murmured.

"And please silence yours," came Campbell-Scott's retort.

"Damn you, then, you condescending prig! I shan't sit here to be humiliated!" Freddie slammed his chair back and strode unevenly toward the door—before remembering that he had left his glass, thus necessitating a rather less effective retreat to collect it.

Lady Westbury let out a sigh of relief. Mercifully, Edward and Stephen's dramatics had been upstaged this time.

Dinner passed unremarkably from then on, and the theatrical flouncing-out was soon forgotten. The marching of Europe toward disaster had been outlined at length by Edward, despite Lydia's best efforts to silence him. Lady Westbury had rescued Campbell-Scott from the Freddie fiasco by regaling him with the gruesome details of the Lady Cranshaw cause célèbre while Rosalind Ashwell looked on with a presumably wine-induced vacancy to her pale-blue eyes. And Anthony de Havilland had found himself finishing sentences for an increasingly beleaguered Lord Westbury, who was visibly laboring under the strain of conversation.

A rattling at the door indicated that Angela had returned to serve port. The sherry decanter earlier had, Lady Westbury knew, been a strain for her maid, whose one shortcoming was her almost pathological aversion to carrying glassware. Not for the first time, Lady Westbury held her breath as Angela slowly—painfully slowly—made her way around the room bearing a load that stretched her abilities fearsomely: a bottle of port and eleven port glasses.

Angela's progress was steady, and Lady Westbury's concerns fluttered away with each glass successfully poured and placed in front of its recipient. De Havilland, Lord Westbury—*success*—Lydia, Edward—*keep going*—Rosalind—*marvelous work*—William—

"Blast it, girl!" William Ashwell's voice cut the air.

"B-b-begging your pardon, sir, I—" a meek reply met his rebuke.

"Are you a half-wit? A moron? Speak, girl!" he demanded, imbuing his words with a vehemence quite out of proportion to the situation, Lady Westbury noted.

"William, it was an accident, it's not her fault," Rosalind said, attempting to assuage the inexplicable ire of her husband.

"Well, whose bloody fault is it if it's not hers? No, people need to take bloody responsibility for their actions!"

His reaction was baffling the other occupants of the table, rendering them speechless, but David Campbell-Scott attempted to assume the role of their spokesperson.

"I say, William, go easy on the girl. We all make mistakes. Nothing that won't come out in the wash," he offered in a clear, incisive tone.

William Ashwell paused. A glance around the table.

"Mr. Campbell-Scott," as if through gritted teeth, "I can assure you. Some things do not 'come out in the wash,' as you so gracefully phrase it."

A nod from Lady Westbury prompted Angela to continue her round, inwardly thankful that tomorrow her only duties lay in preparing breakfast.

Port glasses drained, Christmas Eve salutations exchanged, bedchambers were, in due course, all occupied.

5

While the dinner guests slumbered, that other Christmas visitor, the snow, continued to make itself at home, taking up residence most brazenly in every eave of Westbury Manor. No rest for the falling snow, just as there is no rest for the wicked, so goes the unabridged saying. And indeed, come morning, snow and wickedness found themselves uneasy bedfellows.

By daybreak, anyone drawing their curtains to survey the grounds of Westbury Manor would be met with the sight of a pristine white blanket stretching across the gardens.

Pristine but for one besmirchment.

A fallen branch?

Perhaps a doe, luxuriating in the early-morning tranquility?

Surely not a body.

A human body.

A human body bordered by a crimson outline.

A crimson outline that, as the winter sun rose, was still seeping outward, leaving a stain that would mar Westbury Manor long after the snow had melted.

6

For the moment (that moment being precisely a quarter past eight on Christmas morning), however, let us grant the denizens of Westbury Manor an interlude of tranquility, prolong the period during which the gravest concern for Lady Westbury is whether or not Mrs. Smithson overcooks the carrots again (one of the less enjoyable traditions of a Westbury Christmas), and the highest calamity possible is Freddie dousing himself in whisky during charades.

A banquet of kidneys and bacon had been arranged in the dining room, where three pajama-clad revelers were already in the grips of Christmas merriment.

"A *vegetarian*?" Stephen nearly choked on a recently speared kidney at his sister's announcement.

Lydia's well-practiced eye roll was deployed as she exasperatedly confirmed Stephen's question. Hugh, his rakishly angled and comfortingly old-fashioned nightcap still atop his head, grinned and waved his buttery knife in the air.

"Oh yes," he offered. "It's quite *au courant* in these modern times, fleshless diets, raw-food consumption emancipating women from the slavish confines of the kitchen and so on and so forth. In fact"—excavating some bacon rind that had most inconveniently lodged itself between his canine and his incisor—"I have some fascinating reading material on this, fellow from Iowa—"

"God's teeth, these queer fancies of yours, sis. First suffragism, now vegetarianism…whatever next, spiritualism?" Pausing only to shovel in another forkful of flesh, Stephen continued, "Mother and Father had better be careful. I daresay you'll be charging entry for seances before they can say 'Madam Lydia's Mystical Chamber of Flim-Flam and Flumdubbery'!"

At this, the table began to dramatically buck, crockery rattling and kidneys slopping back and forth in the serving dish.

Stephen, fluttering his eyelids maniacally and swiveling his head in a most disconcertingly arrhythmic manner, emitted a wail: "Spiiiiirits, who goes there? Name yourselves! We mean you no harm!"

Opposed to and unimpressed by her brother in almost every conceivable sphere of life, even Lydia Westbury struggled to repress a giggle at this performance. Stephen's rare breaks from unpleasantness reminded her that, beneath his offensive exterior, there might be lurking a hint of a charming younger brother. Perhaps.

Palms upturned and eyes closed, Stephen intoned, "You say you have visited us from Christmas past, spirit? You are the ghost of—"

"Grandfather, galloping down from heaven on a steed to punish you for cheating at charades?" Lydia suggested. (Not one instance of Stephen's questionable charades tactics had been forgiven or forgotten by his sister.)

The dining-room door creaked open, and Stephen opened one eye to identify the new arrival, then firmly clamped it shut again. "No, I do believe…it's the ghost of Eddy's sense of humor! It's seeking revenge for its callous murder at the hands of…wait, it's coming…at the hands of Eddy's sense of self-righteousness!"

"Oh Stephen, you wag, you master of japes, you shining beacon of high wit and high intellect." Edward's slow handclaps were met by flamboyant bows from his older brother.

"I'd say that I try my hardest, but that of course would be a fraudulent claim—my ingenuity is effortless," Stephen added before savoring a particularly juicy kidney.

"I come bearing terrible news, though, brother dearest." Edward had sloped his way over to Stephen and, arm resting around his shoulder, stage-whispered, "I'm afraid that both the tea leaves and the ectoplasm are unequivocal in their judgment—you shall be trounced at charades tonight. Trounced to kingdom come."

Hugh's mouth hung open, butter coagulating just above his upper lip. Lydia's teacup remained suspended in the air. Stephen, for whom glib words were as easily spun and hurled forth into the world as money, was speechless. For here was a true Christmas miracle. Edward Westbury, self-styled prophet of doom and martyr for the downtrodden; Edward Westbury, partial to provocation and prone to paroxysms of outrage; Edward Westbury, making a joke?

Hugh was the first to break the incredulous silence. "I for one am with you, Eddy. Your 'winning' streak is at an end, Mr. Stephen Westbury."

Edward's unexpected gaiety gained momentum as he trotted to his seat, ruffling his brother's hair (Stephen couldn't remember the last time that had happened, if in fact it *ever* had), kissing his sister, and swiping Hugh's nightcap from his head in a fit of jollity hitherto unimaginable.

"Permit me to offer you all my warmest Christmas greetings and salutations," he trilled as he flumped down in his chair and tucked his napkin extravagantly into his shirt.

"And permit *me* to ask why you're flouncing around like a Dapper Dan at this hour of the morning? Haven't seen him all a-puff like this since he gave old Miss Norcote the slip in Selfridges that time, eh, Lydia?" Stephen looked to his sister for confirmation of this anomalous behavior.

"Christmas is but once a year, et cetera et cetera. And as for this"—Edward fingered his crisp white shirt—"Mother requested that I smarten up owing to the presence of Most Reverend His Excellency Monsignor de Havilland, so far be it from me to upset the applecart."

Lydia snorted into her Earl Grey, exchanging bemused glances with Hugh. "Sorry, Eddy, but since when have you been worried about—"

A thud outside the dining-room door, a muffled groan. The Westbury children knew better than to be alarmed. When their father's episodes had begun at Easter, any concern gave rise only to embarrassed mutterings from Lord Westbury and dismissive placations from Lady Westbury. As the months had drawn on, what could once be tactfully termed vacillations in health had become undeniable failings in health. After a particularly prickly interaction at Edward's birthday supper (Lord Westbury's temper, habitually snoozing within a cave of docility and jocularity, had reared its head at the suggestion that Dr. Shepherd's advice might well carry some weight), the three siblings came to the silent understanding that any changes in Lord Westbury's movement, memory, or moods were to be neither commented nor acted upon. Hugh's instinct to bolt out of his chair to offer assistance was subdued by a pat on the hand from Lydia.

"Oh, look at you all. The picture of Christmas bliss," beamed Lady Westbury, surveying the scene from the doorway. "Good morning, darlings."

Lord Westbury, endeavoring to conceal both slightly breathless wheezing and an ominous bruise forming on his right temple (or was it a fresh bruise overlaying an old one?), let out a *ho, ho, ho* before assailing his children and honorary child with clasps on the shoulders (Edward, Stephen, Hugh) and a kiss (Lydia).

"Tucking into the breakfast already, I see? Growing chaps, growing chaps," he chirruped contentedly before turning a mischievously glinting eye to his daughter. "And, Lydia, didn't Mrs. Smithson go and unearth any nasturtium roots for you? No preserved pine-cone soufflés or conifer-seed stews to start your day?"

Lydia returned his wink with a jovial, "Fear not, Father, my fragrant cedar-bark soup with cyclamen confit has *quite* sated my appetite."

"Surprised you're not still a-slumber," Lord Westbury

commented as he eyed the kidneys, "what with those nocturnal ramblings of yours."

Lydia's smile faltered momentarily and a variety of expressions chased themselves over her countenance.

"I keep telling her," Lord Westbury continued, easing himself into a chair, "a sleeping draught a day keeps the…keeps the…" Incognito, was it? Infernal? No…he almost had it. If only these words weren't so confoundedly slippery…

"Keeps the *insomnia* at bay?" Hugh interjected, grinning affably at Lydia. Was he imagining it, or was she suddenly disinclined to direct her eyes anywhere but at her teacup?

Clearing her throat, she replied, "Thankfully, my habitual afflictions granted me a night's respite—jolly generous of them, Christmas gift. I slept like a baby."

"Splendid news, darling." Lady Westbury handed her husband a napkin. "Has anyone seen our other guests?" A resounding "no" was the answer, though Stephen added that he shouldn't care a deuce whether he saw any of them at all.

How prescient Stephen's boorish words were to be. For there was one guest, of course, who would not be seen again by him. Or by any of the Westburys, for that matter.

7

"Oh, thank goodness you're here!"

Entering the dining room at quarter to nine, the Ashwells were met with exclamations and outpourings from all assembled guests. "A quarter to nine is when I have my breakfast, I'll not be cajoled into any other time," had been William's sour rebuttal of his wife's suggestion that they accommodate the half past eight breakfast time Lady Westbury had posited.

Hugh addressed them. "It's a mess. A frightful mess. I'm so sorry, Rosalind, William, but we need your help."

"Oh Hugh, whatever has happened?" Rosalind's concern was matched only by her husband's air of disengaged impatience.

The furor suspended, Hugh took a deep breath.

"Yesterday's crossword is putting us somewhat through the wringer. Nine across. 'In Greek tragedy, the startling discovery that produces a transition from ignorance to knowledge.' We're all at sixes and sevens about it: I say *anagnorisis*, Lyds is batting for *hamartanein…*"

A vinegary smile from William Ashwell, a curling of the lip that served only to underline the mood of airlessness that accompanied him. "Classics not my forte, a lot of overblown rot if you ask me. Lascivious and lurid, all of it. Cradle of civilization my elbow."

Rosalind emitted a polite titter. Turning to Hugh, she said, "You did have me most worried, Hugh. You always were a prankster."

The Ashwells, who, at William's behest, had ignored Lady Westbury's encouragement to join breakfast in their nightwear ("A frightfully indecent proposal, and one I shan't entertain") and were instead dressed for lunch already, seated themselves.

Lady Westbury frowned and glanced at the gold clock upon the mantelpiece. "No Freddie, no David, and no Mr. de Havilland yet…"

"Freddie'll either be soused already or unconscious," Stephen remarked. "The other two are probably discussing world domination over cigars, away from the hoi polloi."

William Ashwell was tucking his napkin into his shirt collar (a habit that Rosalind had attempted, fruitlessly, to curb some years ago) while his wife exchanged Merry Christmases with the Westburys and Hugh.

"I trust you slept well, Rosalind?" Lady Westbury asked, prompting a *hmmmf* from her husband.

Another edgy titter from Rosalind. She really had become quite the Nervous Nelly, thought Hugh. As a child he had never, of course, questioned the union of William and Rosalind, for the Ashwells and the Westburys had always been an immovable fixture at the dinners hosted by his parents. The passing of time had, however, led him to question their compatibility. Rosalind still glowed with an inner benevolence and bore the traces of a beauty that must surely have marked her out as "a catch" in her youth. She had been a kind and gay visitor to his family home, that rare adult who had sought out opportunities to play hide-and-seek with him, who had listened with a natural attentiveness as he recounted the latest detective stories he had torn through. Her husband, on the other hand, appeared to have determined frivolity and light-heartedness to be his sworn nemeses. Where Rosalind quietly savored socializing, William never seemed anything less than mildly put out when surrounded by other people; around him, one was hard pushed to enjoy one's cake and ale. Hugh couldn't help but wonder what it was that had compelled Rosalind to dedicate her life to a man so unerringly serious. As a result of his oppressive solemnity, she seemed to have retreated, lying dormant within herself in a resigned acceptance of what Hugh could only conclude was a life disappointed.

Rosalind stirred her tea, scraping the side of the cup as she did so in a most teeth-setting manner.

"Olivia, remind me," she casually asked Lady Westbury. "Mr. Campbell-Scott and Mr. de Havilland, will they both be joining us for the entirety of the festivities? Remaining here until the twenty-seventh?"

Her friend informed her that yes, both would be attending the Boxing Day shoot, with Mr. de Havilland returning to London the day after and David staying on a little longer. "Malaya, you see, is considerably far, and of course it's unlikely that David will be setting foot back on home soil for quite a time—so, naturally, he is eager to bed in here, as it were, for a spell," Lady Westbury explained, adding, "and I understand that he wants to attend to some business while in the country, ensure that his solicitors are seeing to everything satisfactorily in his absence."

Rosalind ignored the *pah* emanating from Edward Westbury and continued her questioning. "And his…family, I suppose they're still here in England. They miss him awfully?"

"Family? David?" Lady Westbury replied. "Oh goodness me, no. We're the closest to family that David has. Quite the confirmed bachelor."

"Shouldn't wonder he has a bit of stuff secreted away somewhere," Stephen contributed, "languishing in a flat in Barons Court for the better part of the last decade, living off gin and a healthy allowance from Davey."

Lydia interjected, "Please subdue your obscene imaginings, Stephen. Not everyone is covertly engaged in Caligulan depravity, you know."

"Well, it'd be devilishly aggravating for you if he did have a faded flapper stashed away somewhere, depleting your inheritance by spending it all on mother's ruin down at the local gin palace," Stephen retorted, dipping a chunk of bread in the aftermath of his kidney breakfast.

Rosalind glanced at Lady Westbury quizzically.

"David is Lydia's godfather, you see," she explained. "An admirably doting godfather at that, and so—"

Lady Westbury was interrupted by another thud in the hallway. A scratching at the door. Baffled glances around the table.

Hugh sprang up to investigate, to be met at the door by a sodden Labrador trailing a leash.

"Bruno? What on earth are you up to, boy?"

Further puzzlement around the table. A crashing, followed by the appearance of a particularly red-faced Jim.

"Begging your pardon, milud, milady. It's just—there's—I found something—when I was taking Bruno for his walk…" Jim's faltering invited a mixture of alarm and impatience in the dining room.

"Jim, what is it?" Lady Westbury's voice calmed Jim into eloquence.

"He's dead!"

Impatience vanished; alarm prevailed.

"*Dead*? Who's dead?" Lord Westbury demanded, laying a protective hand on Bruno's drenched head.

"Mr. Campbell-Scott, sir."

8

The very room itself seemed to be holding its breath, suspended in a hinterland of uncertainty. Silence was hanging heavily over its inhabitants, as if all were fearing what elucidation of Jim's statement would bring: an irrevocable and unthinkable change to their lives.

The previous scene of comfortable mundanity gave way to a tableau rich and varied in its elements. An observer would note a palpable sense of Lord Westbury groping for words as he tightened his grip on poor Bruno's nape; would puzzle at William Ashwell's ability to ignore the oddly unsettled demeanor of his wife, prompting Lady Westbury to reach across to take her friend's hand; would perhaps take in Lydia Westbury's eyes darting toward Edward's, only to be met with a sphinx-like inscrutability.

While digesting all of this, our observer might have failed to notice de Havilland appearing behind Jim in the doorway.

Indeed, Hugh started abruptly when the politician asked what he had missed.

"Ah, Mr. de Havilland…yes…something rather dreadful has happened. Jim here, he says that David Campbell-Scott is…well, dead," Hugh explained in a somewhat garbled fashion.

In that determined yet unruffled manner so well cultivated by men of his standing, de Havilland approached the beleaguered footman.

"Someone get this fellow some tea, some hot tea," he intoned, placing a robust hand on Jim's shoulder and exerting a pressure that was at once reassuring and vaguely reminiscent of a schoolmaster coaxing a confession before producing a cane. "Now… Jim, is it? Tell us exactly what happened."

What followed, between splutterings and stutterings, was an account of Jim taking Bruno for his morning walk around the grounds (earlier than usual, it being Christmas, and Jim's mother expecting him in time for a cup of tea before church). Bruno had dashed off ("he likes to dash off, he's a scallywag, he is"), Jim following him (even though the snow was quite deep round there, and Jim's shoes would need seeing to after this), and there it was… There *he* was. More splutterings.

De Havilland's wealth of experience in dealing with important matters enabled him to identify that Jim was now beyond the point of conveying information intelligibly. He handed him the cup of hot tea that Lydia had shakingly poured and said, "Lydia, telephone the police—they'll need to be alerted to a death."

Scanning the room for an appropriate helpmate, de Havilland's eyes alighted on Hugh. "Come with me. We'll need to be able to show the police where it—where *he* is when they arrive. We can't be dillydallying when they get here."

Hugh nodded his assent. Was Lydia all right, though, should he stay? He looked at her, communicating his thoughts wordlessly, but she shook her head. "No, I'm fine. Go with Mr. de Havilland, he's right. I'll stay here and make sure…"

Casting around the room, following Lydia's gaze, he saw what she was referring to: Lord Westbury, enfeebled and flooded with confusion; Lady Westbury, composed; Rosalind Ashwell, decidedly less composed; the blank coldness of William Ashwell compromised not a jot by the unfolding events; and the Westbury brothers, Edward grimacing (for surely he couldn't be sneering?) and Stephen patently flabbergasted yet perhaps suppressing a smirk. Surveying such a scene, Hugh could very much see why Lydia wanted to stay and make sure.

"Right-o, of course, let's."

As de Havilland and Hugh approached the door, the powerful strides of the former offset by the trotting of the latter in a pairing, which, in other circumstances, would have been comical, they were met by yet another of our players returning to the scene.

"Miss me, everyone?" came Freddie Rampling's bleary-eyed warbling. "Damned nasty head this morning. I hope Mrs. Smithson hasn't overcooked the kidneys—dripping in blood, I like 'em!"

To say that Freddie's reappearance was both ill-timed and ill-judged would be the kind of tactful understatement usually reserved for Lady Westbury. Such tact, however, had no place in an environment so saturated with unarticulated questions and unprecedented emotions.

"Jesus Christ, Freddie, you know how to make an entrance." Lydia hurled her words across the room (met, it should be noted, with neither a wince nor a flinch from her mother, who was otherwise engaged in attempting to decipher Rosalind Ashwell's current demeanor).

"Some rather grim news, Rampling. It appears that Campbell-Scott has died," declared de Havilland as he led Hugh (increasingly concerned about being snowbound in only his flannel pajamas) out.

Freddie's face, already destitute of color thanks to the inordinate volumes of whisky consumed the previous day, drained into an even more unsettling pallor.

"This…what? I'm not sure I follow," he said, to nobody in particular. "What the deuce was he talking about?"

Lydia strode toward the door, casting a disdainful glance at Freddie, leaving Stephen to address his inquiry.

"Freddie, remarkable as your swivel-eyed-mouth-agape vaudeville act is, it grew stale some time ago, and now is most certainly not a time for it to make a revival. Let me outline it in terms even you can comprehend. Campbell-Scott. Outside. Dead." Accompanied by dramatic gesticulations, Stephen furnished Freddie with the facts of the morning.

Freddie shot looks at the others in the room. Dead? Outside? Campbell-Scott? How did that…? It hadn't been…? Freddie reeled back through the somewhat hazy actions of last night. After storming out of dinner he'd gone upstairs, hadn't he? He hadn't come back down? Hadn't…?

A multitude of inchoate questions scrambled around

Freddie's addled mind, none of them crystalizing into anything that could sensibly be uttered. Concluding that silence would be his most reliable recourse on this occasion, Freddie shuffled to an unoccupied place at the table. Eyeing up the kidneys, he found himself struck by a feeling of nausea, which left him sinking into a torpor, only to be disturbed when Lydia came back into the room.

"The police are on their way. Didn't sound best pleased to be disturbed on Christmas Day," she announced tightly, "so I apologized from the bottom of my heart for there being a death in the family at such an inconvenient juncture. How thoughtless of us."

She tugged at her stripy pajama sleeve, a movement that prompted a queer little giggle.

"Absurd, isn't it?" she said. "Here I am in my dressing gown, all the presents are under the Christmas tree in the drawing room... and outside...David's lying dead."

Knitting her brow, Lydia seemed uncertain about how to arrange her hands, what function they should be fulfilling. Eventually, she settled upon clenching them by her side.

The ticking of the gold clock seemed impertinently, insensitively loud as the room appeared to be alive with uncomfortable shifting and uneasy motions. A head being scratched, a leg being crossed, throats being cleared: all took on a dimension of disquiet.

Lord Westbury was opening and closing his mouth, as if on the verge of saying something that insisted on fluttering away at the last moment.

Finally, he mumbled, "But what was he *doing* out there? What *happened*?"

Stephen decided to offer his opinions on the matter: "Well, old bugger like that, living in a balmy climate for years, not used to the cold—heart probably conked out during a walk at the crack of dawn." He paused for dramatic effect, before adding, "Unless he spotted something scandalous and shocking in a window that frightened him to death. Lyds, none of your pathetic would-be paramours climbing the trellis to serenade you?"

"Shut up, Stephen," Lydia replied, no energy to spare on crafting a scathing reply. Meditatively, chewing her fingernail, she said, "He must have been out for a walk, yes, must have wanted to get some air. That's the only logical explanation."

Lady Westbury, mindful of the importance of etiquette at times of turpitude, suggested that Stephen and Lydia retreat to change out of their nightwear. Her gentle instruction was gratefully received not only by said pajama-clad siblings, but also by the other inhabitants of the room, reinstating, as it did, some air of fleeting normality.

Just as Stephen was heaving himself out of his chair and depositing his napkin on the bloodied plate before him, Hugh and de Havilland returned. Blue-lipped and shivering in his dressing gown, Hugh appeared to be concentrating on suppressing the chattering of his teeth, while de Havilland wore an expression of sturdy solemnity.

"Well?" Lydia blurted.

"Well, *what* precisely?" Stephen countered with a smirk. "Not expecting them to tell you that it was all a terrible misunderstanding? That David's happy as Larry out there building an elaborate snowman? Young Jim's a regrettably—if entertainingly—dense specimen, I'll grant you, but I suspect even he can discern between a man in rude health and a corpse."

Lady Westbury softly enjoined, "Not now, Stephen; not now."

Her husband half-raised himself from his chair to ask, "Gentlemen, is…can you…?"

De Havilland stepped forward. "I'm afraid it's as the lad said. Mr. Campbell-Scott has died."

Lord Westbury emitted an odd, animal-like sound, not dissimilar to the whimperings of Bruno as he cowered under the table.

"Poor David," Lady Westbury murmured, "to drop dead on Christmas morning."

"The…the pity of it, Olivia, the pity of it." Lord Westbury regained some level of composure.

Stephen, betraying his customary bluster with a demonstration of tenderness toward his father, said, "Well, had a jolly good innings of it, eh, Father? And at least he was here, decent last supper with lashings of Sussex's finest port, then pottering around on Christmas morning, having a lie-down in the snow? Worse ways to kick the bucket, eh?"

Lord Westbury nodded, conceding that his son was speaking sense, and informed his wife that he wanted to go and see David's body, place a blanket over it before the police arrived.

Glances were passed between Hugh and de Havilland. Evidently, Hugh drew the invisible short straw.

"Actually," he began, "that's not quite, um…not quite going to be a viable course of action, I'm afraid. There's…rather a lot of blood. So I might propose that, um, none of us venture outside."

Audible intakes of breath around the table at this revelation: blood?

"What do you mean 'rather a lot of blood'?" Stephen appeared dumbfounded. "Pricked his finger hitting the deck, bashed his head on a rock, what *kind* of 'rather a lot of blood'?"

De Havilland, after a deep breath, furnished Stephen—and the room—with an answer.

"I can't tell you how sorry I am to be bearing this news. Truly, I am. But Mr. Campbell-Scott did not die by natural causes. He died by his own hand. He shot himself."

Lord Westbury collapsed back into his chair, Lady Westbury clutching his arm as he did so. A chorus of muted gasps around the table. Hugh watched as Lydia's clenched fist went first to cover her own mouth, then toward Edward's arm, clutching it for support. Stephen's eyebrows were raised as if pulled skyward by some heavenly string. Freddie appeared to be examining the tablecloth and the creases being born of the tight grip he had on it. William Ashwell had stoically remained with knife and fork motionlessly in hand, while his wife's pale eyes filled with tears.

"That can't be so. That really can't be so…" Lord Westbury began.

"Regrettably, Lord Westbury, it is so," de Havilland asserted. "I wish it weren't, but we both saw the evidence, plain as day. Handgun discarded—well, dropped—beside the chap's right arm. I've seen deaths like this, back on the front. Chaps who couldn't… Well, never mind. The angle of the wound told me everything. I shan't wade into the details of it now, of course. Not decent in company—" He nodded toward the women. "Damned shame, and it's no easier now than it was then. No easier at all."

"A handgun? But why the bloody hell did he bring a gun with him?" Stephen asked.

De Havilland hesitated, while he passed the baton to Hugh.

"He, ah, he didn't. It's, well, it's your handgun, Lord Westbury," Hugh stumblingly said. "I recognized it, you see. Would recognize that Webley anywhere. He must have snatched it from the gun cabinet."

Lord Westbury poured his face into his trembling hands, and Hugh approached to pat his shoulder in an awkward gesture that the Westburys had collectively come to find curiously comforting over the years.

Campbell-Scott, dead.

Shot dead.

By his own doing.

The information crept into the room like a nefarious and unwelcome intruder.

During the moments that passed, Lady Westbury had evidently resolved to salvage some control of the unfolding situation. Falling back on her most reliable of crutches—prudent and reasonable action—she suggested once more that her eldest two children get dressed, while proposing that everyone else convey themselves to the drawing room.

"I think that's sensible," Hugh agreed. "The police will be here soon, I take it, and we ought to all make ourselves available when they need to ask us questions."

"The necessity of any questions seems doubtful, old chap,"

de Havilland said, unable to wholly disguise a patronizing tone. He turned to Lady Westbury. "Please do excuse me for a moment. Without wishing to appear insensitive, may I use your telephone? Christmas though it is, the Minister and I need to hash out a few things."

"Of course, Mr. de Havilland, of course," Lady Westbury murmured, helping her husband raise himself from his seat and gesturing toward the hallway, where de Havilland would find the telephone.

Making way for the somber procession being led out of the dining room, Hugh paused to appraise the happenings and to gather his thoughts. Although Jim's initial news had produced shock and disbelief, the reports from de Havilland and Hugh triggered something ineffable.

Hugh frowned as he tried to put his finger on it: deep sadness, yes; incredulity, a little; but there was something else seeping into the room. An uneasiness. Something was swirling in Hugh's mind, something that would have to wait until later for him to truly dissect its import. He scribbled hastily in the notebook he kept about his person at all times (one never knew when one might be struck by an epiphany that would solve one's latest taxidermical conundrum), returned said book to his dressing-gown pocket, and followed the party to the drawing room.

9

The incongruity of the Christmas tree and its bounty of gifts was striking. In a parallel Sussex, Lord Westbury, as was customary, distributed both presents and festive cheer in abundance. Here, too, the Westbury children laid down their weapons in an armistice, playful squabbles taking the place of spiteful vendettas. Lady Westbury, meanwhile, in this other world, was watching adoringly as Hugh opened the latest volume of detective stories she had bought him.

Such scenes—already imbued with nostalgia and melancholy, seeming so irretrievable after the events of the morning—were absent in the version of Sussex in which we find ourselves. Had Hieronymus Bosch ever turned his hand to depicting domesticity at its most purgatorial (or indeed purgatory at its most domestic), even he might have struggled to conjure the atmosphere of gloom pervading the room. An atmosphere that Hugh, still in his pajamas, had resolved to leaven as best he could, with the limited resources he had to hand: tea and yesterday's crossword.

Having intercepted Angela at the door (the poor girl really shouldn't be exposed to her employers in this state), he had proceeded to furnish every cup in sight with a fresh helping of tea, whether the cup's owner acquiesced to his insistence or not.

"Now, it's a truth universally acknowledged that a single man in possession of a barren crossword must be in want of some brain-boxes," Hugh announced, with admirable amiability, brandishing yesterday's newspaper. "Nine across we can return to later, so let's try eleven across: '1931 Grand National winner, six letters.' Oh golly, never was a horse man. Any ideas?"

Glances around the room revealed a decidedly unforth-coming audience: William Ashwell's opaque stoniness matched his wife's jelly-like quivering, Freddie's hollow-eyed ashenness offset Lydia's flushed visage, while Edward's close-bitten fin-gernails tapped out an increasingly frantic Morse code on the windowsill.

William Ashwell sighed the exasperated sigh of a man who has long since abstained from social niceties.

"Must we go through this charade?"

"Oh, charades are yet to come, old bean! That treat lies yon-der," Stephen delightedly informed him, pointing toward an unseen promised land of parlor games.

Hugh ponderously scratched his chin and frowned as he theat-rically paced the room. "'1931 Grand National winner, six letters. 1931 Grand National winner, six letters. 1931 Grand Na—'"

"Grakle," came the response, uttered in a tone crouching somewhere between contempt and boredom.

"Sorry, come again?" Hugh's pen hovered above the newspaper in anticipation.

"GRAKLE." His tone had scuttled closer to contempt.

"Grackle, no, that's too many letters I'm afraid. Must be—"

"Oh, give me that!" William Ashwell erupted into a state of animation not dissimilar to that unleashed upon poor Angela during the port incident the previous night, snatching the paper and pen from Hugh and scribbling down the answer.

Hugh, oblivious to—or at least conjuring the impression of one oblivious to—his fellow guest's hostility, exclaimed, "That's the spirit! Take our minds off this rotten business. Now, seven down…" Hugh's witterings provided a surprisingly soothing distraction as Lord Westbury turned to his wife.

"Olivia, I'm getting rather fogged by all this," he plaintively murmured. "David, offing himself? It just doesn't tally. Not old Flighty, determined old chap, never thrown in the towel on anything. Damned mulish, some might say—"

"Threw in the towel in Mayfair though, didn't he? Ran for the hills, got off scot-free," Edward snarled, his rat-a-tat-tatting on the fireplace redoubling in pace and force.

"Edward, shut up," Lydia barked. "He's dead, all right? He's dead. He killed himself and now he's dead, and that's that." Then continuing in a softer tone, "One can never wholly know what goes on in another's mind…"

"Pretty plain what was going on in his. 'I rather fancy I'll blow my brains out.' Don't have to be an Austrian shrink to work that one out." A gloomy relish in disaster had always been one of Stephen's more unappealing traits, and here he was displaying it to maximum impact.

Lord Westbury, always reluctant to involve himself in the frequent fracas between his children, grasped his wife's hand as if readying himself for an unprecedented intervention.

Steadily, with palpable determination, and quite without animosity, he said, "You may think I'm a muddle-headed old fool, but of this I am certain—my dearest friend is dead. I'll thank you all to remember that. And to conduct yourselves with some modicum of decorum. Your nonsense has no place here."

A silence that was not altogether companionable descended upon the room.

The unmistakable sternness of Lord Westbury's words even prompted Hugh to look up from his crossword endeavor.

Apologetic murmurs emanated from all three Westbury children, petulant hostility giving way to sheepish embarrassment.

For the first time that morning, Lydia's high color was accompanied by a rush of tears. "I'm sorry, Father… I just… He committed suicide. It's a tragedy, but there's nothing that can be done about it now and it's pointless—*pointless*—rehashing it all."

Edward looked as if he was about to speak, but Lydia caught his eye, almost imperceptibly shook her head.

To the great relief of all, the resounding chime of the doorbell put paid to any continuation of their conversation.

Brightly, though unnecessarily, Hugh declared, "Finally! That must be one of the boys in blue. Let me go and—" Before he had even finished his proclamation, however, voices could be heard in the hallway. Had Jim's shock imbued him with the power of super speed? How had he made his way from the downstairs quarters to the front door with such unearthly alacrity?

The mystery of this newfound agility was resolved forthwith, as de Havilland—not, as assumed, the Westburys' footman—appeared in the doorway of the drawing room, to introduce them all to a Constable Jones.

Before turning his artistic attentions to the rendering of recently deceased rodents, and when he wasn't conspiring with Lydia, of course, Hugh's idle childhood hours were dedicated to elaborately illustrating a town he had imaginatively christened Gavestown. Scrawled on any loose sheaves of paper he could find, including some important legal documents he had chanced upon in his father's study, the settlement was populated with a people notable for their elongated legs, toothsome grins, haphazardly arranged hair, bristling mustaches (Gavestown admitted no females), and eyes just a jot too small for their incongruously large heads.

Shaking hands with Constable Jones, Hugh could not help but feel the power of a deity creator witnessing his vision made flesh: for Constable Jones might well have leaped from the pages of Gavestown directly into Westbury Manor.

Tiny eyes peering around the room, prominent incisors flashing beneath a well-manicured mustache, Constable Jones remarked, "Seems like we have some nasty business here. No disrespect intended to such fine ladies and gentlemen, of course."

Lord Westbury hoisted himself out of his armchair, making toward the gangly officer before him. "Nothing businesslike about a death, young fellow. My dear friend has—"

"I've been apprised of the situational circumstances enacted and upon which we, being myself and you fine people, are to find ourselves. That being"—Constable Jones here referred to a notebook produced from his jacket pocket—"a gentleman, having taken leave of his senses and his right mind, thereupon and whereby issuing a bullet upon himself, thus and therefore concluding in the cessation of life in said gentleman."

Hugh was agog at Jones's proclamation. Had the chap chomped his way through a thesaurus before his arrival? Or perhaps he was laboring—and laboring rather painfully—under the impression that communication with "such fine ladies and gentlemen" required these syntactical contortions.

Freddie broke his silence. "In plain English, man?"

Clearing his throat, Constable Jones began. "Such intelligence as has been furnished, the specifics of which are aforementioned—"

Mercifully, de Havilland assisted in the constable's delivery. "I've told our man here everything we know and everything he needs to know. Campbell-Scott took the gun and shot himself. Damned tragedy of it all."

Winces from Lord and Lady Westbury, as if freshly wounded.

Hugh gestured to the room. "Mr. de Havilland and I can show you the, uh, site of the disturbance, out in the garden. It was Jim, the footman, who made the, uh, discovery, so we ought to call him up so that you can interview him. And of course, we'll all make ourselves available for any questions you need to ask."

"Thank you, Mr...?" Constable Jones said, frowning.

"Gaveston, Hugh Gaveston."

"Thank you, Mr. Gayeston, but such rigmarole and

conflabulatories shall not be necessary. We have here what we in the constabulary term 'an open-and-closed case.'" A reassuring pat to Hugh's shoulder accompanied the pronouncement.

"Open-and-*shut* case, perhaps you mean, Constable?"

"Now, now, don't you trouble yourself with police jargon, Mr. Gayeston."

"It's just I do rather think that we ought to tell you as much as we can about Mr. Campbell-Scott," Hugh insisted.

As he flicked through his notebook, Jones's frown became more pronounced. "Mr. Campbell-Scott?"

"The dead man, you buffoon," Stephen helpfully piped up, bothering to stand.

"Right, yes, Mr. Campbell-Scott, who did knowingly and willfully seek out and then use a firearm in order to injure himself fatally."

"Constable Jones, I do feel rather strongly that, in cases such as this, the more information we can provide, the more you can—"

"Hugh," Lydia cut in, an irrepressible edge to her voice, "the constable has made it abundantly clear that it is, well, it is what it is. David committed suicide."

"I just want to make sure we—the constable here—has all the facts," Hugh replied. "Shall I fetch Jim—the lad who, ah, made the discovery—so that you can speak with him, Constable?"

De Havilland intercepted Hugh's question, explaining that Jim had been in such a state of shock that he had thought it prudent to send the poor boy back to his mother's house for the day. "Senseless prolonging of the fellow's ordeal, after all," he said.

Hugh was taken aback, and persisted. "But surely, Constable, you'll want to speak with the person who *found* the de—who found Mr. Campbell-Scott?"

William Ashwell, scowling and huffing dramatically, interjected, "Gaveston, don't you think it's time to stop bleating on about it?"

"Damned if I want to waste any more time talking about dear old Uncle David." Edward's finger-tapping had now been replaced by an equally arrhythmic knee-jiggling. "If you ask me—"

"Nobody did, Edward, nobody did! So just shut up, will you, just shut up!"

Lydia stood rigid, her fists clenched, nostrils flared.

Lady Westbury reached out toward her daughter, only to be rebuffed by Lydia's upturned palms. "I can't bear this. I can't bear any of it. Everything, this whole mess, this isn't how—"

"Begging your pardon, miss, but please do try to contain yourself. It is my experience that female aversion to unpleasantness can result in fits, swoons, or, in extreme cases, acts of violence. I would ask that you beseat yourself. Have you any pursuits with which you may divert your mind—cross-stitching or a beauty magazine perchance?"

Before Lydia could respond to Constable Jones's advice, Hugh swooped in—the last thing he needed was a case of grievous bodily harm against a police officer.

"Constable, please do follow us. Mr. de Havilland and I shall show you to the scene."

10

In his determination to tend to the Westburys with remedies consisting of Earl Grey and general-knowledge brainteasers, Hugh had not yet attired himself in his daywear. Constable Jones's skepticism about his self-appointed crime-scene tour leader can, therefore, be understood. Traipsing after Hugh, who was absentmindedly swishing his dressing-gown belt in a most distracting manner, Jones turned to an infinitely more reliable source of authority: Anthony de Havilland.

"Mr. Havisham, might I ask what is the nature of your connection to the Westmoreland family?"

"*De Havilland*. Lady *Westbury* is a bastion of hospitality, and she kindly extended an invitation to me when we met at a dinner some months back in town. Naturally, I accepted. The life of an MP is not one of leisure, nor is a Westbury invitation to be sniffed at."

Constable Jones stopped in his tracks. Smoothing his hair, he uttered, "An *MP*, sir? An honorable member of His Majesty's righteous parliament?"

Arranging a patient smile on his face, de Havilland confirmed Jones's inquiry, which prompted a deferential assurance that he would do whatever he possessed in his limited powers as but a mere officer of the law to ensure that Christmas Day was not entirely spoiled by this unfortunate incident.

"Here it—he—is, Constable," Hugh shouted.

And there it—he—was indeed. Hugh's detective stories often dwelt on the lurid details of a dead body, waxed gruesomely poetical about the quality or quantity (more often than not, both) of blood, splayed limbs and ghoulishly distorted faces, and the shrieks and sobs of witnesses. Here, however, one felt oneself enveloped in a scene of otherworldly serenity—which was more than a little unnerving.

There, Campbell-Scott lay.

There, pooled in blood.

There, a pistol beside him.

Jones and de Havilland reached Hugh, who stood five feet or so away from Campbell-Scott's corpse. Jones signaled for the two men to stay put as he made to stride directly toward the body.

"Constable, stop!" Hugh shouted. "Avoid the tracks!"

"As you can see, Constable, one set of footprints in the snow—one set of footprints that stops where the poor fellow did it." De Havilland gestured to the ground. Jones took a moment to register both Hugh's instruction and de Havilland's information before continuing his trajectory toward the body, circumventing the original tracks.

"Hmm, quite so regarding there being one set of footprints, de Havilland, quite so," Hugh began. "But do you perceive a smudging here and there…a blurring almost of the tracks? It strikes me as though the tracks are a little…engineered?"

"I really couldn't say, Gaveston." De Havilland peered down at the prints. "I haven't my spectacles with me."

The MP and the taxidermist watched the policeman at his work, though quite what his work was, they couldn't be certain. He appeared to be tiptoeing around Campbell-Scott as if he were a pickpocket about to loot a sleeping commuter on a train. And a comically inept pickpocket at that. De Havilland and Hugh exchanged dubious glances while Jones laboriously trundled back to them.

"As previously and earlier stated and asserted, it is my incontestable conclusion that leaves no room for doubting or contesting—this gentleman, Mr. Campbell-Knot, has done away with himself," he intoned portentously.

Hugh, mustering all the charm he could, attempted to contend with the constable's conclusions, and said, "To, uh, borrow a phrase of yours, Constable, I mean no impertinence, but, ahh, might that have been rather a…peremptory investigation of the scene? If you look here, you can see the footprints aren't quite—"

"Sir, allow me to cork the flow of your words with a fact, to borrow a phrase from Shakespeare, I believe." Constable Jones twiddled his mustache in self-satisfaction. "You are a gentleman. I am a detective. Granted, not yet formally a detective in rank, but a detective in soul and in experience. And my experienced soul tells me that this"—waving his arm haphazardly toward

Campbell-Scott's body—"is your common-or-garden-variety suicide."

Hugh tightened his dressing gown around him as de Havilland peered over Jones's shoulder at the body.

"It does seem rather unequivocal, old chap," he remarked to Hugh. "He is a policeman."

"That I am, your grace, that I am." Jones half-bowed. "Now all that's left to do is call in Dr. Shepherd—he won't welcome a summons on such a day, but, as we like to say in the business, *habeas corpus*. And said *corpus* shan't make it to the mortuary without assistance. Gentlemen, I, most humble operator of justice, extend to you my gratitude for your forbearance under these situational circumstances. I will make my way to the station."

Having shaken hands with Jones, Hugh and de Havilland turned to make their return to Westbury Manor.

"Oh, hang it, gentlemen, stop!" came a bellow from Jones.

Hugh spun round. "What is it? What have you found?"

"I forgot to wish you both a Merry Christmas!"

11

After Hugh and de Havilland had returned from their excursion with Constable Jones to deliver the definitive news, the guests had become listless. William Ashwell had muttered some response before going upstairs (presumably to check on his wife, who was still out of sorts); Edward had torn from the room, eyes blazing; Lord Westbury announced that he would retire to bed for a time; while Lady Westbury escorted de Havilland to the library—he should like to see the first editions of Tennyson that she had mentioned at that dinner in town.

An hour had passed, during which Hugh, in his bedroom, had taken stock of the situation so far, as he understood it. Which, he concluded, was very poorly indeed.

Hugh was on the point of knocking on Lydia's door when a bell sounded: a bell that had only ever previously been used to signal the end of a game of sardines. Upon hearing it, Hugh knew that the guests were being summoned.

The bell had indeed been sounded with impressive resonance by Lady Westbury, who was now waiting in the drawing room with her husband.

"Not having a moment's silence, are we, Mother?" Stephen asked. "Frightfully sorry, but on point of principle I disagree with that sort of thing. Lot of pomp and hooey."

Lydia followed her brother, snapping, "You disagree with that sort of thing because it's physically impossible for you to shut up for sixty seconds."

Lord Westbury, sitting in his chair in as upright a posture as possible for a man of his health, surveyed his family and his guests, while Lady Westbury stood beside him with her hand on his shoulder. Evidently, the onslaught of this morning's tragedy had forced them to retreat to the sanctuary of domestic unity. While it might be impossible to entirely vanquish the distress waging war on them, Lord and Lady Westbury were resolved to keep outright anguish at bay for as long as possible.

"Your mother and I have been talking," Lord Westbury began, clearly contending against a tremor in his voice.

"Oh crumbs, here it is—taking each other to the highest court in the land for an ugly and scandalously public divorce? Please don't fight too much over who'll have sole custody of me," Stephen replied.

Were he to glance around him, he would see no suppressed smiles at his "joke"—for nobody was in the mood. "Stephen, please," Lady Westbury said. "This is important."

"As you all know," Lord Westbury continued, "a terrible thing has happened. A terrible thing indeed…really, very terrible.

Your mother and I…we…it's not something we take lightly. So terrible."

Lord Westbury had evidently exhausted what eloquence he could muster, and so his wife once more assumed the reins.

"David has died," Lady Westbury pronounced, "in awful circumstances. And we are, of course, inexpressibly sad. He was our friend. Our dear friend."

She paused, allowing the solemnity of her speech to permeate the room.

"However, having discussed matters between us"—she nodded to her husband—"we have decided that we will proceed with Christmas. Everything will go ahead as usual—today's lunch, tomorrow's shoot. It will all happen as planned."

"You—you can't be serious?" Lydia said.

"Quite serious," Lady Westbury replied calmly.

"Everything will go ahead as planned? Crackers and charades today, waving guns around and shooting pheasant tomorrow? This is a joke—Stephen's put you up to this, surely?" Lydia was aghast.

The other guests remained silent. An observer slipping into the room at this juncture would be forgiven for thinking that the guests had lost the power of speech entirely. Indeed, an observer might wonder whether the guests' collective power of hearing had been compromised, given the looks of blankness fixed on their faces.

"Pardon my bluntness," de Havilland uttered, "but continuing with Christmas…it does seem rather ill-advised, after what we have all endured this morning. Might it be better to rethink this suggestion, Lady Westbury?"

"Mr. de Havilland, I admire and am grateful for your frankness," was Lady Westbury's reply. "However, put plainly—Lord Westbury and I see no other way to…go about today."

Rosalind began to sniffle again, while her husband rolled his eyes and straightened his tie.

Stephen shrugged and said, "As long as I get fed, I really don't care what happens today."

"Mother, I must insist. 'Go about today'? How can we sit around eating turkey and playing games when David is dead?" Lydia was doggedly maintaining her stance on the matter.

Lady Westbury sighed deeply.

"It is precisely because David is dead that we must continue. Your father and I—we loved David. Dearly. And we are not ready to sit with the sadness that we feel—not just yet. Allow us this. Allow us to pretend that this is just…Christmas."

Lady Westbury sighed again. And once more, her guests were wordless: this expression of emotion was most unexpected.

Hugh spoke now. "Lady W…I can only imagine how you and Lord W must be feeling. I for one will respect your wishes and say that we all do our jolly darnedest to have as nice a day as possible."

Stephen scoffed. "Oh, a very nice day indeed…"

"I'll be plain," William Ashwell's cold voice stated. "I'm in no mood for any of this, but there are no trains back to town today and I'm damned if I'll go hungry. So be it then—I'll get on with things, but I shan't do it happily."

"As opposed to all the other things you do with a smile on your face and a spring in your step, William?" Stephen was enjoying his Christmas very much.

Lydia hadn't spoken for some moments.

"Mother, I can't pretend to like it," she began, glancing at her father, "but…well, perhaps there is no alternative. Fine."

And so it was decided that the morning's tragedy must be overcome: Christmas lunch, overcooked carrots and all, would be served as planned. Angela and Mrs. Smithson would then be sent home for their own Christmases with their families. (And Lord knows they were thankful for it: Mrs. Smithson never thought she'd live to see the day that bad came to Westbury Manor.)

Lady Westbury was suggesting that everyone use the intervening hours to rest, to reflect, to regather strength for celebrating Christmas—but was interrupted by the doorbell ringing.

"Who the devil is that?" Lord Westbury asked.

De Havilland answered that it must be the arrival that Constable Jones had told him to expect: Dr. Shepherd coming to collect the body.

12

"So that's that then," Stephen languidly drawled as he watched Dr. Shepherd's somewhat clapped-out mortuary vehicle beat a lumbering retreat along the gravel drive through the fast-melting snow. "I'll give him this—old Campbell-Scott went with a bang. Quite literally. Never thought he had the sense of humor to do it like that though." Stephen concluded his verdict by raising his glass in a solitary toast.

Lydia glared coldly at her brother. "Just when I think you've reached your apex of beastliness, you manage to surpass yourself, Stephen."

"No, I mean it, Lydia. Got more respect for the dry old codger now he's blown his brains out—on Christmas Day—than I ever did when he was lecturing us all on the importance of shrewd investments."

"What a blessing it is that Mother and Father have gone

upstairs. Were they to hear you spouting such abhorrent sentiments, they might think twice about leaving their fortune and
their good name in your despicable hands." Lydia went to pour
herself a glass of sherry.

"Well, well, well, Mother Superior stooping to our ranks, eh?"
Freddie slurred. "Rampling and Westbury, united in morning
drinking at"—he hiccoughed—"last."

"Oh, decided to pipe up, have we, Rampling?" Stephen commented, a sneer stamped on his face. "I was beginning to think
that you'd entered a period of mute mourning for Campbell-Scott.
Oh no, my mistake…a period of mourning for the money that
you were so cravenly trying to claw out of him last night."

Freddie's volubility dissolved back into sulking as he folded
his arms and sank down into the armchair. Hugh glanced
around him: he wondered what the other residents of Westbury
Manor were up to while he sat here, watching once again as
Stephen and Lydia engaged in combat and Freddie drained
every glass dry. It was a scene he had witnessed innumerable
times before now.

"Queerest thing is, though," Stephen continued, ignoring
Lydia's increasingly dagger-like glares. "Those shrewd investments
of his—he was rolling in cash, practically a millionaire, I'd wager.
Squirreled it all away in umpteen businesses over here, never mind
what he was raking in over there in Malaya with his rubber enterprise. Pig-rich, he was. So why the devil would he kill himself?"

Stephen's assessment of the situation provided yet another
shock in the day's proceedings: Hugh couldn't help but agree with
him. He was, however, not quite ready to admit to this.

"Believe it or not, brother, there are factors in a person's life just as or more important than money," Lydia answered.

Stephen scoffed. "Says Sister Lydia, paragon of spartan self-denial. 'I forsake all worldly goods! Oh, except the money I'll inherit from Uncle Davey which'll mean I don't have to marry a country squire or live off my pitiful monthly allowance anymore.'"

Under usual circumstances, Lydia would have trotted out her performance of disapproval with what might—just might—be construed as a certain degree of masochistic relish in the role of downtrodden sister to a scandalous dilettante brother. These were, however, not the usual circumstances—and her eyes betrayed no relish in Stephen's ongoing speculations.

Stephen held up his hands in mock affrontery. "I am merely pointing out some deliciously salient truths. Campbell-Scott, money coming out of his…ahem…ears, returns to England a victorious and illustrious walking monument to fortune-hunting, only to—what, shoot himself in the head? On Christmas Day? At his best friend's house? Come, come, sister, you must admit it's an outlandish yarn."

Lydia clutched her sherry glass tightly. "Stop it, Stephen. Just stop it. Before—"

"Before Mother Superior boxes you on the nose and calls you a naughty boy," hooted Freddie from his corner.

Stephen was, of course, reveling in his provocative oratory, bandying his "salient truths" around with the same nonchalance he had bandied around insults when they were children. But Hugh did have to admit it. David Campbell-Scott returning

13

Lady Westbury had known taxing social functions. She had sailed courageously through the choppy waters of dry conversation, engaged in hand-to-hand combat on the battlefield of labored discussions about the class system, nimbly dodged assailants armed with politically incendiary agendas. In short, she was a woman equipped to the teeth with strategies for avoiding or, at the very least alleviating, the strains bestowed by undesirable situations.

This Christmas Day, however, was terrain unknown. Lunch was under way and was fast becoming an unmitigated disaster.

"The fact of the matter is, the whole thing is fishy." Stephen was savoring being center stage and would relinquish his place to nobody. "I smell a rat, I detect foul play, the game is afoot, blah-de-blah-blah."

"You are making extremely heavy weather of this, Stephen, and

I do so wish you'd let sleeping dogs lie." Lady Westbury couldn't quite suppress the edge of irritation in her voice.

"Golly, we really *are* all mixing our metaphors today, aren't we," Stephen hooted.

Over turkey, de Havilland had attempted to jump-start a debate about Mosley's latest pot-stirring, but nobody seemed inclined to participate; the cheese course had seen Hugh valiantly inquiring about everyone's plans for next summer. Now, with mince pies, brandy butter, and champagne punch (a very modish cocktail amongst all the bright young things, Hugh had assured them all), the guests had succumbed to the only subject they all had on their mind: David Campbell-Scott's demise.

Lady Westbury turned to Rosalind as the discussion began, her head inclined at an angle intended to convey solicitous concern. "Dearest, how are you feeling? Has the migraine subsided?"

A snort of derision from William Ashwell.

Rosalind's pale eyes searched Lady Westbury's as she tremulously replied that she was feeling much better.

Loath to give up his place in the spotlight (or, to introduce yet another metaphor into the melee, like a particularly greedy dog with a particularly succulent bone), Stephen marched onward, determined to provoke at least one guest to storm out of the room.

"Lord knows that our dear Davey wasn't short of ne'er-do-wells who might be keen for him to meet his maker and get his comeuppance after all that Mayfair business."

"Now, Stephen, far be it from me to tell you what to do—" began de Havilland.

"Good! Glad that's something you freely acknowledge," Stephen retorted.

"But I really do feel we ought to rein in this slightly tasteless line of conversation. You're in danger of saying something you might regret." In measured and calm tones, de Havilland issued the warning that Lord Westbury wished he could formulate, but found himself quite at a loss as to where to begin.

A moment elapsed before de Havilland, to everyone's surprise, bestowed upon Stephen a most unexpected gift. Or rather, an invitation. Frowning slightly, he asked, "That said…my curiosity dictates that I ask—just what *is* this 'Mayfair business' you mention?"

"Oh, now we're skipping to a sublime treat, de Havilland, utterly delicious," Stephen gleefully exclaimed, rubbing his hands together. "Where shall we start? Perhaps, Edward, you might do us the honor?"

Edward glanced up, shooting a brief look at his sister before saying, "The *Mayfair business*, as it has come to be fondly termed, is an example of the dear departed Mr. Campbell-Scott doing what he does—excuse me, what he *did*—best."

"That being…?" asked de Havilland with a nonchalant swirl of his punch.

"That being, Mr. de Havilland, swindling the vulnerable, cheating the trusting, and leaving everyone high and dry. Everyone, that is, apart from himself." Edward spat the words out with a vitriol that made his mother bridle.

Freddie, at the introduction of something resembling scandal, perked his ears up. "Come again, Edward? Everyone told me that Campbell-Scott was what all us youths aren't—tough, heroic, *honorable*."

"Oh yes. Mr. Campbell-Scott, stalwart of the Somme, quite the convincing cover, I agree," Edward responded, ignoring his mother's injunctions to quieten down.

"Edward, can we just drop this?" Lydia implored in an uncharacteristically plaintive voice.

Stephen yawned. "Yes, come to think of it, Edward, somewhat tedious to delve into all that financial jiggery-pokery. It *is* Christmas, after all. No, let's have some far more light-hearted entertainment. Let's not bother ourselves with all those fellows wronged by him back in London—most of them crooks themselves, I might add. No, let's instead survey the veritable rogues' gallery on our doorstep. Well, around our dining table, to be more precise."

"Stephen, really, you are now being silly," Lady Westbury rebuked in unusually forceful tones.

But Stephen was not to be deterred.

"Look around you, Mother. Freddie, half cut, well, three quarters cut, last night, practically on his knees groveling for a handout from David. Miss Havisham over here clanking her chains over her lost youth, destined to remain alone and penniless until she can be alone and rich. And Little Lord Self-Righteous railing against the Establishment and the Wealthy."

Stephen was enjoying himself enormously: he couldn't remember the last time he'd had such ripe material.

"You're a blithering fool, Stephen. These delirious ravings of yours weren't funny to begin with, and they're certainly beyond a joke now," William Ashwell coldly stated. "I didn't care a fig for the man, but he's dead now and let that be the end of it."

Shrugging off their comments, Stephen turned his attentions to Hugh.

"You're pretty tight-lipped about this whole fandango, Gaveston, but I can tell you agree."

Hugh considered his response. Stephen, he knew, had no interest in whether Campbell-Scott really had killed himself or not. What motivated Stephen was, and always had been, the desire to prod and pinch, to cause discomfort and displeasure, to scandalize and terrorize. On this occasion, however, Stephen's taste for provocation was aligned somewhere with Hugh's nebulous suspicions. Suspicions that he was not quite ready to disclose.

"I…consider that Constable Jones did not, perhaps, conduct the most thorough of examinations of the scene." Hugh's words, in contrast to the callously delivered declarations of Stephen, caused a perceptible ripple of surprise around the table. Lydia stared at her friend. "However, Constable Jones is an officer of the law, and we must put our faith in the law. He made his conclusion clear, and I, for one, believe we must heed his words."

With that, Hugh gulped the last of his punch and proffered a jovial grin to the table.

"Poppycock!" Stephen blurted, to universal eye rolls. "If he killed himself, I'm…I'm Greta bloody Garbo."

"So what, you *genuinely* think someone killed him?" Heads swiveled abruptly to see Edward glowering.

"As a matter of fact, yes," Stephen confirmed, with an authority that surprised even himself. He was unused to cobbling together conclusions and then standing by them, let alone conclusions that had started life as little more than a diversion to keep himself entertained. "I do think that someone killed him."

"And what exactly are you going to do about it, Stephen?" continued his younger brother.

Now here Stephen was back on more familiar ground: incensing Edward.

"What am I going to *do* about it?" he answered. "What a question! Absolutely nothing, of course. He was a sanctimonious, pompous, not to say *hypocritical* old relic—sorry, Father, but you know he was never to my taste—and I don't care if someone killed him or not. I'm just jolly glad there's a bit of intrigue and spark around here at last."

"Typical. Of course you're going to do nothing about it. Why would you trouble yourself to do *any*thing about the world around you? Not when your pockets are lined and your glass is full." Edward, revved up by talk of the Mayfair business, was poised to launch into another of his tirades.

Lord Westbury roused himself to intervene. "Boys, please, not now, not today, not again."

"It's always not now, not today, Father. That's what's the matter with the world, with society. Nobody wants to commit, to act, to *do* anything to change things." Edward was gaining momentum.

"Eddy, stop," Lydia muttered, placing a hand on her brother's arm.

"No, I won't stop. For too long all I've done is write, use words, wait for someone else to do something. Well, not anymore. I'm sick of waiting. Sick of relying on people's decency. Because I'll tell you something—people aren't decent. David wasn't decent, not a bit of it. That death was too kind, too kind by far. I should've—"

"Enough!" Lydia erupted. "What if David was killed, hmm? And what if I did it, to get my hands on that glorious money? What if I decided to liberate myself from the albatross of dependency that's constantly hovering above my head? Seize the opportunity for a life of independent means while I could? What would you do, Stephen? Call in the police? Have me locked up?"

Puzzled stares lined the table. "Lydia, I was only—"

"Only what? Only riding on the coattails of David's death to get a few cheap laughs?"

"Darling, let's settle ourselves down." Lady Westbury was struggling to contend with the multiple fires breaking out around the dinner table today.

"No, no, Inspector Stephen over here thinks he's cracked the case. David was killed, and I killed him. How I shall bask in all my sublime riches. Good riddance, dear David—you died that I might live in the lap of luxury. Amen, blessed art thou amongst recently murdered godfathers." Lydia had, by the denouement of her speech, risen from her seat and was taking bows to the imaginary applause emanating from all corners of the table.

"Crikey, Lyds." Hugh was the first to break the stunned silence. "A star truly is born. Bette Davis had better watch her back—Lydia Westbury, starlet extraordinaire, has arrived."

Hugh's vigorous applause encouraged a rather lackluster accompaniment from the others, astonished as they were by the dramatic flourishes Lydia had delivered.

"Lady Westbury, I'd heard tell of your incomparable soirées, but nothing had quite prepared me for the roster of…entertainment." A polite chuckle came from de Havilland as he joined Hugh in attempting to lighten the mood.

"Speaking *of* entertainment, I do believe the hour is nearly upon us for a spot of charades, is it not, Lady W?" Hugh looked expectantly at his hostess.

"Quite, though perhaps this year…" Lady Westbury gestured at the somewhat sour assortment of faces around her.

"Pishposh." Hugh dismissed her unspoken reservations. "Reconvene in what, half an hour?"

With that, the guests began to disperse, leaving behind the debris of a less-than-jolly Christmas lunch, casting less-than-jolly glances at one another.

14

Hugh bundled Lydia into the library.

"What on *earth* was that?" he demanded.

"You—you heard," came Lydia's stumbling reply. "Maybe… Maybe I—I killed him. Yes, maybe I really did kill David."

Hugh gripped his friend firmly by the shoulders. "Lyds. Look at me."

Although Hugh was just shy of his thirty-fourth birthday, Lydia had never seen him being anything but boyish and charming and jocular. Now, however, he gave the appearance of a responsible adult, a man of deliberation and determination.

"I wanted his money, so I killed him. Simple as that," she stuttered. "Surprised myself, really, but there we go. Desperate times, desperate measures and all that."

Hugh searched her eyes and found them revealing what he knew to be true: she was a terrible liar.

"Lydia Westbury, I've known you since we were children. You are stubborn, you are high-minded, you are dazzlingly brilliant, you are prone to fits of frustration. But you are not a killer."

A pause. A defeated sigh.

"Hugh Gaveston, you are infuriating. You are kind, you are generous, you are stupendously clever, and you are maddeningly right. About everything."

A pause. A relieved sigh.

"Jeepers creepers, you scared me, you awful thing, you!" Hugh wrapped his friend in a tight embrace. "Now. Explain. Everything."

Lydia checked that the door was firmly shut before unburdening herself.

"I think…I fear…I'm almost certain…I think Eddy did it. I think Eddy killed David."

"What? But why? I mean, why would he do that? And why do you think that? Oh, Lyds!"

Lydia went on to explain that last night, Christmas Eve, when they'd all gone to bed, she had intended to take her sleeping draught, but she'd forgotten.

"I was reading in bed, well, rereading in bed—*Orlando* always brings me solace when sleep abandons me—and I heard the floorboards on the landing. There's that one that always creaks— blasted thing, Mother and Father refuse to fix it."

Hugh knew that floorboard well: the cause of its creakiness was, officially, Edward smashing his train set on it during a tantrum. The unofficial—and accurate—version of events was *Stephen* smashing Edward's train set on it during a tantrum. Of course,

Stephen's ability to weave deceit with unerring confidence—even at the age of seven—meant that the accurate version had never been accepted by Lord and Lady Westbury.

"Anyway, I thought it was Father. There are times when he gets…confused in the night, goes walkabout," Lydia continued. "So I got up, just to check on him."

Hugh listened as Lydia went on to explain how, upon opening her door, she had found the landing empty. No Lord Westbury to be seen.

"I thought I must've imagined it, so I was going to get back into bed, but I heard something else—someone being shushed. Naturally, being a nosy parker"—here a nod of assent from Hugh—"I couldn't help but go to see who it was. I peeped out, and there was a figure. It was Edward, at the corner by the top of the stairs. He was whispering, whispering something I couldn't quite make out, but it sounded…"

"Go on."

"Well, it sounded like he said, 'The time for talking is over.'"

"And that's all you heard?"

"Yes, that's all I heard."

"A rather gnomic utterance for the wee small hours. 'The time for talking is over.' What does that mean? Who was Edward saying it to?"

"Don't you see, Hugh? It was a threat. Or a promise, more like, to David. And what Eddy was boring on about at dinner— 'Nobody wants to commit, to act, to do anything to change things.' It smacks of some misguided interpretation of deeds not words. Pankhurst would be rolling in her grave."

Lydia had paced to the poetry and was thrumming her fingers against the spine of *Paradise Lost*.

Hugh frowned. "Lyds, I rather think you're jumping the gun—pardon the expression—to go from one riddling whisper, in the middle of the night, after all parties, you included, had availed of sherry and port and wine…Well, to go from *that* to the suspicion that Eddy *murdered* David."

Lydia fixed him with one of her renowned glares; a glare which told any unfortunate recipient that they were in danger of getting on her wrong side.

"Give me some credit. It's not *just* that. It's that in conjunction with the fact that Eddy's always hated him, always. Has it in his head that David's wicked, that we're all oblivious to some nefarious hidden depths he conceals—concealed. It's all because of that blasted hoo-ha ten bloody years ago. I had thought—hoped—that David's departure to Malaya would see the back of Eddy's senseless vendetta. But it just seems to have made it worse," Lydia explained—not without reason, Hugh had to concede.

Hugh ruminated. Eddy *had* been uncharacteristically sprightly at breakfast this morning. As though Zeus had plucked the load from Atlas's shoulders. Edward's palpable relief when he'd appeared in the dining room was like nothing more than a man unburdened, a man purged of some immense strain. On the other hand, of course, would such levity be the primary characteristic of a man who has just committed murder and knows that his victim's body is sure to be discovered before too long? Hugh was on the point of airing this counterargument to Lydia when she cut in.

"I think—I think he did it."

"We don't know that *anyone* aside from David did it—" he attempted to contend but was stopped short by Lydia's plain opprobrium.

"Hugh, if even *Stephen* has caught the whiff of a rat, we ought to be downright unconscious, knocked out by smell."

"Fine, fine. For the sake of argument, and argument alone." Hugh, although certainly alert to a puzzling element, a discomfiting element, of the day's occurrences, was also alert to his friend's state of nervous agitation. As such, he had decided that presenting her with a cool, dispassionate opponent was far the better option than immediately becoming an eager colluder in her theories. "Let's suppose that David *was* killed. And let's suppose that Eddy *did* do it. Mark that these are two rather heady suppositions already, having been formed based on scant to nonexistent evidence. That doesn't explain one thing. Why did you just put on that show in the dining room?"

"Oh Hugh, you can be an idiot sometimes. Stephen was goading him mercilessly. Eddy was on the point of saying something stupid—I know my brother. And I couldn't let him do that. I *can't* let him do that. He's my little brother. I have to protect him," she explained.

"Lyds, sorry to repeat myself…but I do rather feel that you're making several large—gargantuan—leaps at this point," Hugh countered, pacing toward the biology section of the library. "Firstly, as I said, we don't know that David *was* killed. Secondly, again, as I've said, if he was, we don't know it was Edward. In fact, we don't even know he was threatening David on the landing last night…he could've been saying that to…well, to your mother, about…bringing your father to Dr. Shepherd, for instance."

Lydia raised her eyebrows. "*Now* who's making several rather large leaps?"

Hugh sighed. "The point is that, to be frank, your theory is somewhat flimsy. It would be shredded to pieces if any lawman got within—"

"Flimsy? *Flimsy?* Well, excuse me for not couching it in more robust terms for your law-men. You see, us women, we do enjoy flimsiness and listening to our waters, and in fact why don't I go and put a hex on you all and while I'm at it make an offering to Mother Circe?" Lydia, impassioned now not only by the specific matter in question (her godfather's potential murder at the hand of her brother) but also by her favorite topic in general (the belittling of womankind at the hand of mankind), was, thus, unstoppable.

"Yes, I know, down with silly women, go and have a lie-down before hysteria strikes, et cetera et cetera," Hugh quipped. "But listen, this is serious—"

"Oh, thank you, Mr. Sensible Important Wise *Man*. Thank you for clarifying that this is *serious*."

Hugh considered his options. Lydia was evidently hell-bent on discovering whether Eddy was involved in David's death, and any attempt to derail her would be both futile and counterproductive. For to attempt to derail Lydia Westbury was, in his ample experience, to aggravate her into digging her heels in even more obstinately. No, dissuading her from this would not do. Additionally, Hugh reflected, he was of the mind that there was something amiss with the death. Something rather drastically amiss. And to unleash Lydia upon the situation unsupervised would be disastrous: if there *were* a wrongdoer among them, Lydia's aversion to tact certainly would yield no fruits. No, uncovering the truth—whatever that truth might be—required a thorough and methodical touch. Hugh's specialty.

Lydia had exhausted her tirade against condescension and was focused afresh on the particulars of their circumstance.

"In conclusion, Hugh, I don't give two figs as to whether you believe me or not about this being queer. If Eddy's gotten himself into trouble, I need to do something about it." And so adamant was she that she nearly stamped her foot at this.

Hugh threw his hands in the air in a gesture of surrender.

"Right-o, but before you go charging in all guns blazing deciding to martyr yourself, hadn't we better ascertain whether Eddy *does* have blood on his hands? If he doesn't, your Joan of Arc act will be a little premature," he reasoned.

"So what are you proposing?" Her curiosity was piqued by the latest turn in Hugh's argument.

"I'm proposing that I do a little rummaging around. A little snooping. A little…sleuthing into Eddy's movements last night."

"*You* do a little rummaging around? *You* do a little snooping? Why not me? Typical, that is, bloody—"

Hugh held firm. "Lydia. Remember when you thought someone had stolen your ted? The one you'd had an embarrassingly long time, the one with the fallen-off eyes and the bloodstained arm from when my nose had bled all over it?"

She nodded mulishly, knowing where Hugh was leading with this digression.

"And do you remember your strategy for uncovering the thief?

A jolly lot of storming around, shouting, accusations being flung right, left, and center?"

Another nod.

"You've come a long way since then, but I fear that your diplomacy isn't quite equal to this task. Bulls in china shops are not known for their ability to entice secrets out into the open."

"I resent the analogy but, reluctantly, I agree. Fine," she relented.

"You promise you won't go blundering in? I'll do a far neater job with some well-timed wheedling than you would, I promise," Hugh reassured.

An exasperated *ugh* was emitted, followed by, "All right, no need to make such heavy weather of my apparent inability to sweet-talk anyone into anything. Just promise me one more thing—the second, I mean the *second*, you discover anything at all, you'll tell me?"

Hugh hesitated, but nodded.

"If Eddy has done something stupid, I want to be able to help him," she said.

"If Eddy has done something stupid, Lydia…we'll need the police," Hugh replied.

The silent stare from his friend gave rise to a quizzical glance in him.

"That's a bridge we can cross when we come to it, Hugh," she stated, replacing the Milton brusquely in the shelf. "Right, nearly charades time!"

As she strode out of the library, Hugh found himself deciding that perhaps sharing any discoveries with Lydia ought to be deferred until he himself had landed on a plan of action.

15

The December sun had concluded its half-hearted skirmish against the December clouds and, in a not unexpected turn of events, had found itself cowering in ignominious defeat. As the clock struck three, the scant light began to beat a weary retreat, allowing a cold twilight to take its place. Any guests ascending the stairs might be tempted to peer through the window to gaze upon the snow that carpeted the grounds. Of course, any such guests would find their eye drawn naturally, inexorably, to the blot upon the scene. A blot nearly indistinguishable from the encroaching shadows, were it not for the knowledge of what had caused this indelible stain.

The only guest, however, ascending the stairs at that moment was one determined to make the most of the twenty minutes or so remaining until the agreed charades assembly. A guest whose path brooked no meandering or dillydallying. A guest whose intent required a lightness of gait and swiftness of step designed to attract no unwanted attention.

So it was that Hugh Gaveston soundlessly and speedily made his way upstairs, leaving the other guests to mill around in the library or the billiards room. His destination was a room that should, by rights, have been visited by Constable Jones that morning: David Campbell-Scott's bedroom.

The family bedrooms and guests' chambers were all located on the same floor, branching off a wide corridor decorated with framed still-life drawings and shelves of books not quite pristine enough to be housed in the library. Hugh made his way past his own room, past Lydia's, stopped to check that the Ashwells weren't occupying theirs (a brief ear to the door ascertained that the room was empty) and, glimpsing this way and that, turned the handle, wincing, to let himself into David's room.

Arranged in the same unfussy homely manner as the other guest rooms (except his own, for Hugh had always insisted on sleeping in the Blue Room, so called because he and Lydia had daubed one wall with their blue watercolors during a particularly boring summer holiday some years hence), the room seemed to watch Hugh as he stepped into it. The handsome, solidly built bed sat to his right, the bedcover inexpertly turned in—David had been a bachelor, after all, so his turning-in prowess was not to be judged too harshly. To the left, a bureau, atop which sat a vase of dried hops. A handful of pennies were strewn around the vase and a leather-bound notebook.

The window overlooked the herb garden to the rear of the house, populated now by dormant sage and mint plants, encrusted with jewel-like snowflakes that glinted in the bluish haze of the twilight. Hugh startled himself out of his poetic reverie—no time to gaze upon the ethereal botany, with clues to be hounded down.

He opened the wardrobe door—spectral shirts and suit jackets hung there, garments divested of their owner forevermore. Another reverie from which Hugh had to extricate himself. His poetic nature really did get the better of him from time to time.

Frowning, he retraced his steps to the leather-bound notebook: surely it would contain a clue that might lead to his uncovering unequivocal evidence of some wrongdoing? Flicking through it, however, Hugh was bombarded with equations, figures, profit-margin extrapolations, and complex calculations. Reams and reams of numbers. Endlessly mind-numbing stuff. How very disappointing, he thought. No cryptic allusions to enemies; no illicit correspondence betraying an ignoble foible; not even a botched calculation, as far as Hugh could decipher. In his detective stories, notebooks belonging to the recently deceased invariably offered endless value to the inspecting eye. Alas, alack: he was fast realizing that his stories were but trifling frippery.

Surveying the room again, committing to memory the exact position of every item (details that might be crucial at some later point), Hugh's scrutiny fell upon the fireplace. Expired kindling littered the grate, but was there something nestled amongst the debris?

He checked his watch—still ten minutes before he was expected downstairs for charades—and, using the utmost care, lifted an almost-disintegrated piece of paper from the ashes.

"Hello, what do we have here?" he whispered to his finding. "What might you be?"

What indeed. Placing the paper on the bureau, Hugh turned his attention back to the grate. Any further remnants? Why, yes—two in fact.

Carefully laying them next to the first piece, Hugh read the scraps, eyes widening:

> *The tru*
>> *oid any nasty surprises, mee*
>>> *oney, I might be forced to reveal your little se*

"Bingo," he murmured. "You little beauty, you. 'Nasty surprises,' 'forced to reveal'…I detect a spot of blackmail. Now the question is—what were you hiding, Mr. Campbell-Scott?"

His soliloquy was interrupted by a barely perceptible tread outside the bedroom door: another snooper interested in Campbell-Scott's chambers? Hugh's instincts dictated that, at this crucial juncture in his investigations (he had already determined to name them as such), to be found in the dead man's bedroom would be an error. Scooping the scraps of paper into his jacket pocket, he leaped with surprising agility through the open wardrobe doors, nimbly shutting them behind him.

Crouched in the wardrobe, he strained to hear any clues as to who was now in the bedroom. A clink of ice in a glass would reveal Freddie Rampling; a bewildered sigh, Lord Westbury; a self-satisfied snigger, Stephen. What he heard, however, was the insipid and watery sniffling of Rosalind Ashwell.

Hugh adjusted his position so that his eyes were aligned with the crack in the wardrobe doors. Sure enough, there she was, perched on the edge of the bed.

"Oh, David," came a whimpering from the room. "What have you done? What have you done?"

She hung her head before producing the handkerchief that had been her constant prop all day.

"All these years"—she sniffed—"for this?"

A disconsolate sigh. Rosalind gathered herself, glimpsed around the room and then left it, walking with the solemnity of a pallbearer.

Stepping noiselessly out of the wardrobe, Hugh revolved the perplexities in his mind: Rosalind Ashwell, crying in the bedroom of a dead man she'd met less than twenty-four hours before? Fragments of a letter containing malicious sentiments, almost indubitably issuing threats to Campbell-Scott?

Christmas Day was growing more and more baffling by the moment. Further delving was required, and the perfect stage was set for such delving: the notoriously heated Westbury charades tournament.

16

"Tell me, Mr. Rampling, what exactly is it that you *do* with your time?" William Ashwell's words wriggled out of his thin lips with all the venom and calculation of baby snakes.

Stephen scoffed, contributing, "Freddie Rampling, sole proprietor of the Rampling fortune and all the prestige that carries, can oftentimes be found in dingy dog-tracks, where he enjoys nothing more than throwing his money away on mongrels and perpetuating his record-breaking losing streak. Failing that, Mr. Rampling also enjoys humiliating himself by begging for cash from family friends on Christmas Eve."

Freddie, demonstrating his habitual dedication to the role of inveterate inebriate, let out a hoarse honking, calling to mind a sozzled goose.

"That's right"—*hic*—"Stephen"—*hic*, he began falteringly. "Laugh while you can. You're just jealous."

"I shan't even dignify that with a response, you poor, *poor* deluded boy," Stephen replied.

William Ashwell shook his head in revulsion at Rampling, at Stephen, at the whole lot of them. He was a man of propriety, and here he was being enmired in impropriety of the most shameless variety. Even Rosalind couldn't be relied upon. Ever since she had set foot in this blasted house, she had come over all queer. It would be embarrassing were it not for the fact that he didn't care two pins what these people thought of him. No, it was his Rosalind who needed sheltering; her reputation that needed preserving. If only she hadn't—

Hugh galloped into the billiards room, ebulliently greeting the men as though they were long-lost compatriots separated by decades, reunited here in brotherhood. William Ashwell was suspicious of this bounder. Never trust a man who smiles too much, that's what his father had taught him. What's more, William Ashwell was a man of instinct, and his instinct had always told him that there was more to this Gaveston chap than met the eye. At least with that Rampling boy and the Westburys one knew exactly what one was getting—but Gaveston was an entirely different proposition. He and de Havilland, both fellows one ought to watch one's words around.

"Here you all are! The ladies are waiting in the drawing room—shall we join them?" Hugh cheerfully started to rally the men.

Stephen gulped down the last of his whisky, while Freddie hauled himself up from his chair, and William Ashwell, meanwhile, seemed to be drawing upon his mental strength before rejoining the group.

"Chaps—Eddy, Mr. de Havilland, coming?"

Edward and de Havilland were on the far side of the billiards table, the former clutching his billiards cue as though he were a drowning man grasping a life-ring, the latter using his to lean on in the manner of a Victorian dandy. Evidently, the two had been engrossed in conversation; Hugh had to beckon them a second time before they concluded.

"What were you two bellyaching about over there? Looked delightfully hush-hush!" Stephen yelled at a needlessly high volume.

Continuing to lean slightly on his cue as he ambled over, de Havilland cleared his throat and placed a hand on Hugh's shoulder.

"Gammy leg, de Havilland?" Hugh inquired, having realized that the cue was not so much a Dickensian prop, but almost a crutch. Curious, Hugh thought to himself, that he had singularly failed to notice this before now. Whatever next, neglecting to spot that Lydia was sporting a prosthetic nose?

"Comes and goes, comes and goes. Souvenir from the front," de Havilland answered, patting his thigh and straightening out his leg. "In any case, let's move to the drawing room, Mr. Gaveston. Before we do, however, might I propose that we collectively strive to maintain levity this evening? Failing that, civility at the very least." His stentorian tones succeeded in emitting both warm sincerity and a distinct sense of unyielding authority.

Stephen issued a ferrety grin, directing de Havilland's attention to the wobbling Freddie Rampling. "Look around you, Mr. de Havilland. We are the very image of civility and levity."

"Quite so, Stephen, quite so. I must ask you, in particular, to, shall we say, curb your insistence on distasteful speculations about the late Mr. Campbell-Scott. It is a subject very clearly— and very understandably—upsetting for many here today, not least your own parents."

Stephen startled the men by stamping his foot on the floor with unexpected force. "Yussuh!" Saluting de Havilland and standing rigidly upright, he transformed his face into one of grave severity. "Lead the charge, captain. Once more unto the breech we go, over the top, allezoop, *dulce et decorum est pro de Havilland mori*."

"How very droll, Stephen," Edward muttered. "De Havilland is speaking sense. We've all had quite enough of your nonsense, so let's just uphold the pretense of making it through the rest of the day. And what's more, you all kowtowed to Mother on it this morning—didn't hear you piping up then, Stephen."

"Censorship! Censorship! I'm having my fundamental right to speech stripped from me, on *Christmas Day* no less!" Stephen wailed, quaking his knees together.

William Ashwell clapped a hand on his shoulder, with no artifice of avuncularity. "Stephen, the histrionics have become insufferable. I have no wish to be here, any more than you do, nor have I any desire to know whether Campbell-Scott shot himself or was shot by someone else. I simply want to endure this evening with as little disturbance as possible, wake up and endure this infernal Boxing Day shoot tomorrow, then catch our train on the twenty-seventh, leaving this forsaken place behind us. Will you please make this process less excruciating for me by buttoning your mouth?"

"Oh my, Mr. Ashwell, seeing as you asked so nicely!" Stephen giggled and removed William Ashwell's hand from his shoulder. "I really don't see why everyone's asking me to behave myself. Have we forgotten that we're in the presence of Master Rampling?"

A nod toward Freddie revealed that the wobbling had stopped, to be replaced with a curiously soothing swaying on the spot.

"I'd be vigilant if I were you, Mr. Ashwell, Mr. de Havilland. Once old Rampling gets the whiff of money, he's on the scent like a bloodhound. And look what happened to the last old bugger he tried to squeeze for a bob or two…"

"You're a bastard, Stephen."

To the shock (and perhaps awe) of the men, Freddie's unslurred speech was laden with vitriol and heavy with intent.

"A sneaky, self-serving, smug bastard."

"I do believe, Freddie, that's the most coherent sentence I've heard you string together in years," Stephen responded. "And deploying some rather effective alliteration too. Bravo."

"One day you'll know what it's like, know how it feels. And when that happens, I hope people laugh at you too. And I hope nobody lifts a finger to help you. Then you'll see what it drives you to. What it *reduces* you to." Freddie spoke slowly, enunciating every word as if at pains to carve each one out of the thick air that hung between him and the others.

"Freddie," Hugh began gently, "let's not, eh, old chap? Think of Lady W. De Havilland's policy of levity. Civility is tailor-made for her. Please?"

Freddie relented and grunted some reply (evidently his revealingly coherent soliloquy had exhausted his supplies of eloquence), allowing Hugh to shepherd him out of the billiards room.

Once Freddie was safely on his way, Hugh turned to Edward, who was shuffling, hands stuffed in his pockets, along the corridor.

"Keep meaning to ask, Eddy—what's the name of that fellow you mentioned the other week in town? The writer chap, making noise about the underclasses and whatnot."

Edward's face lightened—the very thought of a fellow scribe dedicated to scraping away the facade of societal mores always chased off some of his gloom. "George Orwell, that's him."

"Oh, that's right. I've a terrible brain for names." Hugh tapped his head to demonstrate. "Yawning great chasms in there where people's names ought to go, but instead I find my cranium populated almost exclusively by the names of my specimens. Give me a George and I'll give you a *Gyrinophilus porphyriticus*. Best scribble it down for me."

Edward took the scrap of paper Hugh produced from his pocket and used his own fountain pen (which he kept in his trousers at all times: a writer never knows when duty might call), and jotted down the name.

"Many thanks, Eddy," Hugh beamed. "This'll be terribly helpful. More helpful than you know."

17

Like one staggering across a desert, parched and ravenous, so Hugh approached the drawing room, seeking a respite from the uncertainty that beleaguered him. And, as an explorer of arid lands might find himself fortunate enough to stumble upon an oasis of cooling water and soothing shade, so too Hugh Gaveston stumbled into the room and was met with a scene that elicited quiet delight.

Lydia was embroiled in a board game with Rosalind, who seemed to be making a steady recovery from her earlier state of discomposure, while Lady Westbury was chattering away in near gaiety.

The specter of the morning's discovery and subsequent… episodes…seemed to have retreated. Or so it seemed to Hugh upon first glimpse.

Let us, however, pause for a second glimpse. A glimpse that

would allow a beady-eyed spectator to be reminded that those staggering across the desert almost invariably stumble upon not an oasis but a mirage. Further scrutiny of the board would lead to the discovery of one unaccountable strategic mistake from Lydia (to point it out would be a mortification to her), and the sight of Rosalind—a veteran at the game—struggling to execute the simplest of moves. Our observer's gaze might stray to the sherry glass beside Rosalind which, were it to be judged by the smudges around its rim, could be said to have been very well used over the course of this interlude.

Lady Westbury clapped her hands together. "Oh splendid! Are we all here?"

Lydia glanced up and snorted. "Deigned to join the little ladies, have we? Quite finished our port and pomp and terribly important discussions?"

"It's for your own safety, Lyds," Hugh began slyly, an arch grin appearing on his face. "Was reading just the other day about a terrible case in Kensington, I believe it was. A poor young woman by the name of Miss Walker, if I recall, insisted on joining in a conversation with some menfolk about politics. Well, all ended in catastrophe of course—poor Miss Walker's feeble female constitution was unable to withstand the force of the men's intellectual discourse, and she fell into a trance of some sort. Then died."

Hugh's elaborate (and wholly improvised) anecdote of course prompted an expertly aimed cushion to be thrown in his direction. Lydia's powerful bowling arm was only ever called upon under two circumstances: the summer rounders game (she was also a dab hand with the bat, the 1926 thwack that resulted in

Stephen's bloody nose being an event of Westbury family legend), and whenever Hugh joked about the feeble female constitution.

Lady Westbury had always enjoyed every element of Christmas Day—the sibling squabbles, Hugh's easy charm, her husband's unabashed sentimentality at this time of the year, even Freddie's efforts (imperceptible to all but her) to be less…Freddie—but charades was the component she savored the most. It was the one occasion during which her three children discarded their grudges and disagreements; or rather, channeled the energy usually reserved for these grudges and disagreements into the unifying purpose of vanquishing each other in the game.

Naturally, she had questioned the propriety of indulging in (and, one could argue, enforcing) this frivolity after the events of the morning. Lady Westbury knew very well that proceeding with charades could be condemned as being gauche, macabre, callous, but the alternative—her guests morosely festering in corners—was too bleak to consider. And so it was that she had decided that yes, charades would go ahead, and yes, they would all enjoy it the best they could. A perfect distraction.

The question of teams was raised then resolved: the Westburys favored small teams, to ensure that no two siblings were faced with the dreaded prospect of working together. Lydia had chosen de Havilland, Stephen was lumbered with Freddie, Edward and William Ashwell made for an unhappy pairing, and Lady Westbury had thought it wise to remain with her husband, all the better to assuage any befuddlement that might occur during the game. Hugh had selected Rosalind, with his eyes fixed decidedly on a certain prize.

The area in front of the fireplace was cleared, the chairs haphazardly arranged into what one might generously describe as a circle—were a circle to be punctuated by a sofa, a footstool, and two small tables. Hugh ensured that he situated the chairs for himself and Rosalind as far from the stage as possible; for what he intended, relative seclusion was required. Diversions were a valuable investigative tool, and what better diversion than the spectacle of ill-judged mime.

The first round began.

As Edward took to the stage and all eyes were upon his surprisingly convincing rendition of an ape, Hugh turned to his teammate.

"Quite a brute of a migraine that smote you earlier, Rosalind—so glad that you're feeling more chipper now," he said gently.

A hesitation, a brief darting of the eyes in the direction of her husband across the room. "Yes, quite, quite horrendous. They afflict me only very occasionally. Such terrible timing."

"Hmm, yes, though I suppose a day like this must be ripe for migraines getting their claws into one," Hugh replied. Softly, softly, he thought. Softly, softly.

"Yes, Christmas indulgence is something of a catalyst." Rosalind forced a meek smile, gestured toward her sherry glass, and then fixed her eyes back on the charades game. Hugh was quite accustomed to evasion: it had taken ages to draw out any tidbits from Lydia about her secretarial course.

"Well, Christmas comes every year. One becomes used to it, I suppose! A stranger found dead outside one's window—that's something I hope none of us shall become used to."

Rosalind paused, as if Hugh was informing her of the discovery for the very first time. She blinked rapidly, rearranged her left hand on her lap while rotating the neck of the glass with her right hand. Hugh sensed that no utterance was forthcoming, so pressed on.

"It's the Westburys I feel sorry for—the people left behind, as they say. Aside from them, I don't think he had anyone else. Lydia paints him as quite a solitary soul." Hugh had started down this track, so he was jolly well going to finish. "I get the impression, reading between the lines, that he was something of a miser. Scrooge-like, really. No time for anything but money-making, by all accounts. Lord W blind to it, of course, always sees the best in—"

Charades was becoming heated: Stephen was very loudly berating Freddie for failing to decipher his—to his own mind—excellent depiction of the Spanish Inquisition. De Havilland and Lydia were about to take their round; Hugh would have to hurry if his objective were to be achieved. Stephen was still grumbling vociferously, and Bruno had made a barking reappearance. Short of cornering Rosalind in a stairwell—which really would be most unsavory—this was the closest to a quiet moment alone with her that Hugh could hope for.

"Anyway, as I was saying—David sounds like a bit of a rogue, all things told." Hugh was delivering his line in what he hoped was a disarmingly jaunty tone.

"Your guess is as good as mine, Hugh—really couldn't speak to the man's character," Rosalind replied, her voice unmistakably brittle now, her eyes refusing to meet his.

Hugh took a moment. His approach was deficient: Rosalind

was not going to budge, clearly. Which was perhaps fortunate, he reflected, given that the charades drama was subsiding slightly, not quite the attention-grabbing spectacle it had been initially.

He sighed. Cornering in a dark stairwell it would have to be, then. Perhaps after the game? No, that would risk being discovered. Rosalind was partial to a glass of warm milk before bed; Hugh could use that as his opportunity for a second bite of the cherry.

While Hugh was considering his next move, however, Rosalind had evidently been contemplating her own countermove. In a steady voice at odds with her recent countenance, she stated, "David wasn't like that, you know. Not really, not deep down. He had such generosity, he cared for people, he wanted so many things—too many things. But he was never mean. Never cruel, not when I…"

Her words came tumbling out, a cascade that had been unplugged and wouldn't stop. Not for the first time that day, Hugh was agog.

"Things could have been so different, so very different, but David…he…"

Rosalind stopped. She realized that no longer was Lydia in front of the fireplace pretending to be Frankenstein's monster. No longer was everyone focused on outplaying each other. Instead, all eyes were fixed on her.

Her husband closed his eyes and brought a hand to his face, rubbing his chin wearily.

"There we have it, Rosalind, there we have it," he said. "Who wants to go next? The next round is 'the cat's out of the bag.'"

Lady Westbury looked baffled; Lord Westbury was still asleep, but Stephen nudged him.

"Father," he stage-whispered. "You're going to want to hear this—sounds supremely juicy."

Hugh cast around the room: this had not been his intention, not his intention at all. A discreet conversation while everyone else was diverted, that was his plan. Sherlock Holmes would never have committed this elementary error in judgment.

"What are you talking about, Rosalind?" Lady Westbury asked, an expression of puzzled amusement on her face. "I fear I may be exposing myself as inexcusably dense, but…I was under the impression that you and David made each other's acquaintance yesterday?"

Rosalind's lip quivered. The cavalcade of emotions scrambling through her mind were almost visible to the onlookers: panic, confusion, sadness. The latter settled on her face, as tears sprang to her eyes.

"Oh, Liv. I'm so sorry. Deceiving you was the last thing I wanted to do."

"*Deceiving* me?" Lady Westbury could not conceive of anyone—let alone her oldest friend—intending to deceive her.

William Ashwell let out a noise, somewhere between a scoff and a snort. "Heaven forfend you deceive dear Olivia Westbury. No, that wouldn't do, would it, Rosalind?"

The bitterness in his voice caused Lydia to wince. "Speak wisely, Mr. Ashwell. Your tone is veering perilously close to the unacceptable."

Hugh glanced at her; that protective spirit was part of her strength of character. Though it could yet prove her downfall.

Rosalind was crumpling and uncrumpling the handkerchief in her hands. Then she discarded it, as if manifest in it was the untruth she had been burdened with.

"There's no use hiding any longer," she began tentatively. "I—I didn't know how to tell you, Liv. I was knocked for six, truly."

Stephen's attempts at waking his father had finally succeeded, as Lord Westbury snuffled back into animation just in time to hear Rosalind unfold her story in earnest.

"Yesterday, when you introduced me to David...I—well—we...already knew each other."

Hugh had to exercise every ounce of self-restraint to not burst out with a triumphant "aha!" He had perceived some charge between the two, some current of recognition. He'd make Scotland Yard yet.

Rosalind continued, explaining that years and years ago, back in the mists of time when she was younger, so much very younger, there had been...a suitor. A suitor who had captivated her youthful heart, promised her the world, swept her off her feet and showed her the possibilities of life, who had—

"Rosalind, please confine yourself to the facts. This florid extravagance is unnecessary and, quite frankly, infuriating." Her husband's words barely inched out of his mouth, so clenched was his jaw.

Stephen took the opportunity to steal some of the spotlight. "Hmmmm, who on earth could this mystery suitor be?" he said, shrugging his shoulders in mock perplexity.

"David Campbell-Scott was my first love," Rosalind continued. "We were...engaged. To be married."

Lady Westbury's face expressed more shock now than it had when David's body had been discovered. Spluttering, she managed to blurt, "You and David were *engaged*? There must be some mistake. Why was I unaware of this? You told me nothing of this, Rosalind…"

"Lydia was just four years old, Stephen still little more than a babe in arms… There was so much for you to think about, and this, well, this was my adventure, my secret adventure. David wanted it that way. I didn't know why, not at the time. I was so naive, I had barely spoken to a man without a chaperone. And here was this worldly man, this gallant man who was so alive, so vibrant. Wanting to marry me, Rosalind Marsh from Leatherhead."

William Ashwell abruptly stood up, began pacing to the fireplace.

"William, I'm sorry, you know I am. But I never lied to you. Not once."

The bitterness in his voice was even more acute now. "No. Never have you tried to hide the truth from me. I have always been aware, painfully, torturously aware of my place—second fiddle to the coward who broke your heart and ran away."

Stephen Westbury let out an "oh my" while his parents exchanged bewildered stares. Hugh had never witnessed Lady Westbury receiving news with such alarm; indeed, "rattled" would never have been an adjective ascribed to her, but evidently today was hell-bent on flinging precedent unceremoniously out of the window. Even Edward appeared riveted by the unfolding tale. De Havilland had put on his glasses and was leaning forward in his seat, one hand on his knee. Hugh had the distinct impression of sitting in the stalls at the Haymarket Theatre.

"He did. He did break my heart. He did run away. He made me so many promises, then left, without having the decency to say good-bye to me," Rosalind concurred with her husband. "But it is not a life without David Campbell-Scott that I regret, William. How many times must I tell you that?"

"Right, that's quite enough now, Rosalind, you've given them all the Christmas pantomime of the season. It's plain who's been cast as the villain, certainly not the debonair Mr. Campbell-Scott. Well, let me tell you, he wasn't half the man you all think he is. He was a selfish, cold-hearted cad, and I for one am—" Here William Ashwell cut himself off, leaving the remainder of the sentence dangling in mid-air.

Lord Westbury stood, approached him, and gently said, "I think that'll do."

"Oh, that will *more* than do, William! Bravissimo to both of you!" Stephen blew kisses to each in turn. "I'd throw some roses at you, but unfortunately I used them all up at the matinee at the Palladium last Saturday."

Rosalind had reclaimed her handkerchief and was clutching it to her breast, taking deep breaths. Hugh made to say something, he didn't know quite what, but she gestured for him to stop. Lady Westbury came and laid her hand on Hugh's shoulder, and he stood to allow her to comfort her friend.

"Blimey, Hugh, you really opened the floodgates there," Lydia whispered.

Hugh glanced awkwardly back at Rosalind. "That was

decidedly not how I had envisaged that conversation, Lyds. Poor Rosalind, in front of everyone…"

Lydia pulled him over to the sherry decanter on the round table by the lamp. "Did you see the jealousy in William, the rage? If he's like that today, one can only imagine his reaction yesterday…"

"That hadn't escaped me."

"That means he might have…it might have been—"

"There you go, jumping the gun—pardon the turn of phrase—again. Just because David was Rosalind's first love and now, decades later, he reappears replete with a mountain of wealth and a swashbuckling reputation, and is reunited with a woman who has, one might argue, settled for a rather different sort of life… Well, that doesn't mean to say that William *killed* David."

Hugh frowned and reflected on the picture he had so vividly painted. "Fine, I take your point…when couched in such melodramatic terms, it is a rather convincing story. In fact, I may have just convinced myself of William's guilt. But listen here, there's still no evidence of anything—anything at all."

Lydia's infamous eye-roll made another appearance, her whispering becoming less hushed all the while. "Hugh, you're supposed to be finding out whether I need to worry about my baby brother being a murderer. So far, zippo, *nada*, *niente*. I don't know why I'm not just doing this myself…"

A glimmer of a grin from Hugh. "Because, darling Lydia, you are far too prickly and combative to coax anyone into unspooling even the mildest and most anodyne of secrets. Thus far too prickly and combative to tend to the delicate business of finding a killer."

Lydia couldn't help but agree. Fine, she would leave him to it, but he'd better—

De Havilland, replacing his glasses in his pocket, strolled over to their spot in the corner. "Well, quite the series of spectacles we're being treated to today. What's your take on events?" Nodding at both Hugh and Lydia, he was clearly, in true parliamentary style, directing his question into the ether, waiting to see which party was more eager to snap it up.

"My take? Well, Mr. de Havilland," Lydia coolly asserted, "my take is that a man was found dead in my garden on Christmas morning, and now my family and our closest friends are being dragged through one of the outer circles of hell."

And not for the first time, Hugh was grateful for Lydia's gladiatorial approach to most aspects of life. For he couldn't help but notice that de Havilland had been looking expectantly at him, waiting—or hoping—to hear his theory about the various incidents.

18

The tension of the Ashwell incident having abated somewhat, the subsequent hours had passed unremarkably enough. Prudently, the party had come to an unspoken agreement neither to partake in any further organized divertissements, nor to mention any of the day's events.

Any onlooker would see the ten inhabitants of the room (eleven, if one includes its canine denizen, who was still snuffling in some doggy dream at the feet of Lord Westbury) engaged in inoffensive conversation. Sherry was being sipped at a moderate pace and cheese was being nibbled politely (for Hugh had fetched an unwieldy block of Wensleydale and a hulking slab of Caerphilly from the larder).

Any onlooker might feel the tentacles of boredom creeping toward them, and thus move on to scout out a more interesting scene. Such a spectator, however, would be mistaken and myopic in their assessment, and roaming onward would be a failure in intuition.

Fortunately, a spectator possessed of diligent perspicacity was, in fact, in attendance: Hugh Gaveston. Who, at this present moment, was listening as Lady Westbury and de Havilland discussed that most pressing of topics: the Future of the Country and Empire.

De Havilland, of course, delivered his analyses and projections in an unhurried and well-practiced oratory, to many nods and considered *mmm*s from Lady Westbury. Hers were not the only indications of approval: in a decidedly unusual development, Edward seemed suspended in a state of smiling silence, vigorously nodding as de Havilland spoke of the need for a gradual recalibration of societal hierarchies, a vision for a future in which a man's path through life was not determined solely by his father's bank balance.

Stephen had been chipping in with the occasional facetious remark, but the absence of any reaction had soon rendered his project tedious, so he had retreated to his father's side, where they appeared to be deep in conversation about tomorrow's shoot. Freddie had relapsed into sulking, staring most offputtingly into the fire. Lydia and Rosalind had reconvened their game; glancing at the scoresheet, Hugh perceived it to be a tight battle of wits—a battle of wits that had, mercifully, distracted Rosalind from shredding her handkerchief. William Ashwell was watching his wife from an armchair, his posture uncharacteristically slouched. If Hugh didn't know this to be impossible, he would have said that the man's eyes were infused with something approaching tenderness. De Havilland, meanwhile, was holding forth:

"We live in modern times, Lady Westbury, modern times in which we must liberate ourselves from the constraints of our Victorian forefathers. Our friends across the pond with their American dream, their belief in the ability of us all to be self-made, to haul ourselves up by the bootstraps. We must look beyond our provincial and petty prejudices, redefine what it is to be English." His speech had taken a passionate turn, his words delivered with a bombast and depth of feeling not often witnessed in the House of Commons.

"If I didn't know better, de Havilland, I'd say you were a Bolshevik." Lord Westbury chuckled while administering some fond pats to Bruno's head.

De Havilland appeared taken aback by the interjection, as if he had unwittingly given away his hand in a game of rummy. He returned Lord Westbury's chuckle, reassuring him. "Well, I'm not quite at the point of running round Westminster with a placard asking God to save us from Old Etonians."

"Now, speaking of running round, this old boy needs to stretch his legs." Lord Westbury indicated Bruno, whose tail was wagging insistently. "And *this* old boy"—gesturing toward himself—"is rather pooped. Any takers for Bruno?"

Hugh recognized an opportunity when one arose, and was never shy about seizing it.

"I need to walk off some of that Wensleydale. Freddie, I am no man's judge, particularly in the matter of fromagerie fondness, but I suspect that you might regret heading straight to bed after chomping on that Caerphilly." Hugh jabbered amiably in the manner he adopted when at his most inane and harmless.

Or, at any rate, when he wanted to appear at his most inane and harmless. "My dear old Great-Aunt Fanny—before she shuffled off this mortal coil, Lord rest her soul—always swore—and she swore like a trooper, mind you—that an abundance of cheese, or in fact any dairy substance, directly before bed leads to the most horrific onslaught of night terrors. Anecdotal evidence supports her claim, and I'm minded to gently suggest that you—"

"All right, Gaveston. God's teeth, I'll come with you—as long as you put a cork in the cheese-and-Great-Aunt-Fanny blether-ings," Freddie grumbled, lurching out of his chair.

Lord Westbury patted Bruno, sending him trotting toward Hugh. Lady Westbury suggested that they borrow the heavy tweed overcoats hanging in the small hallway by the side entrance (newly dubbed the Hobbit Hole last Christmas after some fantasy book or another Hugh had engulfed; a name that had, despite Lady Westbury's best efforts, stuck). And so it was that Hugh took Bruno out for his evening walk—and Freddie out for a little fact-finding expedition.

19

Bruno, straining at his leash, led the pair through the walled garden, an enclave of the Westbury grounds that in the summer provided a shaded sanctuary for those less accustomed to the sunshine. Adjacent to the walled garden, running parallel along the drystone wall (erected some thirty years ago by a ruddy-faced fellow from the village who had been renowned for subsisting on two sources of nutrition: milk and baked beans), was the herb garden, while beyond both these carefully manicured areas lay the greater expanse of the grounds.

Hugh had fond memories of their games in the walled garden, horseplay that sometimes ended in tears or, on that one occasion, the catastrophic destruction of Lady Westbury's dahlias. It was, however, the copse at the perimeter of the grounds that had been the children's true haven in the long summer holidays. Under logs and inside tree trunks Hugh had found the specimens that first ignited his passion for the examination of nature; of course, as he entered adulthood he came to the realization that examining dead specimens was a mite easier than examining scuttling, live ones. He and Lydia had constructed a particularly robust fort there in July of 1917, was it? They had toyed with the idea of setting up camp in the disused stables that lay on the other side of the trees. Exploring them one day, however, had put paid to that: the wooden structure, rotting in parts, was infested with cobwebs and an air of gloom that had given them both an irrepressible case of the heebie-jeebies.

The copse loomed now in somewhat gloomy darkness, the trees themselves having a faintly wraith-like appearance. The moon had succeeded in tearing a sliver through the clouds, providing just enough light for Hugh and Freddie to see the path stones down the garden.

Hugh negotiated the icy path carefully, entirely aware that he would also need to negotiate his conversation with Freddie carefully if it were to yield any illuminating information.

"Daresay it'll be almost melted by morning," he trilled. "Shan't halt the Westbury Boxing Day shoot, that's for certain." Although, Hugh thought to himself, while the wintry conditions might present no obstacle, the fact of a man killed by one of Lord Westbury's own guns could hamper the spirit of the occasion somewhat…

Freddie did not deign to offer a reply.

A change of tack might be necessary, Hugh inwardly reflected. Freddie had always been a remote figure, insulated against the world by wealth and alcohol, but impenetrable silence had never figured quite so heavily in his repertoire of moods.

"Awful lot of brouhaha today," Hugh tried again. "You did a nifty job staying out of it all."

Freddie glanced at him, an odd look of understanding tinged with mirth. "Well, Gaveston, despite the theatrics, I couldn't neglect my dear old friend, whisky. Never let me down a day in my life," he added. A reluctant smile edged its way on to his face.

"In fact, Freddie, I ought to make a confession," Hugh stuttered.

"Oh yes?" Freddie replied, the smile becoming less reluctant. "Better be a terribly scandalous one."

"Well, I have brought you out here under false pretenses. With undisclosed intentions."

"My, my, Hugh Gaveston, you swine!"

"With all the kerfuffle of the day, I haven't had the chance to ask you a favor, Freddie. It's about time I stopped rattling around alone and launched myself upon society." Hugh hoped that he had mustered enough conviction to sound plausible. "And the club in London that you and Stephen frequent and speak of so... highly, well, I thought that might be a sterling starting place."

Freddie's eyebrows were raised. "Lordy Lordy, Gaveston, this *is* a ripe surprise."

"Yes, yes, I know. But New Year and all that." Hugh shrugged. "Anyhow. Favor is…"

"Say no more, Gaveston, say no more. Of course I'll endorse you," Freddie graciously announced.

"Oh splendid!" Hugh exclaimed. "Stephen's already written a brief few words for me"—producing a piece of paper from his trouser pockets—"so you can just add your glowing second to his."

Handing Freddie the paper and the pen, Hugh glanced down

at Bruno, who was growing impatient with this hiatus in motion and was attempting to lurch forward.

Having scribbled on the paper, Freddie returned it to Hugh and the trio began trotting at a reasonable pace, clearing the drystone wall and emerging onto the open ground beyond it.

Hugh's eyes were drawn immediately to the spot where Campbell-Scott's body had been lying. Freddie had followed his gaze—which was precisely what Hugh had counted on. He knew that Freddie's reaction to seeing the spot would be telling.

"That where the old miser was found, was it?" Freddie questioned.

Hugh nodded his response. The area was zigzagged with a hectic crisscross of tracks, the result of Dr. Shepherd (with the queasy assistance of Hugh and de Havilland) hastily hoisting the corpse on to a stretcher and ploughing its rattling wheels through the snow. Hugh frowned. Something about those first tracks irked him. Something he couldn't quite put his finger on.

"S'nice of you to ask me to assist your entrance to the club, Gaveston. S'really nice. I do know what everyone thinks of me, you know," Freddie said, in a tone entirely lacking in malice. "I know everyone laughs at me, pities me, says I've gone to the bad."

Hugh, unaccustomed to such candor from Freddie, remained silent.

"And so I play up to it. Freddie the Fool, Rampling the Reprobate. Acting the perfect devil is better than the truth— that I get so damned blotto so I don't have to think about what a failure I am."

Crouching to let Bruno off his leash, Hugh reflected on the new role in which the guests seemed to have cast him: chief confessor, receptacle of hitherto interred truths. Perhaps he ought to have considered more seriously a life as a man of the cloth.

Freddie took a swig from a hip flask he had evidently brought with him for the extensive journey around the grounds, then continued. "And oblivion is delicious, old chap. Makes one feel decidedly invincible. Helluva lot of power and not a jot of responsibility. So I'd rather be Freddie the Fool than Freddie the Upstanding. Least that way nobody ever expects anything. Never calls me to account on anything. Can rave like a loon, swing from the chandeliers, guzzle away the money my father left me. Can get away with anything I like." Freddie seemed to be delivering his meditative monologue in an almost trancelike state.

Bruno broke the spell, barking and bounding back across the white ground before them. The look of strangely narcotized tranquility receded from Freddie's face.

"What've you got there, boy?" Hugh called to Bruno, who was hauling something behind him.

For an instant, Hugh's more gruesome instincts overcame him and he fancied it to be a human leg; regrettably (for he had to admit that the prospect rather piqued his excitement), it was only a tree limb.

As Bruno approached with his thoughtful gift of moldering timber, Hugh looked back to the path he had just cut across the ground. His tracks distinct on the right side, distinctly smudged on the left side, where he had been dragging the branch.

Smudged tracks which called to mind those peculiarly not-quite-right tracks from this morning.

20

Hugh always found Christmas exhausting; pleasantly exhausting in a manner that ordinarily left him contentedly sipping hot cocoa in the Blue Room on Christmas night, reflecting on the gifts and merriment and warmth shared with the Westburys. Tonight, however, he was waylaid by an exhaustion of an altogether different ilk. The gifts had been neglected, festering under the tree. Goodness knew when, if at all, they'd be salvaged; there was something unseemly at the thought of opening them now. Merriment and warmth, meanwhile, had abandoned Westbury Manor, shooed out of the door by disquiet and distance.

Now, Christmas Day over, the guests had been released from their obligations and had, with a mixture of relief and weariness, returned to their rooms. Hugh was perched cross-legged upon his bed, eager to examine the happenings of the last twenty-four hours.

As the day had worn on, Hugh's amorphous suspicions had begun to shift, to gather themselves into something resembling a hypothesis. A hypothesis in its embryonic stages, but one that had left him in no doubt about one fact: David Campbell-Scott had been murdered.

Returning to his home shores after an absence of eight years, eight years during which whispers of his fortune had reached a cacophony, eight years during which his name—already commanding the immense respect owed a war hero—had taken on even more gilded a status, it made little sense that Campbell-Scott would then pick up a handgun and shoot himself.

Why would he have taken his own life?

Hugh had decided that no, David Campbell-Scott had not taken his own life.

The question now, however, was an even more troubling one: why would any of the guests have wanted him dead?

Lydia was consumed by the worry that Edward might have had a hand in the death. Edward certainly made no bones about his dislike for Campbell-Scott, but, Hugh reflected, he certainly was not alone in bearing complicated feelings toward the deceased man.

Hugh felt sure that the key lay in the fragmented epistle he had recovered from the fire grate in Campbell-Scott's bedroom. He had placed the torn remnants on his bedside table, and examined them once more:

> *The tru*
> > *oid any nasty surprises, mee*
> > > *oney, I might be forced to reveal your little se*

Who had written it? The author behind the missive was, it was surely clear, engaged in the business of blackmail. What "little secret(s)" had Campbell-Scott been hiding? Who had disinterred them?

Hugh turned the possibilities over in his mind. Somebody had tried to blackmail Campbell-Scott; Campbell-Scott had refused to cooperate; things had turned nasty and the blackmailer had shot him? Of course, the blackmail could be incidental, a coincidence, a red herring, a wild-goose chase, a dead end, a nugget of fool's gold.

But then again, how *could* it be merely a coincidence?

Confusion mounted. The more intently he considered the situation, the more diverse and complex the questions that etched themselves into his brain.

And therein lay the problem: Hugh was caught in a closed loop in his enquiries. He felt like an ouroboros, doomed to be perpetually trapped in a cycle of suspicions.

He would disentangle himself from the cycle now, however, thanks to the collection of *objets* he had accrued today.

Strewn across the eiderdown were the only trinkets he had received this Christmas—or rather, the only trinkets he had *taken*, through various instances of subterfuge and happy accident. Frowning, he made a mental inventory:

* Item: Crossword puzzle, 1931 Grand National winner, six letters, completed by William Ashwell
* Item: Score sheet, alternately recorded by Rosalind Ashwell and Lydia

* Item: Christmas card, message crafted by Lady Westbury, signed by her and Lord Westbury
* Item: Name of radical writer, scrawled excitedly by Edward Westbury
* Item: Prized handwritten note of acceptance bestowed upon Lady Westbury by Anthony de Havilland (hopefully its absence from the mantelpiece would not be noticed)
* Item: Ringing endorsement for club application, duly signed by Stephen Westbury and Freddie Rampling

An impressive haul. Hugh had to congratulate himself: Scotland Yard couldn't better him in the swiftness with which he had obtained handwriting samples from all the "personages under the roof" as Constable Jones might say, meaning all of the potential suspects in the murder of David Campbell-Scott.

Of course, as Lydia wanted to ascertain her youngest brother's innocence—or guilt—then the obvious and least laborious option would be simply to eliminate Edward: examine his handwriting, *et voilà!* One way or another, Edward's place in all this would be determined. Hugh Gaveston, however, was never a man to plump for the obvious and least laborious course of action. Besides, placing all suspects under his microscope was far too delicious a treat to deny himself. If the back catalogue of *Mystery Magazine: True Crime Sensations!* had taught him anything, it was that murder investigations were excessively enjoyable larks. And thus he would pursue the far more laborious course of action: examine and eliminate any and all other possibilities.

Now, if he could just match the fragmented blackmail letter to one of the samples, he might inch closer to unraveling this tawdry tale.

Armed with his magnifying glass (essential paraphernalia for any self-respecting taxidermist-cum-detective), Hugh assessed the samples individually, taking note of any kinks in the cursive writing, any telltale sloping ascenders, the odd uncrossed *i* or looping *d*.

Now, the fragments themselves.

He scrutinized each letter, once, twice, thrice, straining his eyes in the dim light of the lamp beside his bed. The devil was in the detail, he was convinced of it. And this was a devil of an undertaking.

Thirty minutes passed, forty minutes.

Again and again he pored over the various notes and daubings and lines.

Nothing.

No match.

Could the author have disguised their writing, composed the blackmail note with their nondominant hand?

Hugh was flummoxed. He would have staked his fledgling detective reputation on the note unlocking everything.

Unless…

But no, he mustn't entertain any more outlandish ideas. No, like the rational man he was, he must make a logical survey of the events as they stood. Discarding his Holmesian magnifying glass, he drew on another of his heroes: What would Carl Linnaeus have done? He would undoubtedly have devised a system of irrefutable logic with which to classify the participants, thus clarifying this most opaque of kingdoms.

And so it was that Hugh, trusted notebook in hand, set about compiling his *Systema Suspectae*. Who had a motive to kill Campbell-Scott? Who had the means to kill Campbell-Scott? Who had the opportunity?

Chewing his pen, Hugh considered the various motives one could ascribe to the guests. Money. Jealousy. Long-standing antipathy. Alcohol-induced reckless abandon.

His pen hesitated before committing his first name to paper. Could he? Yes, he must. Objectivity was crucial to any investigation, be it scientific or criminal. And Hugh Gaveston prided himself on his objectivity in all matters. *Lydia Westbury*, he wrote.

21

A tentative tap sounded at Hugh's door the next morning and, in response to his sprightly "Come in!" (for Hugh had already been awake some half an hour or so), the door swung open and Angela entered. As precariously as she had carried the sherry decanter on Christmas Eve, she now tottered into the chamber balancing a tray perilously laden with a teapot, a milk jug, and a cup.

"Thanks ever so," Hugh began, grinning amiably. "Angela, isn't it?"

A deep (and deeply unnecessary) curtsey was the only answer the timid girl proffered as she maneuvered herself toward the window in order to draw the curtains—maneuvered herself without turning her back to Hugh, in a peculiar performance of deference that made him feel as formidable and regal as the Virgin Queen herself.

"Anybody up and about downstairs?" he inquired while pouring himself a cup.

A barely audible issuance from Angela's mouth.

"Sorry, come again? Left my ear horn at home!" Hugh joked.

Angela flushed and replied, "Just Mr. Rampling, sir."

Hugh frowned. Freddie, vertical at eight o'clock in the morning? It was the Boxing Day shoot, but even still.

"Oh yes, and what's old Freddie up to? Gobbling down toast and guzzling tea?"

"Not as I know of, no, sir. He's on the telephone again," came Angela's response.

Hugh's frown deepened. Awfully early to be telephoning anyone, wasn't it?

"Lummy, I wonder who he's talking to?" he pondered aloud.

Angela darted her eyes briefly around the room, as though confirming no other witnesses were present.

"I'd never eavesdrop of course, sir, but it sounded to me as he was conversing with the same person as Christmas Eve. Being as he seems all sixes and sevens again," Angela imparted cautiously.

Now this might be a helpful tidbit. Hugh's instinct told him to press on.

"Dearie me, sixes and sevens, you say? In what way?"

"Well, sir"—a momentary hesitation before the words poured forth—"before dinner on Christmas Eve Mr. Rampling, well, he was using the telephone, like I said, and he seemed terribly distressed. Whispering like, but you've heard Mr. Rampling's whispering. Quite easy to hear. Quite hard *not* to hear, I should say. Anyway, he was telling the person on the end of the line something about getting it, that he would get it."

"That who would get what, Angela?" Hugh gently probed.

"That Mr. Rampling would get it. I didn't rightly know as what 'it' was, but he seemed awfully keen to get it. Said the other person ought as not do anything silly. That there was no need to get dramatic, something to that effect. Then he lowered his voice a little, so I had to listen hard—not, sir, that I was eavesdropping—and then I heard him say, as clear as day, 'I'll get it. Mark my words.' I remembered that bit because it sounded like something Jimmy Cagney would say."

"Quite," Hugh replied. "And he's on the telephone now, you say? Mr. Rampling?"

"Oh yes, sir, he was down there while I was coming up. Right het up he was. I would have stayed to listen, but I had your morning tea with me. And I'm not one for eavesdropping, sir."

Hugh set his teacup on the bedside table and slid out from underneath the eiderdown and the tray.

"Your talent for *not* eavesdropping is exceptional, Angela. Thank you!"

With that, Hugh scampered out of the bedroom, leaving the maid to wonder at what a strange young gentleman he was. Asking her all sorts of questions—in his pajamas no less!—then galloping around like a giddy mare. She liked Lord and Lady Westbury, but they didn't half keep some queer company.

22

Skulking was never a pursuit that Hugh engaged in lightly or willingly: he far preferred sauntering or bounding. Yet needs must, and here he found himself skulking with aplomb along the corridor (minding that infernally creaking floorboard) and down the stairs.

The mahogany banisters were conveniently bulky; bulky enough to obscure the sight of a pyjamaed skulker listening in to the conversation occurring on the telephone at the bottom of the staircase.

Angela's appraisal of Freddie's whispering was an entirely accurate one, and Hugh had no difficulty in catching the words Freddie was flinging at the telephone receiver:

"I know, I'm aware of that… No, I'm not being… Listen, it went wrong, the whole thing went wrong, I hold my hands up… No, that won't be… I just need a bit more time… I know you've already… This time I'll make sure of it… No, don't… Don't do that… Luxton? Luxton, are you there? Damn you, Luxton. Damn you to hell."

The receiver was dramatically clanged back into its cradle, and Hugh could hear Freddie's heavy breathing resounding through the hallway.

A supplementary annotation to *Systema Suspectae* was needed, and Hugh conveyed himself back upstairs to do so posthaste.

23

Lydia's tea had gone cold. The jam was slowly congealing on her toast as she picked carelessly at the crust. From time to time, she was overcome by the reality of this most unreal scenario: the reality that David was dead. And this was one of those times. The entirety of the preceding twenty-four hours had been something of a blur; had it really happened? Lydia had spent much of her adult life willing her lot to be different, wishing for her future to be less prescribed, praying to be less preoccupied with and hemmed in by brothers—hemmed in by the tedious cruelty of one, the worrisome fragility of the other. David's death meant that her lot would be different now; her future was hers to prescribe. Yet here she was, cold tea, sickly jam, Edward and Stephen still foremost in her mind whether she liked it or not, it seemed. If only the cards had not fallen the way that they had…

Bruno's barking abruptly brought Lydia back to the here and

now; a here and now in which a din of trundling and clattering could be heard as the guests of Westbury Manor readied themselves for the Boxing Day shoot.

As with every year, it would be hours before any shooting commenced: first the interminable process of kitting everyone out; then the irritation of having to listen while Stephen argued that he shouldn't be made a beater because he was too good a shot for such a lowly position; next the trudge to the shooting peg, where Lydia had to stand around with any other women present, pretending to be interested in which of the menfolk had successfully hit which pheasant, thus proving their superiority over the others.

Lydia was certainly in no rush to join them, especially not this year: she had made her feelings about this quite clear to her mother just before breakfast. Everyone picking up guns and waving them around, the day after someone—no, not just someone, after *David*—had been found shot dead? Stephen, of course, had thought the whole enterprise hilarious. It was just the sort of distasteful event he savored. What a pity, Lydia reflected, that her mother was apparently blind to the lack of sensitivity this shoot displayed; to Lady Westbury, it was yet another instance in which carrying on as usual demonstrated fortitude and forbearance.

Lydia had resigned herself to the futility of battling against the masses, though, and thus abandoned her already partially discarded breakfast to make her way to the Hobbit Hole, overstuffed with welly boots, walking boots, and sou'westers. She despaired of its increasingly haphazard appearance. Why did they even need to store that many accoutrements anyway? The usual refrain to this was, of course, that one never knew when the urgent need for shooting paraphernalia might arise. One never knew indeed, Lydia reflected.

The smell of damp dog contended with the whiff of ginger wine (had Freddie already uncorked the bottle?) as the guests attired themselves appropriately. William Ashwell had come fully equipped, of course ("I shan't be going cap in hand to the Westburys begging for a welly-boot loan"), so was standing over his wife as she togged up in tweed. Rosalind had always enthusiastically embraced the role of Provision Purveyor. Tucking her scarf (well, the scarf she had borrowed from Lady Westbury; she could have sworn she'd packed hers) into her coat, she sat down on the wooden bench in the hallway to triple-check that she had indeed packed the pork pie and the crackers.

Stephen was braying about the shotgun cartridges and loudly grumbling about having had to collect the guns from the cabinet. Despite his protestations, he was engrossed in the business of propping each gun against the wall by the door, ready to be collected by the men. No guns, of course, for the little ladies, Lydia reflected: God forbid a woman should be trusted to participate at any higher level than that of meek observer.

Freddie was lost in a fit of giggles in the corner (really, he was the most preposterous boy, Lydia noted, for perhaps the thousandth time in her life), while Edward was helping de Havilland into his coat like a squire assisting a knight, and Lord Westbury and Hugh were burbling contentedly. Stephen continued to bleat in the background, battling as ever to gain everyone's attention.

Lydia watched as the scene unfolded; it was one that she had observed with boredom or slight irritation innumerable times over the years, in various iterations, yet today the banality of it made her smile. It was almost—almost—as if this was an ordinary Westbury Manor shoot, almost as if they need only trouble themselves with finding hats and making sure everyone had even swigs of the ginger wine. Her smile was tinged with pathos; it was a smile that she saw mirrored in her mother's face as she too observed her friends and family.

"I can't find it, Mother!" Stephen, at the grand age of twenty-nine, was whingeing as if he wasn't a day over eight. "I've looked *everywhere*. You must have put it somewhere after the last shoot in September; *I* haven't moved it…"

"Oh! Your jacket? I think I bundled myself into it last night when I went out with Bruno!" Hugh solved the mystery. "It must be upstairs, Stephen—how remiss of me! I do apolo—"

"Trying to pilfer my jacket, eh, Gaveston? Times hard, funds low? Hopefully not as hard or as low as Rampling's!" Never one to miss the opportunity for a jibe, Stephen winked at Hugh as he passed. "Don't you trouble yourself. Stay here, keep my father entertained, and I'll be back in a jiffy with what's rightfully mine."

The gloom that had so forcefully descended upon Freddie yesterday had seemingly dissolved and, though his stifled giggles had subsided, he still wore the look of one slightly dissociated from proceedings, endlessly amused by some private joke. As such, he shrugged off Stephen's parting shot and called over to Rosalind to quadruple-check that she'd packed the ginger wine. She reassured him that yes, she had—as well as the crackers. Crackers, however, Freddie couldn't give two hoots about.

Lady Westbury and Lydia joined the melee, pulling jackets out and ensuring that their socks were tucked into their breeches beneath the boots.

A curiously long interval elapsed before Stephen returned, long enough for all members of the shooting party to have emerged from their general state of dither and to be standing, poised to depart.

"Sis, have you finished that latest penny dreadful of yours?" came Stephen's voice, as he casually approached the group.

"It's not a penny dreadful—it's *experimental fiction*, you philistine." Then she added, "Why? Since when do you take an interest in my reading habits?"

Stephen allowed himself a smirk, like a conjuror relishing the moment before the grand unveiling of a trick. "Oh, nothing, no reason really. Just thought you might enjoy some new reading material—something that might appeal to your taste for the sublimely bonkers."

At that, Stephen nonchalantly threw a book toward Lydia. A notebook, in fact. A notebook that, squinting over the top of Edward's head from the other end of the Hobbit Hole, Hugh recognized to be *his* notebook.

Oh crikey, he thought. Now Stephen's really gone and done it.

24

"Um, Lyds, I think you'll find that's—ah—my notebook, for notes on my specimens, on taxidermical musings, and so forth—"

"On the contrary, Lydia. I think you'll find that's Hugh's little black book of snooping and spying and suspicions," Stephen interjected, sporting his most malevolent of sneers. "Jolly fascinating reading; plot a bit sketchy at times, but thrilling stuff—*sensational* stuff. Oh, and we all have starring roles in it! Destined to be next year's potboiler of choice, Gaveston. Might be a bit too racy, too off-color, though—should brace ourselves to be witnesses at an obscenity trial."

Hugh blanched as Lydia flicked through the book, and he jostled his way along the hallway to his friend. Really it was an insupportably narrow hallway—Bilbo Baggins would struggle to find it spacious.

Lydia began scanning the pages—Stephen had helpfully

turned down the corners of those not pertaining to curing otter skins or cotton-wrapping wire bones. She glanced up and caught Hugh's eye before, in her best impression of being unruffled, saying, "This—this is just a little joke that Hugh and I were indulging in."

Stephen laughed. "A little joke? Well, I do think it's rather entertaining, that much is true."

He turned to the baffled spectators—his mother and father scrutinizing Lydia in a bid to decipher the meaning of her reaction, Edward and de Havilland peering over the heads of the perplexed Ashwells, Freddie slumped against the wall yawning—and explained, "Old Gaveston here has been keeping *quite* the eye on us all, recording our every movement in his very droll way. Turns out he thinks at least one of us is a murderer!"

Stephen's mirthless laughter was met with assorted gasps and suitably shocked faces from the party.

"Oh yes, you all thought I was clowning around saying that old Campbell-Scott had been offed—but Hugh's been with me this whole time! You secretive little scoundrel, you!"

Lady Westbury turned and asked, "Hugh? Is this true? You really think David was…was killed? By someone here?"

Hugh gathered himself. Little use trying to wriggle out of this particular pickle.

"I, well, Stephen is…"

"Hugh," Lord Westbury murmured. "Tell us."

Hugh sighed.

"Stephen is right. I think that Constable Jones was…hasty in his conclusion, and I think, well, I am *convinced* that David

Campbell-Scott was killed. Deliberately killed. Murdered, I suppose, to use the more precise nomenclature." Here he threw his hands above him in a gesture of either universal accusation or universal absolution.

A moment passed while the guests digested this morsel. Stephen making a song and dance about it yesterday was one thing. Everyone viewed Stephen as a jester; of a superior breed to Freddie, but a jester nonetheless. Hugh Gaveston, however, was a different proposition. He was sensible, clever, astute in his judgments. Hugh was someone to be listened to.

Lady Westbury was the first to speak.

"But Hugh…Westbury Manor simply isn't the sort of place where *murders* happen," she asserted. "Not on *Christmas Day*. Not to our guest. It simply isn't possible. Who would do a thing like—"

"Oh Mother, do shut up," Lydia barked. "Of course it's possible. This isn't some kind of sacred ground upon which no blood shall be spilt, no misdemeanors committed. It's entirely possible. And according to Hugh"—she held the book up for all to see—"it could have been any one of us."

"Now, listen here, Hugh," de Havilland began. "This is all very upsetting for everyone, as you can see, so I think it's best if we just put this to bed once and for all."

Lord Westbury rose to his full height, an imposing height that had rarely been seen in recent months as a result of these blasted pains he kept getting. "De Havilland, I know you're a man of some substantial authority, and for that I respect you. But please remind yourself that you are in my house. And I for one would like to hear what Hugh has to say."

Hugh nervously pulled at his earlobe. He was quite unaccustomed to anything but warmth emanating from those around him, and felt his color rising as he started. "Well, I am of the mind that David Campbell-Scott, by all accounts and from all observations, was not a man on the brink of suicide. Far from it. He was a man reaping the rewards of hard work, basking in an exotic life in sunny climes, returning here to visit his oldest friends. To shoot himself...it makes no sense, there's no logic to it, no reason he would commit such an act in such a way. The spectacle of it, the timing of it...I find it extremely difficult—no, I find it *impossible*—to believe that this was a simple suicide."

Hugh had become increasingly impassioned over the course of his explanation, surprising both the onlookers and himself.

"I think you'll find that suicide is rarely simple," commented Lady Westbury. "You barely knew David, and we, his oldest friends, hadn't seen him in eight years. There could have been any number of reasons behind it..."

"Olivia, stop." Lord Westbury motioned to his wife. "We both know. We all know. We've all known since yesterday. There's been something not right about this from the off. I might have my dotty moments, but I can still sense when something is amiss. And something is amiss, Olivia—something is very amiss. David and I were in short trousers together. A man knows a chap, when he's seen him at his best—and at his worst. And by jove, I *know* David—and I know that he would never—*never*—have pulled that trigger."

Lady Westbury looked tenderly at her husband and began to cry. Stunned, the Westbury children exchanged looks. Their mother had never cried in front of them before; their father, all the time, old softie, but Lady Westbury's impeccable veneer of politesse had always proved impregnable.

Hugh moved to put his arm around her, and she leaned against him, allowing herself to surrender to her tears.

"This is *exactly* what I said yesterday!" Stephen blurted. "But did anyone listen? Did anyone *cry*? Did anyone take me *seriously*? Did they *heck*. Bloody typical. Gaveston, I retract my endorsement—bloody better not darken the doorways of the club," he finished sulkily.

Lord Westbury, sinking slightly at the sustained effort of maintaining his superior stature, continued. "One point, though, about which I disagree."

"Yes?" Hugh replied.

"Certainly was nobody here. And certainly isn't your job to investigate it, my boy. I've been mulling it over, and I don't have a notebook but I do have my eyes and my noggin"—Lord Westbury tapped his head—"and I think I know what happened. There's been talk of poachers in the village again, dastardly fellows passing through from village to village, after whatever they can get. Had 'em a few years back—had the cheek to bunker down in the stable. Ask me, it must have been a poacher. David no doubt disturbed them and…well, there you are. In any case, this is a police matter. We'll call 'em up, we'll get 'em out here again. They can see to it all. Find the rogues who did it, lock 'em up."

Hugh nodded. If that was what Lord Westbury wished, then that would be their course of action.

"Good chap, good chap." Lord Westbury had settled the matter and jolly satisfied about it he was too.

"Lord Westbury, allow me to telephone the police again," de Havilland said. "I rather suspect that they might harbor some resentment about being summoned once more. I'm loath to flaunt my parliamentary privilege, but I may well be able to pull some strings—chivvy things along a touch, get this nasty business seen to. If Mr. Campbell-Scott really was killed by these poachers, then we ought to get the police on the scent as soon as possible—before the swine leave any more dead bodies behind them."

Lord and Lady Westbury agreed to this most sensible and generous of offers; it confirmed Lady Westbury's view of de Havilland as a truly valuable acquaintance, and reinforced her husband's notion that the chap was really a good sort.

Lord Westbury nodded at Hugh once more.

"Let's forget all those wild suppositions," he said, a forgiving warmth to his tone. "You always were one for the fantastical, you silly old bean."

With that, he let out a brief rallying whistle and led Bruno out the door. Rosalind gathered her provisions and followed him, accompanied by Lady Westbury, clutching her friend's wrist.

A pause in the procession, however, revealed to Hugh that, although Lord Westbury appeared satisfied that the topic was closed, he was alone in that verdict.

"So we're all suspects, eh, Inspector Gaveston?" Edward asked. "Ought I to seek legal advice?"

"Edward, you heard your father. This is all entirely outlandish," de Havilland remarked as he squeezed past on his way to the telephone. "Hugh is clearly a man in possession of an admirably wild imagination. Give Mr. H. G. Wells a run for his money in these tales of the improbable."

William Ashwell, meanwhile, was staring stony-eyed at Hugh. "Careful, young man. Throwing accusations around might get you into all sorts of trouble."

At this, Stephen chimed in. "Ladies and gentlemen, you heard it here first—there's a murderer amongst us, a grisly, evil, demonic murderer, and only Hugh Gaveston can save us!" Adopting a mock Southern belle accent, he finished with a flourish: "'Oh dear handsome Mr. Gaveston, I do declare that you are my hero, my true hero!'"

Freddie laughed uproariously but could not quite muster his own witty barb to hurl into the arena.

Hearing the ongoing mirth, de Havilland's head reappeared from around the corner to interject once more. "We've had quite enough entertainment for one day. What say we put these she-nanigans to one side and get on with this shoot. I'll make this telephone call and be with you directly."

"I say, de Havilland," Stephen, hoisting on his jacket at last, quipped after the retreating politician, "I'd watch your back if I were you. First he's after the constable's job, next he'll be elbowing you out of the beeline you're making for Number Ten."

Freddie, William Ashwell, and the Westbury brothers all strode outside, throwing dismissive glances at Hugh as they collected their shotguns. He was, however, struck by a feeling of strain behind their collective reaction, a certain hollowness to their assertions that his investigation was ridiculous.

He sighed and made to tuck in his socks, only to catch sight of Lydia, standing stock-still, notebook grasped in her shaking hands.

"'Lydia Westbury—frustrated, impatient. Stands to inherit £££. Could the fears about Edward be a ruse? A double bluff?'" Lydia began reciting.

"Lyds, please—"

"Please what, Hugh? Please pat you on the back for dissecting us under your looking glass like we're so many of your dead frogs?"

"But you want the truth as much as I do, you said so yourself!" Hugh protested, appealing to his friend.

"No, all I wanted was for you to tell me that my baby brother didn't do anything stupid, hasn't ruined his life because of some mulish and idiotic gripe against David," Lydia exclaimed.

"But to do that, I have to conduct a thorough and methodical—"

"Oh, Hugh!" she said, clutching her hair, exasperated. "And what exactly has this thorough and methodical analysis yielded?"

He studied her for a moment. Revealing his findings could compromise the investigation. Especially as Lydia was…well, he hadn't struck her from his list, so she was a suspect. Uncertainty, however, flooded his mind. This was Lydia who, when the chips were down, well, jolly well got on with things. Not exactly grinning and bearing it, but bearing it nonetheless. His pal Lydia who, flares of temper directed against Stephen and against the lot of women notwithstanding, had never hinted at reservoirs of violence or desperation.

On the other hand, however, he really ought to continue his detections in an unbiased and unimpeded manner… Oh, hang it all!

"Lydia. Did you kill Campbell-Scott?" Hugh had learned that, unfailing in her own forthright approach to myriad situations, so too Lydia respected and responded to directness.

A pause while she straightened the cuffs on her jacket.

"Of course I bloody didn't, Hugh," she sighed. "I've thought about murdering Stephen many times before, I've thought about murdering *you* on occasion—but both of you are still walking and talking, aren't you? As for David—he was my *godfather*, you know how fond of him I was. I've kept every postcard he sent from his European adventures, every letter from Malaya. And remember all those trips to town—to Hamleys and Harrods and Regent's Park when we were little? He was like a second father to me."

Hugh's shoulders slumped. "I know, I know…but the money, Lyds, the money. You make it plain how unhappy you are stuck here in Westbury Manor, and it was also plain that David was going to leave you his fortune. With him out of the picture, you're a woman of independent means, everything you've wanted."

"Honestly. In many ways, I wish I were the Lady Macbeth of Westbury Manor—she at least had a bit of oomph about her, took her fate into her own hands. But no, I'm just bloody… Ophelia…moping about depressing everyone, talking nonstop about fennel and daisies."

Hugh frowned at Lydia's Shakespearean interpretations, prompting her to fling her arms up.

"The point is, I am not a murderous harridan hell-bent on getting my hands on David's money, snuffing him out so that I can go on jollies to the French Riviera whenever the fancy takes me," Lydia reasoned. "Apart from anything else, it's embarrassingly unoriginal. Give me some credit."

Hugh bit his lip. This entire exchange contravened some of the fundamental rules of detection club: never tell a suspect you suspect them, and when a suspect denies any wrongdoing, never take their word for it. But Lydia had posited a compelling case.

"Fine, very well argued. I don't think you killed David," he said. "To be honest, I never really thought you did. Not really. I was just being—"

"Thorough and methodical, I know," Lydia interjected. "Please let the record show that, while I forgive your lumping me in with your cast of potential killers and tarring me with a brush I care not a jot for… I shall not easily forget it, Hugh. And thus I reserve the right to use it against you in any and all future fallings-out."

Hugh grinned. He had always taken it as a badge of honor that their friendship could withstand Lydia's notorious grudge-bearing tendencies.

She continued, "The question is—what do we do now? The cat's out of the bag, somewhat. Everyone knows you've been snooping around."

"That might work in my favor. Smoke the culprit out, corner them into a state of nervous agitation, they're bound to slip up."

"Or come after you to shut you up," she said, much to Hugh's visible horror. "Oh, come now, Hugh—surely that's just as likely a scenario as the culprit miraculously leading you straight to them? A killer in our midst, who now knows you're sniffing about with your little black book—not exactly a hardened crime-buster who's going to leave a murderer quaking in their boots, are you? No offense, of course."

"None taken," he murmured, reflecting on the displeasing plausibility of Lydia's contention. He really had placed himself in the firing line now, so to speak. So intent had he been in his evidence-gathering endeavor that he hadn't considered the potential consequences of his investigations. Or rather, he had only considered one outcome: uncovering the truth. Now, with his friend rather bluntly presenting her case, he found himself confronted by another possibility: that he had inadvertently lurched into a path leading directly to danger.

Lydia meditatively asked, "Who do you think did it, Hugh? I don't buy Father's poacher guff for a minute—he always *has* had it in for poachers. Besides, they'd have had to break in to get their hands on that old revolver—and I certainly haven't seen any sign of intruders."

Hugh considered it for a moment.

"Don't tell me you hadn't thought of that, *monsieur le détective*?" Lydia laughed. "Next you'll be telling me you haven't also been wondering what any self-respecting poacher would want with a handgun—when there's a spectacular array of shotguns ripe for the picking."

That was Lydia, all right: canny to the last. Already joining dots that were as yet invisible to him.

"Hmm. You have a point there. Two points, in fact. But I do think the poachers are a theory that we can't discount right now. Not entirely," he replied. "It's not beyond any realm of possibility. And it's a damn sight more palatable than…"

Lydia looked at him intently. He caught himself. Not yet: to share any inkling, any hunch, would be premature. Lydia intuited exactly the thoughts running through her friend's mind, and sighed.

"Just tell me one thing," she tentatively said. "Is Edward… Is Edward a…theory that we *can* discount?"

He knew that misleading her on this point would not only be injurious to their friendship, but would also be impossible—deceiving Lydia had never been a talent.

"No, Lyds. It's not. Not yet."

She sighed the sigh of one who is disappointed but decidedly unsurprised.

"Now, before we go outside," he said, "there's one thing I need from you."

"If you're going to ask me for a vial of my blood in order to thoroughly and methodically eliminate me from your enquiries, might I ask that we seek a medical expert for the procedure?" she replied.

"Nothing quite so dramatic, not this time," he answered. "No, rather dull, in fact. Later on, I'd like to have a gander at those postcards from Malaya that you mentioned."

25

The party had made curiously slow progress when Lydia and Hugh rejoined them, and appeared to be taking an early rest stop before even leaving the walled garden. Stephen, Edward, Lord Westbury, Freddie, and William Ashwell, shotguns slung over their shoulders, were engaged in a discussion about how many cartridges each had been allocated. The youngest Westbury was adamant that his brother had stashed an extra handful in his cartridge bag, but Stephen was laughingly brushing off such an accusation. Lady Westbury and Rosalind looked on, indulgent smiles on their faces.

"Glad you two could make it! What kept you? Help Hugh assassinate a vole for his collection on your way out?" Stephen shouted as Lydia and Hugh approached.

"Oh, voles are decidedly uninteresting, Stephen. Rats, now they're the ones to watch. A hybrid of brute force and sly stealth that's fascinatingly reflected in their musculature," Hugh breezily said.

"Gaveston, there ought to be a law against your joining shoots—terribly unsafe for anyone to be holding a gun when sent to sleep by your insights," Stephen said, readjusting the cartridge-bag strap on his shoulder. "Anyway, chop-chop—men's work to be done, these pheasants aren't going to sit about forever."

"Doesn't appear that de Havilland's finished with his telephone call anyway, Stephen, so let's not get our knickers in a twist," Lydia interjected lightly.

Edward, kicking half-melted lumps of snow, grumbled something while Freddie, evidently still suspended in his curious state of gay hysteria, trilled, "Must be having a simply marvelous jaw with the bobbies. Telling them *all* about us, no doubt. Telling them that we're so unbearably boring that someone had to kill themselves to escape us… Oh no, I forget myself—telling them that we're so unbearably idiotic that we didn't notice someone being murdered by a marauding band of poachers. Oh no, no… so silly of me. Telling them that we're so unbearably evil that one of us is a murderer! Yes, yes, that's right, one of us is a murderer. That's it, isn't it, Gaveston?"

The Westburys were, regrettably, extremely accustomed to Freddie's volatile moods: high as a kite one minute, sinking into a slough of despond the next. For a time, Lydia had hypothesized that his episodes corresponded directly with his drink of choice: gin led to wracking sobs and self-pity; bouts of energetic capering were more often than not born of brandy; sherry ushered in ruminative spells of contemplation; whisky engendered a verbosity that was hard to quell; mead...well, mercifully, mead was a drink that never crossed the threshold of Westbury Manor. But tales abounded in the village about the priapism called forth by mead. As such, this little outburst was met with nothing more than a few rolled eyes and a smattering of shaken heads.

The convoy of tweed resumed its march and navigated its way along the path. Emerging from this side of Westbury Manor, one was greeted with the sight of open fields that in summer promised bucolic wanderings. The frost's grip on the landscape was easing, and underfoot the crunch of snow had become a slush of melting ice. A robin bobbed on a post as the shooting party made slow but steady progress toward the shooting peg.

Stephen had overtaken his father and was now leading the group, flanked by an oddly cantering Freddie. The discordant sounds emanating from the pair indicated that Freddie was in the midst of one of his more excitable episodes, an intimation confirmed by a very clear instruction from Stephen to stop his yammering.

Lydia had caught up with her youngest brother, who was trudging along in his terribly Edward-like fashion, his head slightly lowered and his feet scuffing the ground beneath him. He certainly had deflated again since his uncharacteristically high spirits, Hugh thought. Perky, jovial, open-faced—such anomalous behavior. There was certainly something afoot with Edward—he just needed to tease it out of him.

"I say, Hugh, feeling a bit out of puff already," exclaimed Lord Westbury, who had been contending rather unsuccessfully against the slippery pathway for the last few minutes. "Might just sit this one out, have a spot of rest and contemplation here." He gestured toward the somewhat rickety bench that had been installed several decades ago at a vantage point that allowed one a clear view of the fields.

Lady Westbury and Rosalind were trailing behind them, with William Ashwell bringing up the rear. Curious, Hugh thought. The man's aversion to dawdling was as pronounced as his disdain for levity, yet here he was, proceeding at a pace which would engender impatience in a snail. Watching him silently and vigilantly trudge after the two women, Hugh was reminded of scenes familiar to him and Lydia from all the mobster films they caught at the pictures: scenes in which a gangster goes about his business, tailed by a cop determined to neither lose his target nor be caught out. Hugh was given the distinct impression of a man reluctant to allow his wife to stray too far out of earshot; perhaps a man fearful of leaving his wife alone with her dear friend lest she be given the opportunity to disclose anything untoward. Or was this just one of Hugh's wild suppositions, as Lord Westbury had termed them, taking on a vivid life of its own? Hugh frowned: today, no supposition seemed too wild.

"What's the matter, darling?" Lady Westbury asked her husband as she drew nearer.

"Oh nothing, nothing. This blasted ice just getting the better of me is all," Lord Westbury cheerfully replied. "Going to plant myself here and watch you all from afar."

Lady Westbury's concerns about catching a chill were brushed away as Lord Westbury insisted that she trot on, leave him to it.

"Don't worry, Lady W. I'll stay put too, keep my eye on him.

Make sure he doesn't sneak back in and drain the place of brandy, leave us all high and dry," Hugh added. His volunteering seemed to reassure Lady Westbury, who kissed her husband lightly on the cheek before gesturing for Rosalind (and their unwanted chaperone) to continue.

"Don't forget Bruno!" Lord Westbury shouted somewhat croakily after them. "He's torn off somewhere, don't let him miss out on the fun!"

Led by Stephen, the others proceeded, shotguns bobbing over the shoulders of the men.

Hugh leaned his shotgun against the bench, and then plonked himself down inelegantly next to Lord Westbury, commenting on the remarkable ability of tweed (three to four layers of it, of course) to insulate one's extremities against the inconvenience of frosted wood. Lord Westbury returned his rather inane pleasantry with a generous smile. Hugh suspected that his host would have preferred an interlude of silent contemplation without the distraction (or incumbrance) of a companion, but Hugh was unwilling to permit this opportunity to slip by: here was the oldest friend of David Campbell-Scott. Any detective worth his salt would recognize this as a gold mine for useful information. Hugh snorted. Tell that to Constable Jones, he thought.

"What's that, my boy?" Lord Westbury asked. Evidently his snort had been rather more demonstrative than he'd intended.

"Oh, I was just thinking…" Hugh began. "Lydia told me about when David took her to Hamleys at Christmas, when she was, what, ten? At Santa's Grotto she asked for a train set and

Santa promised her a doll instead—she stamped on his foot and marched right out of there."

Lord Westbury chuckled. "Yes, that sounds about right. Our Lydia, ever the firebrand."

"Jolly touching how fond of her David was. How fond of you all he was," Hugh continued.

A sigh from Lord Westbury. "Thoroughly good sort, David. Ever since our schooldays, he's been...he *was*...an upstanding, reliable, decent man."

Hugh tapped his knee. Should he press Lord Westbury at this juncture, risk losing him, or continue with a gentler approach? He plumped for the former option.

"Hmmm, by all accounts it seems as though...certain among us wouldn't necessarily agree with that, Lord W," Hugh ventured. "All due respect, of course."

A sigh of a different quality from Lord Westbury. "Edward, you mean?"

"Well, yes," Hugh nodded. "And I'm not sure that Rosalind would term him upstanding, reliable, and decent. Not after..."

"Hmm, yes, well..." Lord Westbury bridled slightly.

Had Hugh been a touch too forthright?

"I knew nothing of that. David kept certain...aspects of his life under his hat, you see. Not one for offering up tidbits for the gossipmongers. A man has to have his privacy, after all."

Hugh murmured his assent: of course, of course. Lord Westbury appeared to soften.

"I was aware that David could perhaps...shall we say, throw caution to the wind a little in the courtship game. And it was a game really, for him. For a lot of chaps. I, of course, had my Olivia, cared not a jot for gallivanting around, leading the ladies on—leading them astray. Not that David did that, no, no, that wasn't his *modus operandi*, not a bit of it. He was just so gregarious, a charmer, one might say," Lord Westbury continued. "But if Rosalind's right, and I daresay that she is, then he acted the cad with her—leaving her high and dry without so much as a by-your-leave. Had I known about it at the time, I would've had something to say about it, you can rely on that, my boy."

Lord Westbury appeared to realize that he had ventured into finger-wagging territory, and steered himself back to more comfortable—and comforting—terrain.

"David could be single-minded, I'll grant you. Ever since we were in short trousers, dogged in his pursuit of any end he set his sights on. Straight to Oxford, straight to the City, straight to Malaya."

"I take it from Edward and Stephen that there may have been…some casualties along the way?" Hugh inquired.

Lord Westbury glanced at him. "The boys do enjoy dwelling on that Mayfair gossip. I kept my nose out of it. A man's business is *his* business. Certainly none of mine. And if David says it was all aboveboard, then it was all aboveboard."

"Quite," Hugh agreed. He would have to glean any nuggets about David's Mayfair dealings elsewhere, clearly. Then he added, "I have a habit of taking my friends at their word, too."

"And in any case, not a jot of all that Mayfair business came to anything—all talk and rumors. What stands, though, what's *recorded* in black and white, what is *inconvertible*, is that David was a hero of the highest order. You're too young to remember, my boy, but the war told you things about a man. The way a man acquitted himself. His conduct. And David's conduct was unimpeachable, Hugh. Unimpeachable." Lord Westbury was becoming more and more animated in his hagiographical monologue. Hugh's efforts to encourage his verbosity were unnecessary at this point.

"True gallantry is a rare quality. Rare indeed. David had it in spades. Led men into the very heart of darkness and back out again. Came home changed, of course. They all did. But David never festered on it, none of this fashionable hoo-ha about 'shell shock.' A most unbecoming song and dance. No, not David. Like any good Englishman he marched onward."

Lord Westbury was visibly lost in an idolatrous reminiscence about his friend, gazing ahead at the rapidly retreating stick figures that were the participants in the shooting party. He was roused back to the here and now by the greetings of de Havilland, making his way from the house.

"Ah! Speaking of good Englishmen," Lord Westbury exclaimed as he approached.

Hugh raised himself from the bench and shook de Havilland's hand in a quite unnecessary gesture of deference.

"What word from our friend Constable Jones, Mr. de Havilland?" he asked.

De Havilland sighed before explaining that, alas, the constabulary were somewhat skeptical about this poaching theory; according to Jones, the poachers, though a nuisance, were not known to be the violent type.

"Well, that's bloody outrageous!" Lord Westbury could not

contain his indignation. "Poachers not the violent type—my *eye* they aren't!"

"The doctor—Dr. Shepherd, is it?—has yet to examine the bod—to examine David, so no official conclusion has been reached," de Havilland continued. "And, after a certain level of verbal arm-twisting, I convinced Constable Jones to make another visit to Westbury Manor—so we can apprise him of our hypothesis regarding foul play."

"Oh, hurrah," Hugh exclaimed. Despite his misgivings on a number of fronts (namely, Constable Jones's competence, aptitude, and suitability for his chosen profession), relief flooded Hugh: Jones was an officer of the law, and his presence would—at the very least—persuade everyone that this was a serious matter after all. "Well done, Mr. de Havilland—now we can have this all looked into properly. Is Jones on his way? Ought we to rally the troops? Make our way back indoors?"

"I'm afraid that my persuasive prowess only went so far. Jones can only come tomorrow. He went to great pains—as you can imagine—to inform me of the far more urgent police matters he must attend to today. There was a brawl yesterday evening in the Crown and Cat that requires a great degree of 'post-incident interrogative information-gathering,' as he put it. Oh and something to do with a cow gone walkabout as well," de Havilland concluded, raising his eyebrows.

"That'll be Mrs. Slabley, the butcher, with the fisticuffs, I'll wager," Lord Westbury remarked. "They insist on opening the place for three hours every Christmas Day—caused quite the furor the first year they did it, I can tell you—and every Christmas Day there's a misadventure of some description. The mind really does boggle at the antics of that den. Particularly when one considers how unaccountably fond of the place you are, Hugh." Long had Hugh been a patron of the Crown and Cat. The regulars were now all too familiar with the rudiments of mammalian anatomy thanks to the impromptu lessons Hugh had delivered over shandy and pork scratchings.

Lord Westbury continued. "Well, tomorrow it is, then. Let's hope those poachers keep out of mischief tonight. Else Constable Jones might have blood on his hands."

Hugh was frowning, disappointed—although not altogether surprised—by the news of Constable Jones's reluctance. Tomorrow would be forty-eight hours—at least—since the incident. Forty-eight hours was a dreadfully long time. Evidence could be compromised, eyewitness accounts muddled. Not to mention a thought that had been niggling Hugh since his conversation with Lydia: *or come after you to shut you up*. Another night without police intervention meant another night in the company of a killer. And, thanks to Stephen's theatrics, the killer was now aware of Hugh's not-so-top-secret investigations.

A more melodramatic (and less poetically gifted) man than Hugh Gaveston might have proclaimed that every passing hour struck by the grandfather clock signaled the growing risk of the killer striking again. A less courageous man than Hugh Gaveston might have dwelled on the strange sensation swelling in his chest and have concluded that it was fear. Hugh, however, was both pragmatic and undaunted: the longer this dragged on, the greater the danger to him and to the innocent guests of Westbury Manor.

He would simply have to chivvy himself along and solve this blasted thing.

Ruminating further, he happened upon another nasty thought: what was it that Freddie had been saying on the telephone? *This time I'll make sure of it*, something along those lines? This was neither the time nor the place for an epiphany, but Hugh never had been able to master control of epiphanic moments. What if Freddie had done it but had intended another victim? Slaughtered David in error? He *had* been inordinately drunk that night, even by his own standards. Could he have shot the wrong person? Hugh shook his head, as if trying to dismiss this fresh theory—or fear—while in company. He must revisit it later, when he would have the time to assess it more fully.

"Not joining the shoot, gentlemen?" De Havilland moved the conversation along.

"Aching bones at my age, Mr. de Havilland," Lord Westbury explained. "And in all candor, something about holding a gun today left a rather bad taste in the mouth."

"I doubt they've even reached the shooting peg yet, given their rather sluggish pace; you'll make it over there before they've loaded their first cartridges, I'll wager," Hugh put in. "Meanwhile, I'm here to ensure that Lord Westbury has not a moment's peace. We were, in fact, just talking about David's meritorious service in the field. By all accounts, you and he were two giants of the Great War, what with your derring-do."

Lord Westbury welcomed a return to this particular area of discussion, beaming as he said, "Yes, quite the distinguished guest list we have this Christmas, Hugh. DSO, wasn't it, Mr. de Havilland?"

The MP allowed himself a suitably gracious smile before answering, "Indeed it was, Lord Westbury. I shall of course feel eternally humbled that I was deemed a worthy recipient of that honor."

"Pish-posh to all that guff!" Lord Westbury replied, swatting away de Havilland's claims to humility. "Not every man can stand up proudly and speak of his heroism. Plenty of chaps have reason to do quite the opposite."

"The Somme, wasn't it, Mr. de Havilland?" Hugh asked.

"No, no, Hugh—Ypres!" Lord Westbury corrected him enthusiastically. "Tell him, will you, de Havilland? Remind the whippersnapper what was done so that his generation could live without the specter of another cataclysm looming over it. The glory that you snatched from the jaws of doom and all that."

Hugh couldn't help but smile at Lord Westbury's eager jingoism, and his still being called a "whippersnapper."

De Havilland pulled his jacket tighter, as if the mere mention of the war sent chills through his body. "It certainly didn't feel like glory at the time, Lord Westbury. The trenches were a hellish place. Mud underfoot, sound of artillery fire overhead. Men full of fear—boys, a lot of them. We were fortunate in the Fifth; real camaraderie, true brothers in arms."

"A number of whom wouldn't have made it home were it not for your bravery," Lord Westbury pointed out, prompting a reappearance of the MP's humble smile. "Middlesex Regiment would've been decimated!"

A chuckle from de Havilland. "Well, that's possibly a somewhat hyperbolic assessment of my contribution, Lord Westbury."

"Come, come, Mr. de Havilland, I'll have none of this. Your young audience awaits." He gestured toward Hugh.

De Havilland exhaled, the stream of his breath visible in the cold. "It was nothing extraordinary, I assure you, Mr. Gaveston. It might have been anyone who saved those lads, but it just so happened that it was me. Any honorable man would have done the same—two young chaps, marooned in no man's land. It was a matter of duty," he explained.

"I see, I see," Hugh replied ruminatively. "And you were posted for…?"

"Three years. Three infernal years. Three years that changed me, of course. Crystallized my calling, I suppose you could say. It was when I came home that I realized what I needed to dedicate my life to—bettering our country, making a difference, ensuring a war like that never happens again."

"Damned stirring stuff." Lord Westbury clapped him on the shoulder. "Our country needs a man like you at the helm. Not another of these bureaucratic pen-pushing types who wouldn't know bravery if it bit them in the—"

Lord Westbury's endorsement of de Havilland and denigration of his opponents was interrupted by a shriek from the field—followed swiftly by a gunshot.

"What the devil?" Lord Westbury looked in bewilderment toward the shooting party. "Who's doing all that caterwauling? I didn't think they'd even started firing. Has someone been hurt?"

Hugh could not answer, for he had already bolted toward the site of the disturbance, hastily—and not altogether smoothly—dashing across the wet ground.

26

Panting inelegantly, trouser legs sodden from more than one slide on to the wet ground thanks to his panicked sprinting, Hugh arrived just in time to hear Stephen barking at Freddie to put down the bloody gun.

"Why should I, hmm?" Freddie spat back, waving the shotgun haphazardly in the air with one hand, while with the other he retained a tight grip on the ginger-wine bottle. "You've always thought I was a buffoon—all of you, every one of you. And now you think I'm a murderer!" He hooted mirthlessly. "I can't quite decide which I prefer."

"Freddie, please, let's just…" Lydia carefully edged forward, hands toward him.

"You come one step closer and I'll blow your brains out, like I did David!" Freddie swigged at the bottle and emitted a hollow cackle. "Oh, come on. Look at your faces. Petrified, the lot of you!

Murderers like me, we say things like that all the time, don't you know. Oh look, here he is now, our resident Sherlock Holmes!"

Hugh joined the rest of the shooting party, his eyes fixed on Freddie. "What's all this, eh? Causing quite a hullaballoo, let me tell you," he began.

"I rather think I've a right to cause a hullaballoo, given that everyone thinks I'm headed straight for the noose for *murdering David*." Freddie was lurching back and forth now, a surreal grin on his face. "That would suit you all, the Crown dispatching of me, nice and clean. Then you wouldn't have to put up with me anymore."

While Freddie continued to teeter and sway, shotgun balanced precariously in the crook of his elbow, Hugh turned to Lydia and, under his breath, asked what the blazes was going on.

"Lord knows! One moment he's barreling along, next he's waving the gun, threatening nobody in particular, and shooting it in the bloody air," Lydia whispered rapidly.

Freddie's pacing had subsided, and Lydia turned her attentions to him, attempting to reason. "Freddie, nobody thinks you killed David—"

"Rubbish! He embarrassed me on Christmas Eve, ergo I shot him in the face." Freddie laughed. "You Westburys always have enjoyed a good romp. And what better romp than this." He waved the gun again, prompting sounds indicative of panic and fear from his audience.

"Oh, marvelous, a spy from Westminster is here to watch now as well!" Freddie said, as de Havilland reached the group, limping ever so slightly.

"Rampling, what has possessed you? Why on earth are you waving a shotgun around like a lunatic?" De Havilland was clearly not a believer in Hugh's softly-softly strategy in moments of crisis.

Freddie cackled again. "You see, Mr. de Havilland? As I mentioned, historically everyone has *seen* me as a boozed-up fool, so I *played* the boozed-up fool. And the more I played the boozed-up fool, the more convincing I was—until, one day, I in fact *became* a boozed-up fool. Now, however, everyone thinks I'm a murderer, so I might as well play the murderer, hmmm?" He paused, frowned, grinned maniacally then continued, "So by the same logic, mayn't I *become* a murderer?"

This time, the waving of the shotgun had a decidedly more determined air to it. He hovered it in the general direction of Stephen and Edward.

"Perhaps I'll enjoy my debut in this role, eh, boys?" A new, malicious tone to his voice. A tone which prompted Lady Westbury to move, not tentatively or stealthily, but purposefully and confidently, toward him.

"Freddie," came her clear voice. "Freddie, enough. I *know* you didn't kill David. Enough now, Freddie."

Rampling faltered. Lady Westbury had always been his Achilles' heel. She alone, he felt, had always been able to see that which he truly was: lost, alone, a little misguided. While others had laughed at him, egged him on further in his descent, she had tried to extract him from his self-destruction. To little avail—Freddie had rebuffed her time and time again. But her sustained faith in him had been a source of comfort. And now here she was, her head above the parapet once more—all in the name of trying to salvage what was left of Freddie's dignity.

His resolve crumpled, malice fled from his face. But he did not relinquish the weapon. Tears formed in his red-rimmed eyes, and he spluttered out, "It *is* enough. I've done enough. Caused enough…shame."

This shift in tone alarmed Lydia and Hugh. They had both seen Freddie tottering into one of his swamps of self-pity, but he had never done so with a shotgun in his hand.

"This is all senseless. They—they're coming for me anyway. Soon. Today, maybe. Or tomorrow. Don't know," he garbled.

"Who, Freddie?" Lady Westbury's gentle tones came once again.

"The…the…" Freddie began. "I owe them money. So much—money. And I can't—I don't…There isn't any more. It's—it's gone."

Stephen started to blurt out some utterance, but Lady Westbury quickly turned a hard glare upon her son.

"Freddie. My poor dear boy. I told you, we will help you," she said, taking one final step forward and releasing the gun from his weakened grip.

Relief rippled through the party as Freddie collapsed into Lady Westbury's arms, sobbing with an infant's lack of inhibition.

Lydia immediately strode toward her brothers and embraced them both, Freddie's spectacle and threats—however unfounded—having evidently instigated another brief respite in the Westbury siblings' hostilities.

"The sooner this whole garish carnival ends, the better,"

intoned William Ashwell, gripping his wife's elbow in a manner very much noted by Hugh.

"Oh, lighten up, William. This must be the most excitement you've had in *decades*," Stephen replied, swiftly brushing off any sense that he had come within uncomfortable proximity of peril. "I for one cannot *wait* to see what's next."

27

Freddie's episode had put paid to any notion of continuing the shoot—or, in fact, commencing it—and thus the party traipsed back to Westbury Manor, collecting an understandably perplexed and fretful Lord Westbury en route.

Rosalind returned the crackers, uneaten, to the larder, the guests discarded their tweed garb in the hallway, and Lady Westbury escorted an exhausted Freddie to his bedroom.

An awkward interlude played out in the drawing room, where Lord Westbury valiantly attempted to initiate a "relaxing hour or so listening to the wireless, anybody?" His offer was not warmly received: the fleeting relief of Freddie having relinquished his shotgun without causing any harm had given way to a reinforced sense of unease. There was really no escaping it: this Christmas was a catastrophe. Hopes of a slightly more bearable Boxing Day had been resolutely dashed by Freddie's escapades. Goodness knew what lay in store for this evening. Implicitly acknowledged by all, it was a sentiment made crudely explicit by William Ashwell as he barged upstairs. Rosalind apologized for her husband but, unexpectedly, did not scurry after him. Instead, she smiled warmly at Lord Westbury and told him that she hoped they would be in time to catch the Boxing Day program of gramophone records that she had seen scheduled in this week's *Radio Times*.

Edward and de Havilland, newly thick as thieves, Hugh thought, announced that they were going to the library.

Much like children being seated at a separate table to indulge in games and avoid the doldrums of grown-up talk, Hugh, Lydia, and Stephen decided to retire elsewhere for a refreshment. Hugh had suggested they ask Angela to prepare a pot of tea, but this had been met with opprobrium by Lydia: if this wasn't the time for a proper drink, then when was? Concluding that the gin in the drawing room would not be missed, she led the charge to the dining room, clutching the bottle in one hand and a soda siphon in the other, while Hugh clinked his way along the corridor carrying their glasses. Ice bucket collected from downstairs, Stephen proceeded to fix their drinks with a finesse that surprised both Hugh and Lydia.

"Well, isn't this turning out to be a nonstop whirligig of theatrics?" Hugh breezed to the Westbury siblings.

"Ain't that the truth," said Stephen as he distributed the glasses.

"Can we please swear an oath to ensure that next Christmas will be one of tranquility and goodwill to all men?" Lydia proposed.

"Hear, hear," Hugh agreed.

"Thank goodness for Mother and her Freddie-abating ways,"

Lydia remarked. "Else goodness knows how that would have concluded."

Stephen snorted. "You credit the man with more gumption than he actually possesses, Lydia. Freddie Rampling's too spineless to have followed through. I knew he wasn't going to point that gun anywhere that might do any damage."

Lydia arched her eyebrow skeptically. "Stephen, I haven't seen you look that scared since Edward fell out of the tree and broke his wrist. Scared until you concocted your story about his having climbed it of his own accord, certainly not because you had told him Headless Hamish would cut off his head if he didn't."

"Ah yes," Stephen reminisced. "Headless Hamish. A true stalwart of our childhood."

Hugh allowed them to continue their sniping as he drifted into a meditation on everything that had come to pass. Questions were plucking at the edge of his consciousness. Nothing was any clearer than before. He was no closer to an answer. If anything, he felt further away. Distractions and diversions kept popping up. Freddie's theatrics, for one. He had to keep that to one side for the moment. For there was something curious about this whole business. His mind kept returning to the letter he had found in Campbell-Scott's room. Who had written it? What had David been hiding?

"Hellooo, Hugh?" Stephen cooed. "Wakey, wakey!"

Lydia frowned at him. She knew him well enough to deduce that he was entangled in some tricky knot in his thorough and methodical investigation.

"Oh, I was quite somewhere else," Hugh said.

"Allow me to guess where—your musty old study surrounded by stuffed badgers and squirrel skulls?" Stephen ventured. "Gaveston, we really must get you out and about more. Find you a wife to keep you away from cat bones and rotting rodents."

Hugh and Lydia shared a smirk at this suggestion.

"Stephen, 'fraid to break it to you, but Hugh has no more need of a wife than I do of a husband," Lydia replied.

"What I am in need of, however, is your assistance, Stephen," Hugh started.

"Oh Lord, can't you ask your trusted sidekick?" Stephen lazily nudged his head in Lydia's direction.

"I am a man parched," Hugh continued, undeterred, "yearning for that most nourishing of liquors—gossip."

"Oh hello, now this is more my wheelhouse," Stephen answered, sitting up in his chair. "What are you in the market for? Mother's quite the unparalleled expert on Lady Horton's antics, but I can furnish you with a rudimentary synopsis. If you want all the ins and outs of the saga of Viscount Ludlow and the trapeze artiste—well, you have absolutely come to the right place."

Hugh pressed on. "Nothing quite so juicy, I'm afraid. It's this elusive 'Mayfair business' that keeps rearing its head—I feel woefully ill-informed about it. And you appear to be extremely up to speed on the matter. Might you be prevailed upon to enlighten me?"

Lydia started at this—must he rake it all up again? Hugh, however, did not respond to her protestations, merely bestowed upon her a glance that communicated all she needed to know: did she want confirmation of Eddy's innocence or not?

Stephen made a raspberry noise with his mouth, signaling his disappointment in Hugh's selection.

"Well, I've bugger all else to do around here, so might as well," he conceded. Then he added, "For a topic this dry, however, we'll need another of these."

Stephen refreshed their gin tumblers, and launched into the explanation that Hugh had requested.

"Ten years ago this was—by rights it should all be dead and buried now. Campbell-Scott certainly did his best to keep things shtum—butter up anyone who might be able to spill the beans on it. And nobody did, really, nobody *could*—because there was never any evidence. Just a delectable cocktail of hearsay and whispers that was the tipple *du jour* back then. Couldn't smoke a cigar in peace without someone or other asking if you'd heard what old Campbell-Scott had been up to." Stephen paused to sip his gin.

"Really, must you recount this with such glee, Stephen?" Lydia barked. "It's so tawdry, and David always denied every bit of it."

Stephen nearly choked on his drink. "Of course he denied every bit of it! Wasn't going to blithely own up to putting all his high-rolling City pals in something of a pickle, was he?"

"'Putting his pals in something of a pickle?' Golly, that doesn't sound particularly delectable…" Hugh remarked.

"The pickle, you see, was the sort of pickle that can land people in jail, if they're avaricious and blinkered enough to have blindly put their faith in someone a damned sight smarter than them," Stephen continued, clearly relishing his role as raconteur.

"You've lost me, Stephen," Hugh said.

"Jesus, Stephen, get to it, will you, or I will," Lydia interjected.

"As you wish, sister, as you wish." Stephen held up his hands in mock innocence. "These chums of his, wealthy chums interested in making themselves even wealthier. Campbell-Scott, war hero and good all-round chap renowned for his financial nous, was, so insiders say, whispering into his chums' ears about a first-rate opportunity for them to double their investments. So the story goes, he was telling Lord Tom, Dick, and Harry that he had his ears to the ground on an endeavor that would make millionaires of them all—property investments in East London slums. Idea was, shell out on some passably adequate buildings—basic tenement buildings, really—chock them full of families desperate for a roof over their heads, charge through that roof for rent, and you're quids in."

Hugh frowned. "That doesn't sound like a particularly noble undertaking…"

"To reiterate," Lydia stressed, "there is no proof that David was involved. No proof at all."

Stephen picked up the story again. "Admittedly, no proof at all. However, all roads lead to Rome, yes? And once everything went, shall we say, belly up, all rumors led to David."

"How do you mean?" Hugh asked.

"Belly up, in that there weren't any tenement buildings in East London," Stephen explained. "Rumor is that Decent David was collecting their investments and, well, pocketing them."

"This seems rather far-fetched," Hugh murmured.

"Oh, my dear naive Hugh—we live in a world where the far-fetched walks among us," Stephen replied.

"If that's the case, then surely these chums of his needed only to tell the police—tell them that David was fraudulently taking their investments and the whole thing was a sham?" Hugh, ever faithful to truth and justice, persevered.

"Ah, well, here's where it does become a touch more interesting." Stephen grinned. "You see—and those of a delicate disposition may wish to close their ears now—these chums of David's...he'd selected them because they were all patrons of a certain establishment in Mayfair. A certain...high-class establishment, that catered to certain...particular needs. Or shall I say, certain particular *predilections*."

Hugh, clearly puzzled, glanced at Lydia for assistance in this fog of confusion.

"Oh, for Christ's sake, Hugh—please don't be so dense," Lydia snapped. "If you are unable to decipher Stephen's words, then you truly are a ninny of the highest order."

The penny dropped. As did Hugh's mouth. He composed himself and cleared his throat. "I...uh, I see."

"I'm not sure that you do, but I shall continue nonetheless," Stephen said, luxuriating in this more and more with every passing moment. "Such was the particular predilection these gentlemen shared, that when they threatened to expose David's fraudulence—all right, all right, Lydia, *alleged* fraudulence—all he had to do was threaten to expose their patronage of this Mayfair establishment, and that was that. They kept their mouths shut."

"And they ended up in jail?" Hugh was aghast.

"Some of them did, yes."

"But...sorry, I'm fogged again. Why did they end up in jail if there weren't any buildings and David had taken the money?"

"It transpired that, as well as asking his City chums to fork out the cash, he'd been employing agents to rustle up business in Bethnal Green. Slum-lord types of ill-repute who were prowling around, foraging out the most desperate among the East Enders, convincing them to put down 'deposits' to secure homes." Stephen swilled his gin. "And of course—these deposits, after a small cut to the agents, were also going straight into David's pockets. Police got wind of it, but he, clever old blighter, had foreseen that eventuality—so his name was on no paperwork, nothing in writing that could lead anybody back to him. Only the names of his City chums."

It was becoming clear to Hugh now. "So…the chums, they were the ones it led back to? And the East End families…what happened to them?"

Stephen shrugged. "More penniless than they had been before."

"If this is all so well-known, why on earth did nobody come forward?" Hugh's confusion redoubled: surely, justice could be served somehow? "And hang on—why did you never tell me about it before now?"

Lydia defensively snapped again. "Because it's just gossip. You know what gossip can be like—idle pot-stirrers with very little else to do than try to blacken other people's names."

"Oh sister, you know me so well!" Stephen exclaimed.

Hugh turned all this over in his mind. If it was true, it painted a very different picture of David Campbell-Scott. Swindling goodness knew how many monied folk in town—monied folk who might be only too pleased to spend their money on a well-executed murder. Not to mention the legion denizens of Bethnal Green who had been conned out of what little money they had. Ten years to harbor hatred, to cook up a plot for revenge. Ten years. Ten years?

"Wait, ten years ago this happened?" Hugh questioned.

"Aha, has the other penny dropped?" Stephen smirked.

"Ten years ago is when—that's when Edward went to stay with David, wasn't it? When he finished school, I remember that—Lord W said it would be good for him to spend some time seeing an entrepreneur in action…" Hugh trailed off. It was all making sense now.

Lydia sighed. "Yes, Hugh. Mother and Father carted impressionable, idealistic young Eddy off to Uncle David…and he came back hating him and being all fired up about the rich getting richer and the poor getting poorer."

"And since then he's been an insufferable bore ranting on about uprooting the social hierarchy and throwing the aristocracy in the stocks," Stephen added, raising his glass. "Something else we have David to thank for."

Even Lydia must entertain her doubts about David's part in all of this, Hugh thought. Eddy's social awakening roaring into life just after a sojourn with David, suspected of conning the poor and blackmailing the rich? Hugh had always respected David and his generosity toward Lydia, his evident fondness for her. It was a bitter pill to swallow; he could see why she would want to spit it out.

"Crikey…I think I do need another gin," he said, glancing between sister and brother, the former glowering, the latter smugly grinning.

"Hope that's sated your appetite for a lip-smacking pudding of rumor, Hugh," Stephen said. "Pleasure to have been of service to you."

Lydia winced slightly, remarking, "I am entirely aware of how it all sounds, Hugh, really I am. That's why I didn't tell you about it... Mother and Father were, of course, blind and deaf to the whole sordid story—willfully so, needless to say. Mother would just bat it away with that infuriating diplomacy of hers, changing the subject to...Lady Veronica's bunion treatment or Mr. Winsgate's latest prize filly. And I...well, I never wanted to believe it, so I just...made the decision to not believe it. Edward's never forgiven me for that, though."

Hugh nodded, patted his friend's hand.

Poking the lemon in his glass in a manner which would have rendered Lady Westbury speechless with shock, Hugh allowed this new information to take root. He tuned back into the conversation between Lydia and Stephen, which had moved on to speculating as to the nature of the sudden and seemingly irrevocable bond between their brother and de Havilland. It was a question that was also forming itself amongst the panoply of enquiries jostling for priority within Hugh's mind. For the moment, however, he reflected on the unusual cordiality with which the pair were conversing—no excessive snapping, an absence of vitriol. Lydia appeared to be actively enjoying her brother's company, in fact. He was on the point of wondering whether this might signal an evolution in the relationship between Lydia and Stephen, the unearthing of a common ground. Then he checked himself: Lord Westbury had warned him against his wilder suppositions.

As the siblings continued their discussion, several things were beginning to click together in Hugh's thoughts. The sediment was settling. He needed to speak with Lady Westbury next.

28

Westbury Manor appeared to have entered into a peculiar state of limbo. Time had lost its relevance (for the time-conscious, however, the clock had not long ago struck two p.m.) and any semblance of routine was nowhere to be found (a development most galling to Mrs. Smithson downstairs, being as she was perpetually poised to prepare luncheon). Listlessness pervaded the house. Even Angela, never one to bemoan a lack of employment, was growing restless and had chosen to refold the table runners that she had already folded before Christmas.

Hugh, having excused himself from Lydia and Stephen, made his way along the corridor as if traversing an uncanny dreamscape. The grandfather clock, the library door, the strange oil painting with no apparent merit that the Westburys insisted on hanging…all so familiar, yet strangely becoming less so. *Is this what becomes of those engaged in the game of detection?* he asked himself. *Are we doomed to exist in a liminal world where trust, even trust in inanimate objects, recedes? Must I sever ties with those I once held dear, lest they obstruct my discharging my duties in my quest for justice? Am I to—*

"God's sake, man!" came a blast. "Are you in a trance? Do we need to call for an exorcism?"

William Ashwell stood before him, carrying, rather incongruously, an orange in one hand and a half-eaten piece of toast in the other.

"William! I didn't see you there, I was…"

"Lost in a daydream, I know." He softened slightly. "Haven't changed a jot since you were small. Haven't changed at all. The world will see to that. Chew you up, spit you out, leave you to salvage what little you can—with whatever means you have."

It was now William Ashwell who appeared lost in a daydream, albeit an unpleasant one shot through with bleakness. Hugh unpicked his declaration, wondering exactly how his fellow guest had been chewed up and spat out, and precisely what he had salvaged. Hugh's expression of curiosity evidently returned him to his senses.

"Damned near starving, had to make do with this"—he gestured to the pairing of foodstuff he was brandishing—"seeing as nobody else is bothering about their stomachs. If it weren't for the blasted trains, I'd be long gone—shan't be rushing back to Westbury bloody Manor any time soon." And with that, he marched toward the stairs, presumably back to seclusion in his bedroom.

As William Ashwell strode up, Lady Westbury was gliding down. Bingo, thought Hugh.

"Really," she said as she reached the foot of the stairs and noticed Hugh, "that man becomes less palatable with every passing visit."

Lady Westbury, expressing an unfavorable opinion of a guest… in the presence of another guest. My, my, thought Hugh, it really was the end of days.

"Perhaps his orange will cheer him up," he suggested, taking her hand and placing it on his arm.

"I was on my way to the reading room, if you'd care to join?" Lady Westbury invited.

"I should like that very much," he said as they made their way to their destination.

The reading room had always been one of Hugh's most treasured locations in Westbury Manor. He co-owned the copse with Lydia (he had drawn up legal documents to that effect, stipulating the borders of their territories, when he was twelve), the Blue Room was *his* room, the drawing room was the site of innumerable dinner parties, but the reading room—the reading room was a domain he shared only with Lady Westbury. Or rather, which she elected to share with him.

During childhood overnight stays when afflicted by sleeplessness, this had been his refuge. Lady Westbury would prepare him a mug of warm milk (never with honey: warm milk with honey was, to his mind, an abomination) while he inspected the herbs in the kitchen, then they would return to the reading room. It had become their tradition; in fact, Hugh had to admit that on more than one occasion he had feigned the inability to sleep, purely to steal a stint there. The night he received news of his parents' deaths, he came down immediately from Cambridge; he couldn't countenance returning to his own empty house, so it was to Westbury Manor that he went. And it was in the reading room, with the usual mug of milk (supplemented this time by an infusion of whisky), that he and Lady Westbury spoke of his parents, her friends, until Bruno came scratching at the door for his early-morning walk.

It was so named not because its walls were lined with bookcases populated by dusty tomes or well-thumbed potboilers (for that was the function of the library, of course). No, on the contrary, the walls here were bare except for one framed print, bizarre to any onlooker, but cherished by Lord and Lady Westbury: a vivisectional drawing of Bruno that Hugh had labored over for months at the outset of his taxidermical career. Of course, surveying it in the intervening years, he berated himself for several inaccuracies (a rogue kidney here, an out-of-proportion tibia there), but there it still hung.

No, it was named the reading room because that is precisely the pastime Hugh and Lady Westbury enjoyed while within its four walls. An unspoken rule had been established and never flouted: in the reading room, we do not talk. In the reading room we read. Since his initiation into this sacred chamber, Hugh had come to realize that the poise and decorum exhibited in front of company were, while not entirely artifice, not necessarily Lady Westbury's natural state of being. Observing her lost in a George Eliot or a Brontë, Hugh saw the strains of the day evaporate from her face, the taxing business of pleasing others done with until tomorrow.

And so it was now, as Hugh and Lady Westbury closed the

door behind them, shutting out the rest of Westbury Manor, and settled down in their armchairs.

Hugh allowed a few moments of silence to pass. Whether Lady Westbury was contemplating the preceding events, he could not tell. Perhaps she was emptying her mind of the woes that had befallen her house, her family. Was she inwardly assessing the likelihood that her husband's oldest friend had committed suicide? Could she be returning to Lord Westbury's theory about the wicked poachers, callously killing an unwitting bystander? Or might she be examining the possibility that, yes, a murder had been committed, but a murder motivated by something far more grisly than mere happenstance and panic.

Taking a deep breath, Hugh prepared himself to break the rule fundamental to this space shared with Lady Westbury.

"Quite the, uh, day we've had," he said.

Lady Westbury appeared neither startled nor affronted by Hugh's contravention of their dictates. Perhaps, he thought, she had been expectant—or desirous—of a discussion of this ilk.

"Quite the two days we've had, Hugh," she replied, staring at a fixed point on the bare wall. She added, in a slightly softer voice, "And quite the legacy they shall leave us."

"Mmm, quite."

"Whatever befell David—and I shall be clear from the outset and admit that I have no clue as to what truly did befall him—will remain here for some time. Some time indeed."

"How is Lord W, really?" Hugh asked.

Lady Westbury sighed. "This has shaken him, Hugh. Shaken him deeply. This year has been…trying, as you know, and David's visit had come to represent some great milestone. If he could battle through the year's difficulties, all would be well when David arrived. It was as though David's being here symbolized some return of his youth, his sense of self. How excited he was. And now... Well, I cannot quite bear to consider the repercussions of this. The effects it will have on him."

Hugh was unaccustomed to seeing such openness from Lady Westbury; she usually maintained some vestigial level of reserve.

"And the children... I worry about my children, Hugh. They have their troubles. Goodness knows we all have our troubles—but it's the manner in which they negotiate them that causes concern. Stephen, well, Stephen is Stephen. Lydia—you know as well as I that her unhappiness has threatened to overwhelm her at times. And Edward's slipping further and further away from me."

Hugh frowned and preserved an expression of concern on his face. Inwardly, however, he was aware that to continue this thread of conversation—a general assessment of her children and their respective psychological make-ups—would be to wander too far from the matter at hand. Loath as he was to curtail Lady Westbury's clearly cathartic outpouring, Hugh knew he had to retain a terrier-like focus.

"May I ask you something, Lady W?"

Lady Westbury tore her gaze from the wall and looked at Hugh, her eyes flashing with the mixture of amusement and intelligence that made her company so highly coveted.

"I think you ought to, yes."

He returned her oddly forthright yet elusive answer with a puzzled look. She smiled the smile of a benevolent, omniscient sage.

"It's about Freddie, isn't it?"

Hugh nodded.

"About my conversation with him, outside earlier?"

To call it a conversation felt incongruous with the reality of the situation in the field: a negotiation would have been more accurate.

"You said that you *knew* he hadn't killed David. And that you'd told him you would help with his…financial circumstances," Hugh said.

"I knew that you would be listening intently—you always have possessed a preternatural ability to listen and extract meaning where others hear and fail to interpret. An occasionally irksome ability in a child—your mother and I always had to ensure we were at a safe distance from your ears before enjoying our gossips— but an invaluable one in an adult. Particularly a *man*—I have always found men to be wanting when it comes to listening and to understanding precisely what one means." She smiled wryly.

Hugh waited, allowed Lady Westbury to decide the moment at which to provide the explanation he was seeking. He turned his glance to the window, where a robin—the same as earlier?—was peering inquisitively into the room. Perhaps he ought to sidle up to this little chap, he thought, find out what he'd witnessed over the last two days. Although to judge the robin by the same standards as the inhabitants of the house, he probably harbored numerous secrets, had demonstrated some questionable behavior, and had reason to dislike David Campbell-Scott. Another potential culprit was highly undesirable. Hugh turned his attentions from the avian visitor back to his hostess.

"Freddie is a most fragile being, Hugh. Most fragile. Having brought up Edward, I am keenly attuned to sensitivity and vulnerability. Eddy, though of course he'd deny it to the hilt, has always been loved and supported. He has never lacked a welcoming home or a listening ear. When I first met Freddie—he must have been perhaps six or seven, at home from boarding school for some holiday or another—I sensed fragility in him. He was quiet, shy, uncertain of himself. The same age as Stephen, but the difference between them…oh, Freddie was like a puppy, scampering after Stephen, being knocked back time after time. And his father did the same—was so hard on the boy, criticized him mercilessly in front of company, and it only became worse after James died."

James? Who was James?

Lady Westbury clearly sensed Hugh's confusion. "James was Freddie's older brother; older by a number of years. You and your parents moved to Little Bourton in…it must have been 1916, yes. I remember because it was the summer of Lydia's tenth birthday party. The two of you hit it off immediately, constructed some kind of den in the copse, if I recall correctly?"

Hugh nodded, a smile appearing on his face at this memory.

"That would be the year after James died. Over in Belgium. Frightfully tragic: enlisted without Sir Charles's knowledge, arrived in Europe just in time to be killed in a shell attack. Sir Charles, of course, was never the same. Took it out on poor Freddie. Barely spoke to him except to berate him for his schoolwork, or his sporting ability, or his slight frame. As a result, Freddie became more and more…erratic. Shyness became tomfoolery. Acting out constantly, as I'm sure you recall."

Hugh did recall: Freddie had never held a place in any of their hearts, being neither clever enough to spar with, nor kind enough to wholly take pity on.

"All of which is to say, Hugh, that his behavior, though vexing, though galling…one must understand the provenance of it. One must make certain allowances for it—for him."

An intriguing turn in the conversation, Hugh thought. What was she preparing him for?

"At dinner on Christmas Eve, he oughtn't to have behaved the way he did—drunk and pestering David for money. Of course he oughtn't to have behaved in that way."

"Rather unseemly, even for Freddie, yes."

"But nor do I condone David's behavior that evening," she carefully explained. Adding meditatively, "In fact, hearing Rosalind's account of events, I find myself questioning David's conduct in other matters. That, however, is neither here nor there."

On that, Hugh couldn't quite agree: Lady Westbury's ire at David's decisions was both here and there.

"Freddie lives a life untethered to…anything substantial. When his father died, I somewhat optimistically—naively— thought that might allow him to emerge from the maelstrom of alcohol and…silliness…that he had so artlessly constructed. Alas, though; it only served to make him worse. Now he rattles around that house of his, completely and utterly alone—goodness knows what he even *eats* now that the staff have upped sticks."

"Kippers and crackers, as I understand it," Hugh answered.

"In any case, this is all a roundabout way of telling you that there is more to Freddie Rampling than many know…than many *care* to know. After Christmas Eve dinner, I felt appalled by both Freddie and David. Freddie being so inebriated, I was worried about our waking up on Christmas morning to find him sozzled out of his skull—or something worse. Of course, I needn't have worried on that front. I went to check on him—maternal instinct is difficult to assuage—and found him inconsolable in his bedroom. Freddie's always prone to fits of melodrama, but he appeared beyond reason. He's managed to get himself into rather a lot of trouble, you see—money trouble."

This was no surprise: Freddie's wheedling of David at dinner, the telephone call that Hugh had overheard earlier today. Lord, was it really only this morning? How peculiarly time is warped when nefarious machinations are at work.

"He was blathering on, telling me he was useless and everyone hated him and that he was going to go and get a gun—"

A raised eyebrow from Hugh.

"I am aware of the impression this gives, Hugh, but inflicting damage upon himself was the only intention on Freddie's mind. I told him that we would help him—that his debts couldn't be as bad as all that, and that we could stand him a sum—to be repaid, of course. This seemed to placate him somewhat. His sobs settled down, quite like a child who has had a bandage applied to a graze. He looked awful—wild-eyed, pale, shaking. Already incoherent, he became unintelligible. 'Ramblings of a madman' was the phrase that came to mind."

"He does get himself into a bad way, old Freddie," Hugh remarked.

"Yes, he does. I was still fretful about his temperament, so

I decided upon a solution. Lydia keeps her sleeping draught in the bathroom cabinet, so I gave some to Freddie, to soothe him. Poor lamb. He was out for the count like that—" Lady Westbury clicked her fingers.

Hugh understood the importance of this information, understood why she was disclosing this to him: it meant that Freddie, submerged in deep, induced slumber, would not have been capable of killing David. That's what she had meant out in the field: *I* know *you didn't kill David.*

"So you see…" she began.

"I do, Lady W. But forgive me, this begs another question."

Her eyes glinted at him again.

"Why didn't I reveal this rather crucial nugget before now?" He nodded.

"Hugh," she sighed. "I pride myself on myriad things—dinner parties populated by the wittiest and most stimulating guests, conversations that brim with laughter and repartee, a family that presents itself more or less impressively to society. I also pride myself on tactfully massaging challenging situations into more palatable iterations. David Campbell-Scott being found dead outside my house on Christmas morning is perhaps the most challenging situation I have confronted. There is nothing I can do about the facts—he was found dead, here—but what is, was, within my control was presenting the circumstance in its neatest—least messy, in any case—version."

"I think I understand…"

"Let me be plain. To tell you about Freddie and his sleeping draught would have been to, well, frankly, provide him with an alibi. And to provide him with an alibi would be to admit that there was cause to suspect him of foul play. And that, Hugh, is something which I am simply not willing to admit. I am not willing to admit that *anyone* in this house may have taken David's life. Westbury Manor is simply not the kind of place where that kind of thing happens."

Hugh looked at Lady Westbury. Her eyes burned with a seriousness he had not seen in her before; now he could understand how it was that Lydia and Edward possessed such fierce earnestness and ardent ferocity. Her cheeks were quite flushed, but a moment passed and she seemed to recall herself, her expression softening into one of beguiling warmth.

"Oh Hugh," she breezed, far lighter in tone now, "the sooner the police come tomorrow and catch those poachers, the better."

The poachers: that hypothesis once again. She seemed to have adopted her husband's certainty about it, based on precisely not an ounce of evidence. Perhaps, Hugh reflected, it was preferable to imagine their friend being felled by local scoundrels than killed at his own hand—or at the hand of one of their guests. Hugh mentally noted that he must address this poacher idea, and soon.

Now that Lady Westbury had concluded her monologue, it was as though the rest of the house sprang back into life, having been caught in a state of suspension while she had spoken. Outside the door Hugh could hear Lydia's voice, its tone chiding—perhaps the armistice between her and Stephen had been more short-lived than he'd allowed himself to wish. A door opened and closed—the library—and footsteps and murmurs receded along the corridor.

A scuffling at the window drew two pairs of eyes to it, to

observe that Hugh's robin friend—or robin suspect—had been joined by a companion.

"Friendly little chaps," Lady Westbury said benignly.

"Awfully fiddly to mount," Hugh commented. "Bones inordinately brittle—one false move and the whole caboodle is ruined. Delicacy and caution, two essential qualities of a successful taxidermist."

"I daresay. Delicacy and caution are to be commended in many endeavors, Hugh."

The robins bobbed slightly, cocking their heads in unison as if trying to decipher the words being spoken on the other side of the glass.

"I'm a firm believer in such attributes," she continued, "which is why I hesitate before telling you this."

Hello, thought Hugh, *what's this?*

Lady Westbury beamed at him. "Please do conceal your glee at least a little."

"Sorry, I just…that's an awfully promising preamble to dangle before me, Lady W."

"That night, Hugh—Christmas Eve night—I told you I was appalled by both Freddie and David," she said in a curiously tentative way. "I went upstairs to Freddie, as I explained. And then I didn't retire directly to my own bedroom. I came back downstairs."

Hugh couldn't help but emit a sound denoting extreme intrigue: something between an "ahaaa" and a "hmmmm."

"I had no earthly reason to be downstairs—I was neither fetching some cocoa nor extinguishing any of the candles from the dining-room table—but I felt compelled to return. I could see that the lamp in the library was on—the dim one in the corner—so naturally I went to see who it was indulging in some midnight reading. I half hoped that it was Edward. I so rarely have the opportunity to catch that boy alone, to speak with him properly. It was, however, David."

Well, well, well, thought Hugh. *Lady W has been withholding quite the treasure trove of information.*

She went on to detail that David appeared to be standing there empty-handed, neither a drink nor a book to explain his presence there—most curious. She had decorously inquired as to whether his room was to his liking, whether he was in need of anything. David had assured her that all was present and correct.

"Then he merely stood there, most peculiarly, looking at me as though it was I who was misplaced, as if I ought to return to my room. David and I have always rubbed along marvelously, but this...this was a most bizarre interaction." Lady Westbury frowned at the memory of it. "This irked me, Hugh, it irked me tremendously. I had been deliberating over whether to mention his attitude toward Freddie, but the haughty expression he was casting at me made up my mind. I—again, decorously—asked that he please retain a sense of politesse around other guests, regardless of their shortcomings."

"And how did he react to being castigated?" Hugh asked, imagining it to be something of a shock to David—a rebuke from his hostess would be enough to send even the most polished of socialites retreating with their tail between their legs.

"The odd thing was—he chuckled. For a little longer than I would deem wholly acceptable. Then he apologized, reassured me that I need not fear any continued hostility toward Freddie, because…" Here she faltered slightly.

"Because?" Hugh gently said.

"I need not fear any continued hostility toward Freddie, because David had bigger fish to fry," she concluded with haste.

Hugh's mouth hung open. To think, Lady W had been in possession of this information for nearly two days—and had neglected to tell him! *Bigger fish to fry.* Her disinclination to share this encounter indicated to Hugh that, despite her insistence upon the fact that so grisly a crime could never be committed at Westbury Manor, she knew that her midnight exchange with David, a mere matter of hours before he was killed, held some significance. The exact nature of that significance was, of course, still to be determined. What exactly were these *bigger fish* toward which David was turning his attentions?

"A trifle, I know, and I'm at a loss as to why I thought it pertinent to tell you." Lady Westbury's talents were manifold, but disingenuity was notably absent from her retinue. "It's just that you do have a wicked habit of coaxing one into spilling every conceivable bean—however trivial."

Hugh grinned at the chiding, while being acutely aware of the fact that these were no trivial beans—and Lady Westbury knew it too.

29

Drawn by the indistinct aroma of food, Hugh entered the dining room in time to find Lydia consuming a dish of indeterminate mush with all the elegance of a particularly ravenous wolf pup.

"What on earth are you shoveling into your mouth?" he asked.

A moment passed while Lydia swallowed.

"Poached egg and creamed spinach," she answered, tipping her plate toward him so that he could admire the wet mulch slopping around it. "I realized I was famished, so popped downstairs. Never seen Mrs. Smithson so delighted to have a request—she said she'd been twiddling her thumbs down there all morning, waiting for someone—*any*one—to remember their stomachs. The only visitor she'd had was William and, well, you may allow your imagination to inform you how *that* particular interaction panned out."

Hugh was still transfixed by the contents of her plate.

"Would you like some?" Lydia managed to utter, concentrating as she was on loading her spoon with the perfect proportion of spinach to egg.

"I don't think I've seen anything quite so unappetizing in my life."

She grunted something that sounded like "your loss," but Hugh couldn't be entirely sure. He asked her where everyone else was, an inquiry Lydia met with a nonplussed shrug of her shoulders.

"Far as I know, Father and Rosalind are still in situ with the wireless—though I'd wager that Father at least is fast asleep. Last I saw of William, he was wandering along the corridor as if the Four Horsemen of the Apocalypse had rejected his application to join them, on account of his being a little too gloomy for their liking. Stephen went for a lie-down—after you sloped off, he managed to get ever so slightly blotto on that gin. Too early in the day, even by his extremely low standards."

Hugh laughed and frowned again at the damp spinach.

"And Eddy and de Havilland?"

"Eddy and de Havilland, yes. There's a queer duo," Lydia said. Hugh agreed.

"Touch of hero worship occurring, to my mind," she continued. "Someone need only say they'd rather like it if the world were a fairer place, and Eddy's theirs for life. And de Havilland's not just any old idealist—he's an idealist with a seat in the House of Commons. Eddy's positively doolally about him, by all accounts."

"I was under the impression that de Havilland was a bit less revolutionary than Eddy's inclinations—it doesn't strike me that, should he ascend his final few rungs up the ladder, he'll be building guillotines and rounding anyone up."

"Oh, I quite agree—but he's a politician. And politicians are in the business of winning over hearts and minds—and knowing precisely which buttons to press in order to achieve that end. Eddy's buttons are eminently visible to any fool. His sleeve—which is, needless to say, the sleeve of a shirt he's owned for at least five years, because replacing a shirt is tantamount to laughing in the face of the impoverished—is constantly adorned with his bleeding heart." Lydia paused to scoff another egg–spinach mouthful. In a more serious tone, she continued, "He's just so impressionable and impulsive. I hope de Havilland, whatever the content of their conversations, isn't leading him on a merry dance. Anyway—why are you loitering?"

"I'm informing you of my intentions."

"Oh, I say. I never thought I'd see the day—I'm not quite sure you're my type, though, old pal," Lydia quipped.

"Alas, I'm not another rejected proposal to add to your tally, Lyds. I'm going to get some fresh air. Seek some clarity in the outdoors—when the outdoors is not home to Freddie Rampling waving a gun around, that is," he said, glancing out of the window. "Not much of the day left before dark, so I'd best chivvy myself along."

Lydia placed her cutlery in the center of her plate and looked at Hugh.

"Clarity on this confounded mess that's enveloped the house?"

He nodded.

"Truly, I'm beginning to believe Father's poacher theory.

Claptrap though it might be, it's starting to sound less outlandish than the notion that a killer lurks among us. Mightn't it be true? And oughtn't we perhaps to abandon all this detection and skulduggery and just allow Constable Jones to do his job tomorrow?" She looked searchingly at him.

He sighed. "I honestly don't know anymore. Hence the need for a spot of nature and contemplation."

"Give me five minutes to get my jacket, then we can—"

"*Solitary* contemplation, Lyds," he firmly answered. "I need to de-fog myself."

Hearing talk of a meander outside, Bruno came trotting placidly into the dining room, casting his eyes dolefully at Hugh.

"Bruno, stay. Hugh is on a vital de-fogging mission. Zero distractions permitted," Lydia explained.

Distractions had been far too numerous today; Hugh was in danger of failing to see the wood for the trees.

30

Upon leaving Westbury Manor, Hugh headed neither for the copse nor for the fields. Instead, his route took him down the gravel driveway, toward the footpath that would, if he continued along it for a mile or so, lead him to the center—such as it was—of Little Bourton.

He had not decided if he would journey that far, but he felt an urge to extricate himself from the environs of Westbury Manor; it was beginning to feel oppressive. The sense of danger was starting to encroach upon his psyche rather too insistently. He judged that it could only be to the good to take the queries and theories pressing in on him and give them a runaround in the open air to see which had legs; which could sprint, which barely crawled, which ones made it to the finishing line, and which ones limped along, prodded by his guiding hand.

Walking at a brisk but comfortable pace, he listened to the

thoughts clamoring for attention in his mind and attempted to whip them into line. Thorough and methodical, he told himself, thorough and methodical. He gave a backward glance over the gray slush colonizing the driveway—Westbury Manor looked back at him, as if daring him to return sans answers. An epiphany, that's what he needed; a good-old fashioned "eureka," apple-to-the-head moment. He wondered whether Archimedes or Newton had ever turned their attentions to crime-solving; woe betide the deviant who attempted to pull the wool over their—

Hugh stopped in his tracks: he must focus. None of these fantastical musings. What was it that Great-Aunt Fanny used to say? *Stop playing silly buggers, Hugh.* Yes, the profundity and philosophical maxims of Great-Aunt Fanny must be heeded.

To that end, Hugh swerved off the footpath and sat himself on the wall separating it from the field beyond.

He closed his eyes. Inhaled. And exhaled.

Thorough and methodical.

Hugh's scientific tomes and studies had always stated emphatically and unreservedly that assumptions were the stuff of rank amateurs: to rely on preconceived notions was to tumble headlong into the pit of ignorance, from which escape was difficult. And the events of the last two days had been a case study in overturning assumptions.

The question of whether David Campbell-Scott had been killed or committed suicide was now moot: Hugh knew in his waters (and his waters were nigh-on infallible) that yes, David had been murdered. He doubted very much that anyone under the Westbury Manor roof really believed that it had been self-inflicted.

That, he suspected, had been collective wishful thinking: for if it were suicide, it would make life a damned sight more convenient for all involved. The only people who seemed to have backed the suicide argument were de Havilland and William Ashwell, the two people who knew David very little, if at all.

That debate discarded, all that remained—which was quite a lot—was to sift through the various possibilities as to the agent behind his slaying.

Or did that still remain?

Ought he to listen to Lydia—and indeed to everyone else—and allow Constable Jones to pick up the trail tomorrow?

He frowned.

Hugh was a magnanimous, open-hearted man. But he must draw a line somewhere. And entrusting this mystery to that blockhead Jones was that somewhere.

Eddy's having no part in it all was still, regrettably, not a conclusion he could form with any certainty. His contempt for David had been deep-seated and unapologetic in its intensity. To kill him would be to…to avenge the victims of David's allegedly fraudulent activities from a decade ago? A symbolic act—ridding society of one more embodiment of greed? He could well imagine Edward figuring himself as some avenging angel, that much was true. And having executed this offering to the gods of revolution, it would explain his uncharacteristic joviality at breakfast on Christmas morning.

William Ashwell too had every reason to harbor less-than-favorable feelings toward David. It was true that he was a man who seemed devoid of favorable feelings toward many aspects of

the world at large but, stony and naysaying disposition notwithstanding, his disdain for Campbell-Scott was evident. Perfectly
understandable to feel threatened by the man's presence, Hugh
reflected reasonably: here was the robust, charismatic, easy-on-
the-eye chap who had captured his wife's heart years ago, only to
callously discard it. By all accounts, Rosalind was not perturbed
to be unexpectedly reunited with her first love—quite the contrary. Hugh's understanding of women, limited though it was,
suggested that some females were rather predisposed to enjoying
the company of what may generally be termed Bad Sorts. Not to
say that Campbell-Scott was a bad sort as such, but his exoticism
did present something of a brooding Heathcliff to the constancy
of William Ashwell's Edgar Linton.

Now, Freddie. An interesting case, Hugh thought. Freddie's
desperation and volatility were as unswerving and evident as the
other man's dourness. He had bolted on Christmas Eve in a terrible state. But Lady Westbury had vouched for his incapacitation.
Lady Westbury who, by her own admission, strove to iron out
inconveniences, and who had felt protective toward Rampling
since he was a boy.

Stephen was out of the frame, as he entirely lacked the depth
of feeling, the integrity, or the commitment required to murder
anyone. (A triptych of attributes which startled Hugh: it strayed
perilously close to suggesting he *admired* killers. Crikey, he'd
better keep an eye on that.) Similarly, Lord Westbury could be
discounted owing to his frailty: he was so impeded by his health
as to render most physical exertions impossible. His shaking hands
strained with the effort of maintaining a grip on a wineglass for

any prolonged period, never mind holding a gun for long enough to successfully—and neatly—issue a fatal shot.

Which left de Havilland, Lady Westbury, and Rosalind. Rosalind certainly had cause—David had left her high and dry, doomed her to a life of taxes and moderation. Hugh shook his head; no, a *crime passionnel* was out of the question. Rosalind had appeared more eager to reignite her passion with David, rather than to snuff out his life. Lady Westbury he wouldn't—couldn't—countenance. She was averse to mess, to awkwardness, to the wrong kind of attention, and murdering a house guest on Christmas morning was about the most awkwardly messy wrong-kind-of-attention-inducing act imaginable. No, she must be struck from the list also. De Havilland was a slippery fellow all right; he was evasive, his veneer immaculate and his conduct unassailable. Still, there was something Hugh couldn't quite pin down about him. He always had distrusted politicians, though.

The gray sky overhead was darkening; it wasn't yet four o'clock, but the daylight was fast disappearing from sight.

Hugh sighed. The same faces, the same questions. In addition to which, there were now the shadowy faces of all those David had wronged back in 1928—if, indeed, the rumor mill was to be believed. And the poachers—those blasted poachers. It was becoming clear that there was but one way to eliminate that particular line of inquiry.

More questions jostled for attention—who had Edward been speaking with on the stairs that night? What did David mean by *bigger fish* during his exchange with Lady Westbury? Who had written the note in David's fireplace?

"Oh Gaveston, you silly old sausage," he said aloud. "What a royal conundrum you've landed yourself in."

He swung his legs up on to the wall, allowed his head to fall back.

There, upside down behind him, was a sight that had filled him with fear for decades. A sight that had driven him and Lydia to frenzied homeward dashes countless times.

For there, standing behind Hugh, was Mrs. Slabley, the butcher.

Abruptly, he swung his head forward and spun around clumsily. "Mrs. Slabley! I, ah, I didn't see you there—didn't hear you there," he stuttered, leaping down from the wall and approaching the formidable woman, hand outstretched to shake hers.

Mrs. Slabley cut an imposing figure. She cut it almost as impressively as she cut her tenderloin steaks. Amazonian in stature, she had been a mainstay in Little Bourton since Hugh and his family had moved there, some twenty years ago.

She inspected his hand, sniffed, then administered a shake bone-crushing in strength.

"Mr. Gaveston," she uttered, narrowing her eyes as she did so. He was filled with awe, fear, admiration, and more fear. A paralyzing cocktail.

A moment passed. Or was it several? Hugh couldn't be sure. In the presence of Mrs. Slabley, he felt himself become the eleven-year-old boy who had first laid eyes on her as she strung up a beef flank in the window of her butcher's shop. Dark hair scraped tightly—painfully tightly, it always appeared—back into a bun (though the word "bun" in association with Mrs. Slabley was comically incongruous), aquiline features tautly prepared to detect any suggestion of weakness, sturdy legs clad in corduroy slacks: here truly was Mrs. Slabley.

"Happen as there's some nastiness yonder," she stated, nodding almost imperceptibly toward Westbury Manor.

Before he could ask how she was aware of this, she stated, just as matter-of-factly, "Mrs. Smithson. Little chat. This afternoon."

Hugh mentally scrambled for something, anything to say. What had Mrs. Smithson told her? Had she heard anything else? Mrs. Slabley, however, waited for no man to propel her conversations.

"Happen somethin' went wrong."

A woman of reticence, Mrs. Slabley nonetheless managed to convey more in four words than Hugh could have mustered in several paragraphs of unbroken prose.

"I'm sorry?"

"Somethin'. Went. Wrong."

"Well, yes, something…yes…someone was *killed*," Hugh babbled. "So yes, all things considered, one could define that as—"

"Not with that," Mrs. Slabley continued enigmatically. "With *that*."

She gestured over the wall upon which Hugh had been perched.

"Yonder."

"Right-o, of course, yes, yonder. That yonder." Hugh nodded. Then added, "With what yonder?"

Mrs. Slabley did not even deign to roll her eyes, for such physical effort would be to dignify Hugh's question more than it deserved. Hugh interpreted her motionless silence accurately and turned back to the wall. He peered over it, yonder. Straining his eyes against the impending darkness and the all-consuming grayness of the terrain, he spotted something.

A bag, wrapped in something—a scarf perhaps? A blanket?

He turned to look at Mrs. Slabley, who returned his glance with an entirely inscrutable stare. *Don't run, Hugh*, he told himself, *she doesn't really chop off fingers with her butcher's knife.*

He hopped over the wall and made his way toward the bag which, as suspected, was wrapped in a scarf. Picking it up, he returned to Mrs. Slabley.

"Do you…ah, do you know what's in here, Mrs. Slabley?" he asked.

"Happen I do."

Hugh carefully unraveled the scarf, which was soggy from the melting snow in which it had been deposited, and removed the bag. It was unremarkable in every way, except for its contents. For inside the bag lay two items of interest to any burgeoning detective: a pair of black gloves and a gun.

Eyes widened, he asked Mrs. Slabley if she knew who had deposited the bag. It happened that she did.

"Could you…could you tell me who it was, Mrs. Slabley?" Hugh asked, a hint of impatience in his voice.

"Happen it was some fella from yonder." Another nod toward Westbury Manor. Hugh was on the point of seeking clarification on which particular fella that might be, when Mrs. Slabley reiterated that it was some fella from yonder.

"How exactly do you know that, Mrs. Slabley?"

She regarded him as a cat might regard a particularly dim mouse before deciding whether to pounce or leave it be.

"Happen I saw 'em. Yesterday morning."

Yesterday morning? But that was Christmas morning. The morning David's body was found. This didn't add up.

"Happen it was around nine thirty. Happen it's when I go walking. No bother around. No *people* around," she elaborated, becoming positively verbose at this point.

"And you saw them—you saw someone put this bag here?"

"Happen I know where the shooter came from and all." Was it his fancy, or was Mrs. Slabley enjoying these elusive pronouncements?

"And I don't suppose you could tell me where the, uh, shooter came from?"

"Crown and Cat."

"The pub in the village? The gun came from the pub?" Hugh blurted.

A nod whose firmness indicated that she would brook no further converse. And with that, Mrs. Slabley strode forth. Gone just as swiftly as she had arrived.

"Oh lummy," Hugh muttered, inspecting the contents of the bag once again. "Oh lummy."

31

Hugh plodded—for plod really was the only appropriate verb to assign to his movements—back up to Westbury Manor, dejected, confused, and assailed by questions.

He was overcome by a longing to be back in his study—his makeshift workshop—where a question could be answered by simply leafing through the relevant reference book. Oh, to be stitching a mink pelt now; to be affixing a pair of iridescent glass eyes to a stoat. Painstaking though it was, taxidermy bore startlingly tangible and pleasingly real results. Attempting to stitch together the truth and affix a conclusion to what had happened to David Campbell-Scott—such labor did not seem to be promising a satisfying outcome. Quite the contrary; traipsing toward the house, Hugh felt that the situation was unraveling rapidly.

Another gun? Hidden outside? What the deuce was happening? Another killer? A duo of killers? Or merely one ruthless, relentless, fearless killer, with multiple weapons—perhaps multiple targets? Once again, Hugh worried that in revealing his investigations, Stephen had, however unintentionally, succeeded in placing Hugh in a significant amount of danger. Squishing and squelching his way the final few steps to the door, he resolved to take some action. He would eliminate at least one line of inquiry tonight, by hook or by crook.

32

As Hugh divested himself of his boots and deposited the *item* in his bedroom (he would deal with that later), our eager observer of proceedings might take the opportunity to leave him to the unknotting of his bootlaces (most stubborn specimens) and to meander through the rest of the house. Such surreptitious wanderings might take our spectator to the dining room, to find that most intriguing of partnerships, de Havilland and Edward, deep in conversation once again, and finishing what appeared to be another bespoke meal cobbled together by Mrs. Smithson: apple chutney accompanied by sausages and crackers.

Tact being a prized trait of any eager observer, eavesdropping is strongly frowned upon, and thus the mere sight of de Havilland and Edward suffices to furnish our onlooker with food for thought; not for our spectator the uncouth sport of loitering to steal any conversational crumbs. The dining room is, after all, but one room in a house full of nooks and crannies brimming with intrigue. For example, our observer, upon entering the library, would be met with William Ashwell's glassy stare as he clenched and unclenched his fists as if under an enchantment. Or, upon descending the stairs to the kitchen, might overhear Mrs. Smithson explaining to Angela that he was always a wrong'un, from the word go. Quite who was a wrong'un, our observer would be forced to mull over while returning upstairs to find Hugh, boots replaced with slippers, making his way along the corridor.

Despite Lady Westbury's insistence on business as usual, Hugh couldn't help but feel that there was an odd, apocalyptic air to the house. As though the wider world had been subject to a terrible fate that had left civilization razed to the ground—and this merry band comprised the only remaining survivors.

The thought sent a shudder through Hugh. Thank goodness for Mrs. Slabley, a timely reminder that, mercifully, he was not doomed to live out his days subsisting on soggy creamed spinach and half-baked murder conspiracies.

"What ho, chaps?" he inquired, rubbing his cold hands together and approaching the warmth of the fire.

Edward's spirits seemed to have risen again—he really was a most unpredictable fellow, trumped only by Freddie on that front, Hugh reflected—and he appeared unambiguously pleased to see him.

"*What ho*, Hugh, *what ho* is that times are changing!" he beamed.

Oh Lord, Hugh thought. He's all fired up again. Another piece of agitprop drama was coming his way.

De Havilland smiled politely, poured a little more tea from the pot on the tray in front of him. "We were just discussing Eddy's future."

Eddy's future? Hugh had only ever heard Edward countenance this abbreviation within the family bosom—he'd only a few years ago managed to suppress his winces when Hugh used the pet name. De Havilland really did have him in the palm of his hand.

"Oh yes?" Hugh responded, the fire bringing the circulation back to his hands.

"Mr. de Havilland's twisted my arm about a rather exciting matter." Edward's glee could hardly be contained.

A chuckle from de Havilland. "And it did take quite some arm-twisting, I'll grant you."

Hugh waited expectantly, observing the flush in Edward's cheeks and the burning excitement in his eyes.

"I've been chewing his ear off these last couple of days, telling him all about my work in Bethnal Green—the children sifting through rubbish bins for food, the families living seven to a room, the criminals exploiting all of this for their own ends."

Hugh nodded. He had, of course, heard this countless times before—but there was a new tenor to Edward's voice. Not raging indignation, but ardent zeal—a smidgen of…hope in there?

"And of course about what I do for the newspaper—what I *try* to do, when they don't want me to cover 'human interest' stories about school fairs and puppies reunited with their owners. What, I ask you, could be of more 'human interest' than real people talking about their real lives, their real woes, their real sufferings?" Edward continued.

"Unutterably valuable work Eddy has been undertaking—admirable stuff," de Havilland chipped in. "However, the trouble is—nobody's listening. And this is the problem I have seen time and time again. Power stays with those already in power, shutting out anyone who has truly seen the impact of the decisions made in Westminster. Denying entry to all but those who seek to pat each other on the back, make a few speeches, then retire for brandy and cigars."

Edward's glow was radiating more evidently now.

"I've decided," de Havilland continued, "to create a job for Eddy in Westminster. A fact-finder, a man with his ear to the ground who can help me to change policies and make a real difference in this country."

"Crikey, Eddy!" Hugh exclaimed, genuinely surprised by this turn of events. Eddy usually rubbed people up the wrong way to such an extent that they might be tempted to pay him to keep away from them—certainly he had never encountered anyone who would willingly and knowingly pay Edward to spend even more time with them. "This is a turn-out for the books! Stomping around Westminster! When did you two cook all this up?"

"Last—" Edward began, only to be interrupted by de Havilland.

"Last few hours, really. It came to me like a bolt from the blue—why surround myself with chaps who'd no sooner step foot in East London than they would the seventh circle of hell? It's change this country needs, and by listening to the passion and insight of people like Eddy, I hope to bring about that change."

De Havilland was now giving the impression of an MP

finessing his latest campaign speech—which, Hugh reflected, he supposed he was.

"Mr. de Havilland is going to lead England to a bright 1939, a bright future—I know it, Hugh." Eddy was practically foaming at the mouth now. "One where men like David Campbell-Scott will be held accountable for their actions, here and overseas. When Mr. de Havilland becomes our next Prime Minister, the time for talking will be over."

Hugh paused, frowned.

"Oh, you flatter me, Eddy." De Havilland smiled, not entirely convincing in his humility. "But that is my hope, my vision—to lead our country into a new era of equality and fairness and real change."

"Stirring stuff indeed, Mr. de Havilland," Hugh said, helping himself to a morsel of cracker from Eddy's plate. "If you'll excuse me—I have been struck by the most beastly hunger pangs, and rumor has it that Mrs. Smithson is desperate to plate up some chops."

With that, Hugh departed. His stomach was indeed rumbling, but there were more pressing matters to attend to.

33

Boxing Day was drawing to a close in much the same way as it had begun: shuffling along uncertainly, episodes of forced jollity interrupted by moments of uncomfortable candor.

Freddie had emerged from his post-shooting convalescence, whimpering his apologies to everyone in the drawing room before asking Angela—who had already successfully circulated a tray of gin and its various accoutrements around the room—to fetch him some soda water.

This, of course, raised eyebrows and prompted Stephen to mock-faint, then declare that he had spotted a platoon of pigs flying outside the window, then inquire as to when they ought to go ice-skating in the newly frozen-over hell.

Lady Westbury appeared content with Freddie's reappearance and his choice of beverage, while Lord Westbury's wireless nap had reinvigorated his spirits. He was extolling the virtues of peat whisky to William Ashwell, who seemed more interested in watching—monitoring—his wife.

As for Rosalind, she too appeared less doldrum-bound than a few hours earlier, and was uttering a whinnying laugh as she conversed with Lydia and de Havilland about something or other. Hugh wondered whether de Havilland ever stopped canvassing for votes and supporters. Probably not, he resolved.

Hugh's eyes roved around the room, analyzing the smallest gestures of those about him. Observation was the stepping-stone to conclusion, he knew that much. Particularly the observation of subjects who were unaware that they were under scrutiny.

"I say, everyone," he announced, the various conversations coming to a close. "Tomorrow we're all departing Westbury Manor—those of us not fortunate enough to call it home, that is. I wonder—might we take a moment before we leave to exchange presents? Of course, yesterday it would have been…undecorous, naturally, what with…"

He need say no more—nods of assent from around the room.

"But it occurred to me that all these gifts are languishing rather morosely under the tree—it would be a terrible shame to neglect them entirely. I for one am jolly keen to see what color socks Lady W has bestowed upon me this year," he continued merrily.

"You're quite right, Hugh," his hostess purred. "I think that's a splendid plan." The notion of sending her guests away without a present had been plaguing her all day, and she had intended to raise the topic over dinner. A death on Christmas Day was a dire disaster out of her control; empty-handed guests was a faux pas well within her power to avoid.

"Why don't we just see to it now?" Lydia asked. She was ever the iconoclast, Hugh thought; always finding room for objection where no objection lay. "Why do we need to stand on ceremony and make a song and dance of it?"

"Hear, hear, sis," Stephen said, before adding, "That way I can slope off early tomorrow and we needn't see each other again 'til Christmas 1939!"

"We could, I suppose…" Lady Westbury began.

That wouldn't do at all. It wouldn't give Hugh enough time to prepare.

"No, no," he disagreed, rather more sharply than he'd intended. Softening his tone, he said, "We're all a bit pooped after…the events of this morning, and there's dinner ahead of us yet. My proposal is that we turn in early tonight, then have presents and the parting of ways tomorrow. After our interlocution with Constable Jones, of course. What time did he say he would be arriving, Mr. de Havilland?"

"Oh…two o'clock, I believe he said."

"That does it then." Hugh surveyed the room with a grin. "Jones, presents, departures."

Shoulders were shrugged, grunts were uttered, glasses were refreshed. He had had suggestions more warmly received in the past, but this was not a time for concerns about etiquette, Hugh thought.

"Well, let's get some grub, shall we?" Lord Westbury proposed. "Had a pickle and a sardine earlier, no way for a man to live!"

34

The mood was subdued as dinner was devoured with varying degrees of relish by the guests. The efforts of generating and sustaining polite conversation seemed to have taken their toll, and the clinking of cutlery on china was the dominant force puncturing the regular spells of silence.

Even Stephen appeared to have fallen into the clutches of fatigue and, following a handful of half-hearted jibes, he wordlessly finished his salmon.

Angela felt rather redundant, as not only had Mr. Rampling abstained from wine this evening, but all other glasses were slow to be emptied, their owners reluctant to allow them to be replenished. Hugh scanned the room: everyone was evidently still ill at ease, perhaps believing that by not partaking in the free-flowing alcohol with such gusto, they might be able to stave off further incidents.

In short, a bacchanal it was not.

Lord Westbury's plate was the last to be cleared of its load, and the relief as he carefully placed his napkin on the table palpable.

"Right-o, I'm to bed!" Hugh exclaimed, perhaps in too sprightly a manner, he immediately realized.

"It's barely nine o'clock," Lydia remonstrated.

He performed a stretch that he hoped would convey weary limbs and an addled mind.

"Oh, time is but a number, Lyds," he replied. "I'm tuckered, dead on my feet, positively spent, dog-tired." Was he overegging the pudding somewhat?

"All right, all right, get thee to bed then, you decrepit old creature, you," Lydia answered, dismissing him with a wave of her hands.

Hugh absented himself to a general hum of sounds—guests expressing their intentions for the evening before dispersing to an assortment of destinations.

He was confident, however, that he would have no accidental or unwanted companions as he made his way to his own two destinations: the Crown and Cat, and the dilapidated stables beyond the copse.

Confident, of course, because he was trying with all his might to ignore the inner voice reminding him that, if he was correct, there was a killer at large who might be keeping a very close eye on him.

35

Lydia would disapprove of Hugh's plans in the strongest possible terms. He was a bloody idiot, it was a fool's errand, he'd better not come crying to her when he ended up dead too. He could hear her words clattering through his mind as he trundled once more down the path toward the village.

The mile's trudge seemed to take far longer than usual: perhaps, Hugh reflected, it would have been quicker had he resisted the urge to regularly and repeatedly look over his shoulder to ensure that he wasn't being followed. The trip accomplished, Hugh checked his watch: nine thirty. It was, in fact, the perfect time for a swift half.

The bottle-green tiles adorning the outside of the Crown and Cat provided a welcoming sight as he turned on to the high street, such as it was. For the high street of Little Bourton was home to precisely five buildings of public interest: Mrs. Slabley's butcher's shop; a bakery that claimed to purvey England's finest hot-cross buns (a claim to which Hugh could attest); a bric-a-brac shop that was the first port of call in myriad situations, whether one had misplaced one's doorknob or needed a new fountain pen; Mr. Norris's post office (which, in 1932, Mr. Norris had sworn blind was haunted, but it turned out to be a terrible case of rising damp); and finally, the Crown and Cat. A bus stop farther along the street would take one to Great Bourton (once a week, on a Tuesday, any time between two o'clock and five o'clock), and if one was feeling adventurous, one need only continue along the street to reach the train station, whence one could be conveyed to the bright lights of London (when there was neither snow nor leaves on the line, naturally).

Nods greeted Hugh as he made his way toward the bar. He was well-liked in Little Bourton: the eccentric bachelor sitting on a fortune and cavorting around with that standoffish Westbury girl. He was well aware of his reputation, and knew that popular opinion would serve him well in tonight's endeavor.

Having acquired his half and a packet of pork scratchings, Hugh installed himself on a barstool and cast his eyes around the pub. The usual assortment of locals were positioned at the tables, and Hugh fancied that a few voices had lowered since his arrival—word must, by now, be spreading about the Christmas-morning discovery up at Westbury Manor.

"And how was your Christmas, Mr. Gaveston?" Rita, the landlady, inquired.

"Oh, so-so—overcooked turkey, too much sherry, a bout of charades," Hugh answered cheerily. "And yours? I hear tell that there was a spot of bother here—Christmas Day revelers taking their reveling a bit far, eh?"

Rita brushed off any suggestion of there having been trouble; she was a proud landlady, and any besmirchment on her establishment she took as a besmirchment on her character. And she'd have none of that.

A moment passed as Hugh took a sip from his drink. He cleared his throat and turned back to her. *Now or never, Hugh.*

"I say," he began, giving his best impression of a hapless naïf, "friends of mine are down from town tomorrow, jolly keen to get out and about, nab some pheasants."

Rita, or Mrs. Ludgate to newcomers, continued wiping the bar top with her dishcloth, listening to, but not particularly interested in, Hugh's witterings. So far, so bland—*well done, Hugh*, he thought to himself.

"Blasted nuisance of it is, though"—*here goes*, he thought— "I'm short a gun. No fun if we're not all equipped, you see."

Rita's dishcloth motions continued, albeit at a slightly slower pace. *Easy does it, Hugh, easy does it.*

"Don't suppose, ah, you'd know where a man might be able to get his hands on one? At, ah, short notice?" He chanced it, smiling guilelessly as Rita glanced up at him.

Were he a newcomer, this, of course, would have been a fatal leap to have made. Being as he was, however, the harmless dandy from Gaveston Lodge, Rita did not immediately bristle or bridle at his query. Perhaps it was the accompanying wink that ensured his success.

"I couldn't say, Mr. Gaveston, other than to point your *friends* in the direction of the nearest licensed outlet of such accessories, over in Great Bourton," Rita replied.

"Oh, of course, of course," Hugh said. Perhaps this had been a fool's errand after all. "Fire up the motor tomorrow, zip on over in the car…"

"But of course, Mr. Harding might be able to give you directions to a closer shop," Rita continued, her effortless nonchalance matched by the efficiency of her handiwork at the now gleaming bar top. She nodded across the counter, where a thicket of white hair and a sheepdog sprawled on the floor signaled Mr. Harding's presence.

That old scoundrel. He'd been knocking around Little Bourton for decades; Lord Westbury reckoned him to be some twenty years his senior, but he showed no signs of slowing down in his shenanigans. Wiry and wily, Mr. Harding was known to have his fingers in many pies—none of them wholly legal pies. There had been the incident with the stud-farm racket, then the antiques dealing…and now dabbling in firearms? Well, well, well. One had to admire the entrepreneurship of the old coot.

Hugh expressed his gratitude to Rita, explained that his *friends* would be awfully glad of it, and sidled his way round to Mr. Harding.

"Evening, Mr. Gaveston," Mr. Harding croaked amiably.

Hugh returned his greeting and asked Rita to furnish Mr. Harding with the same again. A further nod from Mr. Harding signified his thanks for the fresh stout.

"Am I to understand that…should a man be in need of a certain piece of…equipment, he might be able to procure such equipment from you, Mr. Harding?" he asked.

"Christ alive, Gaveston, no beating about the bush with you, is there!" Harding exclaimed, as loudly as a hushed tone would allow for exclamations. "A by-your-leave might be nice, you know, young fella."

Hugh artfully arranged his most ostensibly artless smile once more. Unstudied naivety would be just the ticket with a rogue like this: a rogue who would cheat his own mother given half the chance.

"Well, I'm a straightforward chap, Mr. Harding—ask anyone who knows me. In fact, my old Latin master used to say, 'Gaveston, you're the most straightforward fellow I've ever encountered.' And he'd led *quite* the life. Spent a year in Mongolia, where he met some old chap he'd known in Oxford, quite the coincidence really. Now what was his name…Dewitt, Dewlitt, Dewinter…oh, it's on the tip of my tongue."

"God's teeth, man," Harding interjected. "What is it that you want?"

Bingo.

"Dewynter it was! Dewynter with a y!" Hugh exclaimed. "That was going to aggravate me all night! Oh, what was it I came over here for?"

He conjured a look of puzzlement as one groping for a memory might have.

"Ah yes! That was it. Chum of mine was here just the other night, told me to come here to see a man about a…about a *you-know-what*." Hugh winked ostentatiously.

Harding looked at him carefully. "Which night would you be talking about, Mr. Gaveston, specifically?"

Another risk. One which, he hoped, would reap rewards. "Oh, Christmas Eve it must have been. Yes, Christmas Eve, that was it."

Proffering this detail appeared to assuage any suspicions that might have been growing in Harding's mind. "That older fellow, he's your 'chum,' is he? Didn't seem like a man inclined to chumminess with anyone, not from where I was standing."

Bingo again.

"That'll be him, yes," Hugh confirmed. "Anyway, my chum. The, ah, equipment he procured from you—" Hugh placed the bag on the floor between the barstools upon which he and Harding were perched. "He thinks there's a fault of some kind with it—sent me to ask about it."

A further glance of suspicion. "Why didn't he just come back himself? Why send an errand boy?"

Now that was a rather excellent question, and one for which Hugh had not prepared an answer. He could have kicked himself. But needs must: improvise or be damned.

"He's gone back to town. Left it here for his next trip, you see." Perhaps not entirely convincing, but not entirely implausible either.

Harding dismounted his stool with a surprising level of agility—if he was, as Lord Westbury surmised, nearing his ninetieth year on Earth, then he was a highly impressive specimen—and, bending down under the pretense of petting his sleeping sheepdog, cast an appraising glance into the bag.

Hugh held his breath. If Harding did not recognize the pistol, then his entire hypothesis was flawed—no, not flawed: failed. If, however, he did recognize the gun, then that confirmed Hugh's theory.

Harding returned to his seat and grunted.

"It's in mint condition—was when I sold it to your *chum*, still is now. Forgive my bluntness, Mr. Gaveston, but a bad workman blames his tools."

"Oh dear, oh dear." Hugh shrugged his shoulders affably. "I understand, Mr. Harding. And I thank you for your time."

He polished off the last drop of his half-pint and clapped Harding on the shoulder as he cradled the bundle in his arm.

"You have been immensely helpful—as have you, Rita!"

Turning on his heel and strolling out of the Crown and Cat, Hugh couldn't help but break into a merry whistle: the fogs were clearing at last.

36

Where he had trudged earlier, Hugh was on the verge of skipping now. The clickings and cog-turnings in his brain propelled him along the path, back in the direction of Westbury Manor. His confabulation with Mr. Harding had provided him with confirmation of one aspect of his investigations, but he mustn't become complacent: there was still another concern niggling away persistently in his mind. The galling thing was that he couldn't quite put his finger on its precise nature.

No matter. That would have to wait until the morning: fresh eyes would attend to it.

For now, there was one final pit stop on tonight's little expedition: the old stables.

As he passed Westbury Manor, the lights in various windows indicated that a number of rooms were populated with occupants who had no mind for sleep just yet. A house alive with festive merriment and a-buzz with warmth, Hugh thought ironically. As a rule, he tended to avoid irony, convinced that embracing it led to cynicism and a callow outlook on the world. But occasionally, he allowed himself to dip his toes into its shallows, careful not to wade further into the murky depths of sarcasm. If, of course, he were a sarcastic man (which, of course, he wasn't), he would almost certainly be thinking that he simply couldn't *wait* to return to the rest and tranquility of Westbury Manor.

Smiling at his own dialogue with himself, Hugh directed his torch into the copse—he ought to pinpoint as direct a route as possible before setting off to the stables. Minimal sludge was required in order to make this mission as swift as possible. He had set himself a ten-thirty curfew in order to collect his thoughts adequately with a mug of cocoa before bed—he was straying perilously close to breaching his own deadline now.

The spindly trees seemed to grimace as he approached. It is always as well to take note of any portents when undertaking a quest such as his, and Hugh had to concede that the rather abrupt arrival of some howling wind and a soggy branch slapping him in the face were undeniably portents of something. Heeding them not a jot, he crashed onward, determined to reach the stables and thus put to bed at least one of the theories ricocheting around his mind.

His torch emitting a somewhat feeble beam, he placed his steps as carefully as he could, taking note of his path so that he might follow it with ease on the return trip.

Hugh was not a superstitious man. He was not a believer in preternatural beings or ghosties or goblins. He was instead a man alert to the empirical evidence of any given situation. A keen observer of the world and the tangible realities that lay therein.

Blundering through the copse, however, he felt his skin prickle.

By the same token, he was not a paranoid man. Baseless worries skimmed from him as water from a duck.

As he pulled his coat tighter around him, however, Hugh heard Lydia's words once again: *or come after you to shut you up*.

A crash up ahead, to the right.

He swung his torch in the direction of the noise.

Was that a figure?

Moving rather rapidly?

Moving rather rapidly *toward* him?

Before Hugh could gather his wits and formulate a rational response to what, he now concluded with alarming certainty, was indeed a figure rushing toward him in a dark wood, he surrendered to his natural impulse. He screamed.

Not a bloodcurdling scream or an ear-piercing scream. More of a shriek, if one were to strive for accuracy in one's description.

Fight or flight being the innate dilemma in situations such as these, fight is, more often than not, viewed as the more honorable of the two options. However, as Hugh knew all too well from his studies of the natural world, flight was an infinitely more reliable option for survival.

And so it was that Hugh Gaveston, aspiring detective, would-be ensnarer of murderers, foiler of nefarious plots, shrieked and ran away.

Crashing through the copse back toward Westbury Manor, he could see the lights of the house glowing, beckoning him onward.

What Hugh did not see, however—and what a more composed, less affrighted spectator would undoubtedly have noticed—was the damp piece of wood upon which his foot slipped.

Such a spectator would, needless to say, have avoided this unfortunately placed piece of wood, thus also avoiding the fate which befell our woebegone, would-be-intrepid nocturnal adventurer.

For in an instant, Hugh was plunging forward, hands clasping the bag containing the gun—hands which he should have put out to protect himself as the plunge continued. For if he had put out his hands, he might have protected his head from the rock peering out from the sludge on the ground.

37

Hugh woke up to a soft murmur of voices and, blinking his eyes, he realized that he was lying on a sofa in the Westburys' drawing room.

"He's come to! He's coming round!" a voice exclaimed.

"Oh, thank goodness!" Another voice, Lady Westbury's.

Stephen's laughter. "Bloody hell, Gaveston, gave us all a fright! What a to-do!"

Hugh adjusted himself on the sofa, raising a hand to his head where an impressive bump was already erupting. Still dazed, he slowly gazed around the room—an array of concerned faces stared back at him. Even William Ashwell looked worried.

"What—what happened?" he asked.

"Good bloody question! I thought you'd been coshed on the head! Thumped good and proper!" Stephen answered. "But no, nothing quite as dramatic as all that—you took a real header, by all accounts."

Hugh remembered running, he remembered falling…and remembered *why* he'd been running.

"Someone was out there! Someone was chasing me!" he exclaimed, sitting upright.

"No, Hugh. Nobody was chasing you," Lydia sternly intoned.

"They were! There was a figure in the copse, they—"

"It was me, you mortal idiot. It was *me* out there."

Lydia? *Lydia* had been out in the copse? It didn't make any sense. "But why did you chase me?" he asked.

A snort from Stephen.

"I wasn't chasing you, I was…just running toward you," Lydia grumbled.

"Why didn't you call my name then?"

"I did. Several times, in fact. But I imagine that you couldn't hear me. What with all the screaming you were doing," she concluded.

Ah.

Stephen burst out into hoots of merriment. Hugh couldn't help but smile too. What a goose he'd been. What an absolute goose. His admission of his own goose-like behavior prompted the tension in the room to evaporate entirely; everyone was united in agreeing that, yes, Hugh had been *quite* the goose.

Lydia explained that she had been out for a walk, had heard a noise that sounded like a wounded bird, and so had, rather foolishly, followed the noise into the copse.

"'Course there wasn't a damn thing there—sorry, Mother." Lady Westbury had flinched at her expletive—a positive sign of normality returning. "And the next thing I knew, you were shining

your torch in there, so I started to dash over to you—only for you to start wailing like a banshee and then hit the deck. Out cold. I came back in here for assistance, and Mr. de Havilland and Eddy helped to carry you in here. Where you've been recumbent for"—she checked her watch—"half an hour now."

Lady Westbury insisted he take some of the hot tea steaming on the corner table beside him. Sipping it, he again touched his forehead and winced.

"Not a scratch on you, old chap—no blood drawn," Lord Westbury reassured him.

"Shan't be needing to administer any Dakin's solution, not just yet," de Havilland added. Lord Westbury's confused glance prompted him to elaborate. "Applied it to minor wounds back on the front. Pungent stuff—trenches in Ypres positively drenched in it, stank the place out."

"What?" Hugh asked, before correcting himself. "Sorry, this bump has really knocked me for six. My head's swimming. I think I ought to get to bed."

"And whither wilt thou wander *this* time?" Stephen inquired. "A trip to bed for young Hugh Gaveston could end in any number of ways these days: daresay in a few hours we'll have word of him speaking in tongues on a Blackpool pier or in a trance in Piccadilly."

"No more walkabouts, Hugh," Lady Westbury lightly chided. "I might have to affix a lock to the outside of the Blue Room if you insist on these nocturnal wanderings."

"Oh—uh—my bag—the bag I had with me…" he began, struggling to conceal his panic. That bag had the gun in it.

"Don't worry—safe and sound over here." Lydia picked it up. "I'll carry it upstairs for you. Now that you're a bona fide casualty, can't be expected to carry your own luggage."

A chorus of good-nights ushered them out, and the pair made their way up the stairs.

As soon as they were safely out of earshot and in the Blue Room, Hugh turned to Lydia.

"What the deuce were you *doing* out there?" he asked urgently.

"Could ask the same of *you*! I thought you were in bed!" Lydia barked.

"I was…I popped to the pub," Hugh replied, in an admission that struck them both as being utterly absurd.

"The *pub*? You *popped to the pub*?" Lydia spat.

Hugh couldn't risk revealing his latest findings to her now; not when he was so close to the truth. He loved his friend, but Lord knew she was a blunderer. And it was crucial that no blunderings occur between now and tomorrow.

"I needed some more fresh air, stretch my legs," he jabbered.

"You had some fresh air *earlier*, and I wasn't allowed to join you on that little escapade either," she impetuously pointed out.

"Yes, well, anyway. Don't deflect. What the blazes were you doing out there?"

"I told you—I went for a walk, heard a wounded bird, went to try to save it."

"Poppycock! Saving a wounded bird? In the copse? In the middle of the night? Pull the other one, Lydia. The day you become the Florence Nightingale of the natural world is the day that—that Freddie Rampling swears off booze." A pause as he remembered Freddie's soda water earlier. "Scratch that—but you know what I mean!"

Lydia sighed.

"Fine. I know you told me to sit tight, to not go charging around," she began. "And I think you'll agree that I've done a jolly good job of that. Been biting my tongue for approximately thirty-six hours now. A woman has her limits. So I thought I'd do something useful that wouldn't jeopardize your...sleuthing."

As soon as the words had left her mouth, Hugh knew where she had been: the stables.

"Don't tell me you were at the stables, Lydia," he said. "Don't tell me you were hunting down poachers."

A flush rose in her face.

"Well, if you can promise me that that's not precisely where you had been heading—before you ran off screaming, that is— then I can promise you that that's not precisely where I had been."

She was infuriating, Hugh thought. Telling her as much, he then conceded that yes, that was precisely where he had been heading.

"Well, there you have it, Hugh. Either we're both geniuses, or we're both imbeciles." Her anger had subsided, he could tell.

"And?" Hugh knew what he had been on his way there to do: examine the stables for any signs of inhabitation by the poachers. After the last bout of poaching, all manner of debris had been recovered there: Lord Westbury had been incensed when Tom (his previous footman) had reported the evidence of a fire, some bullet casings, empty tins of beans, and, inexplicably, a sock. They had clearly set up shop there, as it were, using it as a convenient base for forays out into the surrounding properties. Hugh suspected that, if they were up to their old tricks, they would most likely utilize the stables as makeshift headquarters once again.

"Nothing. Absolutely nothing. Not a sausage. Or even a bean, for that matter," Lydia told him. "And you know what that means?"

He did: it meant that it was highly improbable that David had disturbed any poachers (for if they weren't camped out on the Westbury Manor grounds, there would be no call to be crossing it), and therefore it was highly improbable that he had been killed by any poachers either.

"I was half hoping that I'd find all sorts there—proof that the poachers were there, proof that they'd been disturbed by David yesterday morning," Lydia explained. "At least that way I might have been able to sleep better tonight—knowing that it *had* been poachers, and not Eddy. But now…now I don't know what to think."

Despondently, she plumped down on his bed. There was, Hugh reasoned, nothing more they could do tonight—they were better off getting to sleep and reconvening in the morning.

"Yes. I suppose you're right," Lydia grumbled. "No more troublemaking, Hugh. At least not until tomorrow."

As she closed the door, he himself flopped down on the bed and fell almost immediately to sleep, where he found himself enmeshed in a peculiarly vivid dream: he was punting in Cambridge. Except instead of his college friends, the inhabitants of Westbury Manor were there with him. And every time he plunged the pole into the water, it became harder and harder to extract it. Harder and harder to extricate it from the sludge that lay beneath.

38

Notebook in hand, our perspicacious observer would no doubt be up with the lark to witness Jim returning from his morning walk with Bruno. It would be noted that Jim did not appear entirely at ease and had not, in fact, polished his shoes for several hours: signals that our observer would, with habitual insight, interpret as effects of Jim's happening upon a dead body the last time he was undertaking his dog-walking duties. Reflections upon Jim's state of mind would be interrupted by Hugh's bounding down the stairs. Pen poised, our spectator would proceed to jot down the interaction which left Jim in wordless astonishment: the interaction during which Hugh maneuvered an abrupt about-turn and bounded directly back up the staircase.

Astonished though Jim might be, our spectator would have no such response, for our spectator would follow Hugh upstairs to see him inform Lydia of his plans for the morning—plans which he had only formulated when he woke with a start at the ungodly hour of five o'clock.

"Lyyyyydia," he trilled as he gently pushed open her bedroom door. "Wakey, wakey, rise and shine."

She groaned and flung her body over, so that she was facing the wall, pulling her bedcovers up around her ears.

"Lyyyyydia," came the melodious refrain. "Lydia!"

A grunt came which Hugh interpreted as a request to clarify his presence in her room so early in the morning.

"Lyds, I'm trotting off for a spell," he whispered. "I'll be back for luncheon."

Lydia bolted upright, an expression of irritation and aggrievement slapped on her face.

"What? What're you *talking* about, Hugh?"

"There's something I must do—someone I must see. I'll be a few hours—tell everyone there's been a burst pipe at Gaveston Lodge, something of that ilk. Had to dash off to see to it, yadda, yadda," he quickly explained, checking his watch and already retreating toward the door.

"Oh, and Lyds—don't let anyone leave this house. Chain yourself to 'em if you must—but don't let *anyone* leave."

39

As the 06.13 to Waterloo pulled out of Little Bourton station, Hugh Gaveston felt queasy with trepidation. For this was the step that would seal the outcome of today: this would either confirm his suspicion once and for all, or discredit it entirely. Last night's somewhat embarrassing knock to the head might have left him in a brief stupor, but it had also led to the crystallization of one critical point in his mind.

Upon waking this morning before dawn, he had known precisely what he must do: today, 27 December 1938, would be the making of him. It had been irksome to wait until the first train of the day, and padding about in the Blue Room in his dressing gown and slippers, he had revolved all the possibilities several times over until the only certainty he held was that he was going mad. No, this had to stop: London would see him right.

Rolling—or rather, chugging—through the gray environs

of Sussex, Hugh's train carriage was pleasingly unpopulated; the only fellow travelers were a handful of bowler-hatted gentlemen evidently returning to the City after the festive break. Hugh found the intermittent rustling of newspapers and the occasional throat-clearing a soothing sonic accompaniment to his continued calculations. He sincerely hoped he wasn't going to make a fool of himself; what if this newfound certainty and razor-sharp clarity were, in fact, symptoms of further muddlement? *Well, Hugh*, he told himself, *if they are, then the worst that can happen is the word "ninny" being attached to your name from here unto eternity.* That, he thought, was a consequence he could manage. If, however, he was wrong, then a killer would be walking free—a consequence he might not be able to stomach quite so sanguinely.

The blurred flashes of gray fields slowly became blurred flashes of red-brick terraced houses, and Hugh glanced up from his notebook (for he had been studying it for the umpteenth time that day already) to observe that the train was puffing its way through the suburbs of Greater London. He took a deep breath and was then startled at the gurgling sound emanating from his belly. It had been rash to forgo breakfast; as Great-Aunt Fanny used to say, *Only silly buggers leave the house without a pot of tea and a muffin inside them.* He was, however, an emissary of justice, beholden to loftier imperatives than those of tea and muffins. Besides which, breakfast would have slowed his progress and, checking his watch again, Hugh reminded himself that time was of the essence.

Once safely alighted at Waterloo, Hugh negotiated his way nimbly through the stream of commuters flooding toward the Underground like so many worker bees drawn inexorably toward their hive. Bustling out into the open air, he was assaulted by the hoots of buses, the tinging of bicycle bells, the grumbles of irate pedestrians as they jostled one another on the pavements. Trips to the capital always filled him with a deep sense of relief that he did not have to battle through it every day: no, give him Little Bourton and the Crown and Cat any day.

He hailed a taxi and leaped in, asking the driver to take him to Pimlico, please; 46 Moreton Street, to be precise. At the double. Hugh had always wanted to issue this latter command, but had never found cause: now, having discharged such an instruction, he found it to be quite as satisfying as he had imagined. So far, this day was going sublimely.

The cab crawled its way across town, weaving through endless convoys of double-decker buses. The driver attempted to engage his passenger in conversation, but Hugh had to firmly if politely thwart these endeavors: he had not a jot of mental energy to spare. Westminster Bridge, the Houses of Parliament, Chelsea College of Arts…all peered in the cab window as the vehicle drew Hugh closer to his destination, but he was too engrossed in his notebook (once again) to observe, as he ordinarily would have done, the happenings of London.

"Here we are, sir," the driver intoned as they pulled up to a smart Regency building.

Hugh adjusted his shirt collar and surveyed the street: the bustle of Waterloo was a world away from this gentility and refinement. Approaching the solid black door of number 46, he felt another wave of queasiness, similar in quality to that experienced whenever he was applying the final stitches to a particularly prized fox specimen: trepidation married to an acute awareness that he was about to make a move that would have far-reaching ramifications.

The door swung open before he had a chance to use the handsome wrought-iron knocker. Standing in the doorway was a large man, nearing his late fifties, portly in stature, bemused of demeanor. With one arm he was leaning jauntily against the door, the other hand in his pocket; the top button of his otherwise pristine and crisp white shirt was undone, all of which generated the impression of a louche dandy about to skip off to Liberty for a browse of the cravats before an afternoon vermouth in Soho. It was a persona that Rufus had cultivated with relish since retiring from life as a medical man a few years ago; emancipated from the fetters of bunion procedures and advising on rheumatism, he now spent his hours making house calls to Bloomsbury and weekending with painters.

"Rufus, you old roué, you!" Hugh beamed, opening his arms in anticipation of the firm hug that was always administered upon greeting his old friend.

"I've been on tenterhooks all morning, you tease," he exclaimed. "It's not every day one receives such a deliciously tantalizing telephone call before the milk has even arrived on one's doorstep. Fortunately for you, I had only just returned home." A wink from Rufus told Hugh all he needed to know. "Come in, come in!"

"I'm loath to pussyfoot around, Rufus—time is of the essence

40

The five shillings he paid for the second-class return ticket had been one of Hugh's most prudent and profitable investments yet, and he was still congratulating himself for his own ingenuity as he neared Westbury Manor at just after midday. Never had such a brief excursion yielded such dividends.

Rufus had been only too pleased to assist him with his enquiries, glad to have the chance to deploy his expertise in a matter of intrigue, rather than in dispensing suggestions to elderly ladies on how to avoid bilious attacks. Hugh had had to draw on all his reserves of fortitude to decline the invitation to stay for kippers and toast (the muffins had only mildly assuaged his pangs), and now, ever closer, he bounded back toward Westbury Manor.

"Oh, the rover he doth return!" Stephen's welcome was characteristically bombastic, resounding through the hallway as Hugh hung up his jacket.

Lady Westbury rather inelegantly stuck her head out of the drawing-room doorway, smiling and asking Hugh where he had been gallivanting off to at that hour of the morning.

"Pipes back at home, Lady W—they've been temperamental all winter, and chose today to give up the ghost," he explained, peering into the drawing room to see that the Ashwells, Eddy, de Havilland, Freddie, and Lord Westbury were all present and correct. Where, however, was Lydia?

"Oh yes," Lady Westbury replied with a twinkle. "The pipes. Of course."

A little fib here and there never does anyone any harm, Hugh told himself. *And besides, Lady W will forgive my minor deception once all's out in the open*, he justified.

"Finally!" Lydia called as she plodded down the stairs with what might ungenerously be described as a galumphing gait. "Plumbing seen to, Hughey?"

"Oh, most thoroughly and methodically seen to, yes," he responded.

A benign grin on his face, Hugh rubbed his hands together and announced, "Right, folks, I have exhausted my patience and I am chomping at the bit to open my presents. Shall we?"

41

"You really shouldn't have, Rosalind." Lady Westbury beamed as she neatly folded up the brown paper in which her gift had been wrapped. "I do so adore Turkish Delight—let's open it now."

The Westburys and their remaining guests were assembled around the Christmas tree in the drawing room. Lord and Lady Westbury side by side on a long sofa, Rosalind Ashwell next to them. Hugh and Lydia had positioned themselves on the floor, sitting cross-legged, Bruno's head resting placidly on Lydia's knee. Eddy was perched on the sofa arm by his mother, while Stephen and Freddie were both hovering conveniently close to the sherry decanter. The novelty of soda water had evidently worn off, Hugh reflected. William Ashwell, meanwhile, stood with his arms primly folded behind his back, a cold and impatient eye fixed on the tree as if berating it for some unforgivable misdemeanor.

Mr. de Havilland, afforded the luxury of an armchair, was

placing a bottle of Scotch on the floor beside him—jolly generous of the Westburys to have given it to him, he had told them—they really needn't have bought him a present at all.

Edward's new fountain pen had been a huge success (Hugh had been particularly pleased when that idea struck him), and the amber-hilted letter opener for Lord Westbury had prompted admiring oohs and aaahs from everyone.

"Hugh, thank you for proposing this—I think it a fitting end to this rather…unexpected of Christmases," Lady Westbury commented.

Nods all round, with the exception of William Ashwell, who brusquely added, "Time's a-ticking though—some of us have trains to catch."

"Mr. de Havilland, what time are you due back in town tonight?" Lord Westbury inquired, eager to ensure that the future Prime Minister was not detained unduly.

"Oh, I have no particular appointments this evening, but I'd like to be on the road before dark. Driving on these country roads can be a mite treacherous," he answered, glancing at his watch.

"Constable Jones should have been and gone by then," Hugh said. "If he's prompt about it at two, there'll be ample time for us to explain our collective misgivings about his…verdict."

Hugh decided that the niceties had been allowed to play out for long enough now, and so, retrieving a present that had been carefully placed at the back of the pile, he braced himself.

"William, I think this is for you," he said lightly, getting to his feet to pass it to its recipient.

William Ashwell, whose attempts at mustering a smile during

the present-exchange ceremony had resulted in an unsettling contortion of his features, took the parcel and began to unwrap it. Hugh held his breath.

"What the—" William Ashwell began, before his wife interjected.

"That's my scarf! How peculiar—I knew I'd lost it! Why is it wrapped up?" Rosalind asked, peering at the bundle. "And what's it wrapped *around*?"

Observing the scene unfold, our beady-eyed spectator would be presented with a tableau of puzzlement and curiosity. Stephen's interest had been piqued and he was watching closely lest he miss an opportunity for a dig at someone (it didn't particularly matter who). Lady Westbury's eyes were fixed on her friend— just what was Rosalind going to reveal this time? Meanwhile, Hugh Gaveston was scrutinizing one person and one person only: William Ashwell. And this person blinked hurriedly, glancing rapidly around the room before returning his attention to the parcel, rather ridiculously trying to re-wrap it in the paper—but it was too late, the genie was well and truly out of the bottle.

"It's, uh…must be some mistake…don't think this is for me…" he spluttered.

Stephen, alert as ever to a scene that could be exploited for his entertainment, waltzed over. "What do we have here? A regular pass-the-parcel affair. There's a…what's that? A bag inside the scarf?"

"No, you're quite mistaken—I don't know—" Outright denial had been a foolish move: Stephen was like a bloodhound when it came to detecting discomfort in others, and he wasted no time in plucking the bag from William Ashwell's now-trembling hands.

Ignoring his mother's admonishment ("Really, Stephen, that's William's!"), he trilled, "Don't be coy. Let's all see what's in the bag, you lucky boy you…"

Stephen rummaged at the zip to the bag while William Ashwell, face a deathly pale, stood stock-still.

"Oh my…where did *this* beauty come from?" Stephen couldn't believe his luck: this Christmas was one gift after another for his gleeful delight in drama. Gently, he withdrew his hand from the bag, carefully displaying its contents for all to see.

"Jesus Christ, Stephen, put it down! Is it loaded?" Lydia was the first to speak while the others looked on at Stephen caressing an admittedly rather handsome pistol.

Rosalind let out her peculiar nervous whinnying laugh. "What—is this a silly prank? Stephen?"

He shrugged his shoulders in ignorance. "Damned if it has anything to do with me…"

Lord Westbury suggested that his son replace the gun in the bag; uncharacteristically, Stephen acquiesced with neither remonstration nor hesitation.

Rosalind was now clutching her scarf, staring in bafflement at her silent husband.

"Courtesy of Mr. Harding," Hugh said in a clear, direct tone that startled everyone. He looked levelly, challengingly, at William Ashwell.

"You…you did this?" William Ashwell's eyes narrowed, his fists clenching by his side.

"What are you talking about, William? What does Hugh

mean?" Rosalind was looking panicked at the turn events had taken.

"Harding? That reprobate? What's his part in all this?" Lord Westbury huffed.

"Will you tell them, or shall I, William?" Hugh asked, keeping his eyes fixed on his victim.

"Sorry—don't mind me, you boys carry on. I'm just getting another drink." Stephen mock-tiptoed away from the scene, back toward the sherry.

"I demand an explanation." Everyone had been shocked by David's death. Taken aback by a gun beneath the Christmas tree. But even these incidents were as nothing compared to the improbability of hearing Rosalind Ashwell—timid, mousy, nervy Rosalind Ashwell—issue such a stern command.

It was an utterance that appeared to send a jolt through her husband; his face crumpled and he massaged his knotted brow with a hand.

"Explain yourself," she said firmly.

Hugh calculated his options: explain all, or grant the man himself one more opportunity to do so. The conundrum was wrested from his grip as William Ashwell shakily began.

"I—it's…the gun is mine," he stuttered, his hitherto inviolable state of stoniness rapidly crumbling before them. "I—I wanted him dead."

Rosalind's eyes widened.

"I wanted that cad Campbell-Scott dead," he blurted and collapsed back onto the vacant chair behind him, as if the energy required to make this admission had drained him.

Muted gasps from around the room.

"Come again?" Lord Westbury asked, an incongruous half-smile hovering on his face. "That can't be right?"

"I did. I wanted nothing more than for that man to die." He was becoming more determined now, gathering momentum. "He was a selfish, careless, *heartless* swine."

"Now, now, the man is *dead*, Ashwell, I'll thank you to mind your words. In addition to which, you barely knew him—why the devil would you wish him ill?" Lord Westbury had yet to put the pieces together.

"Because of what he did to Rosalind, all those years ago." He turned to his wife. "Bewitching you, taking advantage of you, *leaving* you like that. I couldn't abide it. Seeing him swanning around, not a care in the world. Inconceivable to him that he had inflicted damage—that he had hurt Rosalind irreparably."

Lydia threw a quizzical glance at Hugh, who returned her look with an expression that instructed her to wait, to have patience.

"On Christmas Eve, I needed to get out of the house—couldn't bear to be under the same roof as a man who had wronged my wife so heinously. I found myself in the village, in the Crown and Cat," William Ashwell continued.

Stephen had joined Lydia on the floor, so keen was he to have ringside seats to the unfolding excitement.

"All I wanted was to have a scotch and some time to think. Alone. But all I could think about was *him*—what he'd done. His misdemeanor had brought no consequences upon him. He didn't carry it on his conscience, that much was plain. He needed to know that what he did was *wrong*. I was full of anger. Mr.

Harding—that's his name, isn't it?—started talking to me. Asking if I needed any last-minute Christmas presents, of all things. He could procure perfumes, rare books, all manner of black-market knockoffs—I told him I wanted to be alone. Then he…then he asked if I had any friends who might like…a gun for Christmas. I'm no fool. I knew he could sense some…desperation within me. So I told him, yes, yes, in fact I did have a friend who would like a gun. And that was that—easy as pie."

Rosalind's hand went to her mouth, aghast at the revelations pouring forth from her husband. Lady Westbury gripped her friend's arm.

"You *killed* David? *You* killed David?" Rosalind's voice was imbued not with shock, not with sadness. But with rage.

"No! I did not kill that man! I wanted him dead, I'll grant you—I wanted to kill him, so help me *God* I wanted to kill him." He rose from his seat and was, incongruously, standing in front of the Christmas tree now. "I took the gun, yes, I took the gun—*bought* the gun. Came back here that night and went to bed. I don't know what I was planning, what I was thinking. All I know is that buying the gun made me feel…back in control. Like a man. Maybe I would scare him, I thought, or maybe I *would* kill him. No more than he deserved, spineless wretch." William Ashwell's anger was reemerging.

"Except it was all to naught—he was dead already. I felt… relieved, glad that he was dead. Regret that it wasn't me—yes, I admit, *regret*. I wanted to show him that it was me who had won, after all these years, not him."

Lydia could confine herself to silence no more.

"How did *Hugh* get hold of the gun, though?"

William Ashwell stared sharply at Hugh. "Quite what I would like to know as well. When that man's body was discovered, I panicked. I had a gun that I no longer wanted—needed—and so my first and only thought was to get rid of it. In hindsight I ought really to have…formulated a better plan, but time was short. So I—"

"So you took my scarf, wrapped it up, and dumped it somewhere?" Rosalind stated coldly, eliciting a sheepish nod from her husband.

"Dumped it not a hundred yards away—by the wall, in fact," Hugh added. "Where Mrs. Slabley spotted you on Christmas morning. Around nine thirty. Happen it's when she goes for her walk."

"My, my, my," Stephen exclaimed. "Up to your old investigative tricks this whole time, Gaveston? Chin, *chin* to you, old boy."

William Ashwell was still looking at his wife.

"Please, Rosalind, it was a foolish urge, but one born of love for you. I wanted him to know the pain that he had caused. I would have done that—for you."

Rosalind blinked slowly, extricated her arm from Lady Westbury's comforting grip, and rose from the sofa to stand facing her husband.

"Very romantic," she began. "Except not a word of it is true."

Stephen whispered to Hugh, "This just gets better and better!"

"What on earth do you mean? Do you think I did it?" William Ashwell asked in shock.

"No, that's not the lie. The lie is that you were angry on my behalf, that you wanted to avenge me and my broken heart from when he left me. You weren't thinking about me, though, dear heart—you were thinking about yourself, your reputation."

Rosalind was speaking in an unsettlingly dispassionate tone, as if reading the Yellow Pages.

"Our argument before dinner on Christmas Eve. You thought I would divorce you and run off with David, humiliate you by turning my back on you, after you had so gallantly stepped in to save me from spinsterhood."

It was apparent that her husband's attempt at spinning himself an honorable motive was futile: he once again gripped his brow.

"It's true. I was afraid. Afraid that you'd divorce me for *him*. Leave me for that…that devil." He looked plaintively at Rosalind.

"You silly, silly man," she began. "Silly, silly man. I wasn't going to divorce you because an old flame had reappeared."

"I can see that now—I can see the folly of my—"

"I was going to divorce you because you are a joyless man who has gone out of his way to void my life of happiness, to flatten me and control me and deaden me," Rosalind explained in the same tone, not a trace of malice in her voice. "That is why I was going to divorce you, William—why I *am* going to divorce you."

With that pronouncement, Rosalind gently sat back down, arranging herself neatly next to Lady Westbury.

Silence pervaded the room. William Ashwell stood motionless, still posed in front of the twinkling Christmas tree.

"It's behind you!" called Stephen from the floor. "Sorry, sorry, how disrespectful of me. Must remember where I am. This is infinitely better-quality entertainment than a pantomime!"

Lord Westbury wearily snapped at his son. "Stephen, please. Enough. I'm tired of it. Tired of this"—his arms flailed around the room—"this ongoing spectacle! Hugh, I trust that there are no more surprises orchestrated?"

"I'm sorry it had to be done like that, Lord W. It was important that we all hear it, and returning the gun was the only way I could guarantee that William would furnish us with the facts," he explained.

"Post-show sherry, anybody?" Freddie piped up from the corner.

"Permit me to interject"—de Havilland stirred himself from his armchair—"but it strikes me that, while convincing, Mr. Ashwell's story begs several questions. How can we be sure that he didn't use this weapon to murder Mr. Campbell-Scott, then discard it and engineer the scene to resemble a suicide? Are we to take his word for it? Forgive my skepticism, but I rather think we oughtn't to let the matter drop quite so easily."

Lydia agreed, nodding her head vigorously, suggesting that the gun, the story, and William Ashwell be brought to Constable Jones's attention when he arrived shortly.

"Without doubt," stated de Havilland.

"Yes, a most sensible course of action," Hugh added. "Regrettably, however, one that won't be possible."

Puzzled faces met Hugh as he surveyed the room. "Because Constable Jones isn't arriving at two o'clock. Because you didn't call Constable Jones, did you, Mr. de Havilland?"

42

"I beg your pardon, Gaveston?" de Havilland uttered, a baffled smile forming. He remained in his armchair, not rousing himself from his rather recumbent position in it.

Several voices joined a chorus of questions. What did Hugh mean? Why would he say that? How was he going to explain this? Was there time to get a snack before the next act commenced?

Hugh stood firmly in front of the fireplace, gesturing for William Ashwell to take a seat somewhere.

"Yes, that's right, William, no nabbing any of Hugh's limelight, if you please," Stephen brayed, though he was just as puzzled as anyone about what would come next.

"Lady Westbury, I have maintained my patience throughout the endless series of theatrics thus far, but I must confess that my limit may have been reached with this…this latest clowning," de Havilland said to his hostess.

"I'm inclined to agree, Mr. de Havilland. Hugh, please sit down and apologize to Mr. de Havilland," she firmly instructed.

Hugh frowned. Distressing Lady Westbury wasn't on his list of objectives, but lamentably, he knew it would be a by-product of his actions.

"I'm afraid that that, too, won't be possible, Lady W," he started. "Not least because…" Hugh paused to take a deep breath. "Because, if I'm correct, then there's nobody here by that name—there is no Anthony de Havilland."

A loud thwack gave them all a fright. It was the sound of Stephen Westbury, beside himself with delight, slapping his thigh.

"Mother, Mother—can we get the maid to bring up the Bolly? We were saving it for a special occasion and that occasion is now—Hugh Gaveston has lost his bloody mind!"

Lady Westbury shot her elder son a disapproving look, while her other son stood up.

"Look here, Hugh, I don't know what you've cooked up in that brain of yours, but this is ridiculous," Edward said.

"Believe me, Eddy, I know how far-fetched it sounds," Hugh replied, "but that's the truth, isn't it? 'Mr. de Havilland'?"

The MP was regarding Hugh with a look of wry amusement. He sipped his sherry, raised his eyebrows, leaned forward slightly with one hand beneath his chin, the other resting on his knee. "You have my attention, Mr. Gaveston. I am intrigued as to just what it is you have to say for yourself. I take no delight in watching a man embarrass himself but, as you seem hell-bent upon this course, please—by all means, enlighten us."

"Yes, we're all ears!" Stephen added. "I'm thrilled by this latest turn of the screw. If he's not Anthony de Havilland, who is he? Wait, wait, let me guess: the last known survivor of the *Mary Celeste*. And for that matter, if our fellow here's an impostor, where's the *real* Anthony de Havilland? Having a jolly somewhere over the Pacific with Amelia Earhart?"

"Just let him tell us, will you, Stephen?" Lydia retorted, before nodding at Hugh. "You are rather stringing this out, Hugh—can we get on with it?"

Hugh composed himself, then began.

"Three key facts must be established before we can go any further. One, David Campbell-Scott had secrets. He was not the thoroughly decent sort that he gave himself to be. Two, David Campbell-Scott did not kill himself. Three, this man"—gesturing toward de Havilland—"is the one who killed him."

"Oh, this is *too* far!" Edward snapped.

"Hugh, please believe me when I tell you that I sincerely hope you know what you're doing," Lord Westbury murmured, gazing at him.

"I do, Lord W. I've been thorough and methodical in my investigations—"

"Pah! *Investigations*?" Edward spat.

"Settle down, Eddy. Let Mr. Gaveston here unfold the text of his bosom to us," de Havilland cautioned Edward, not tearing his eyes from Hugh.

"When we discovered David on Christmas morning," Hugh began, "it was an awful shock, that goes without saying. Upsetting though the idea of his suicide was, I think we all wanted to believe it to be true—it was far preferable to entertaining any alternatives.

But I suspect that we none of us quite believed it—not wholly. Too many questions persisted. Chief among them, why would he come back from Malaya and shoot himself at Westbury Manor? Something was amiss from the off. Something drastically amiss."

Despite their best efforts, nobody could argue with that.

"We were all rattled—all confused. Except you, Mr. de Havilland," he continued, leveling an even look at the MP. "You were so quick to conclude suicide. So unwaveringly certain of it. When we—you and I—went out there in the morning, you immediately judged it to be self-inflicted. Would brook no equivocation. Then, of course, you sent Jim home before the police arrived, dismissing the person who had found the dead body. It seemed a little queer to me at the time, all of it did, but I, like everyone else, also appreciated your taking the lead. We were all so…at a loss, but there you were—war hero Anthony de Havilland displaying cool under crisis, taking the reins and steering us all exactly where you wanted us to be."

A chuckle from de Havilland. "If I'd known that lending a hand to you all would prove so incriminating, I would have left you to flap about like headless chickens."

"At the time, of course, it seemed that you were being helpful, Mr. de Havilland. That's why it took me so long to pinpoint exactly what it was that didn't sit right," Hugh admitted. He paused. The audience was rapt, everyone riveted to his tale. "Something else that niggled at me, something from the scene—that smudged track."

"Smudged track?" Lydia echoed.

"Yes—the footprints supposedly left by David as he paced out to find a spot to shoot himself. I thought that some of them were smudged, and pointed it out to our so-called Mr. de Havilland here—but he told me that he didn't perceive anything odd. It stayed in my mind, though, and when I took Bruno for a walk with you, Freddie, it struck me—the tracks were smudged because something had been dragged slightly."

"Dragged slightly?" Lydia repeated.

"Lydia, if you've nothing useful to say, please hush." Lady Westbury's face revealed no emotion: was she angry with him? Incredulous? He couldn't tell. All he could do was press on.

"As in, dragging a dead body?" Stephen inquired. "No, nothing as substantial as that. Dragging a foot, though."

"Wait…someone *chopped off David's foot* and dragged it through the snow?" Freddie was aghast. He was also at least three sherries in, and his powers of inference were faltering.

Patiently, Hugh explained, "Again, no. Someone was dragging *their own* foot—still very much attached to their body."

"And let me guess—you're laboring under the impression that it was Anthony?" Edward sulkily remarked.

"Aha," de Havilland himself interjected. "My old war wound, yes? My intermittently troublesome leg? I see. Your powers of observation are quite impressive, Mr. Gaveston." Here he stood up, stretched out his right leg. "It is quite true, ladies and gentlemen. I find myself afflicted, from time to time, with an inconveniently gammy leg, as I believe the medical term is. Which does, therefore, lead occasionally to a certain…heaviness of gait."

Hugh maintained his steady eye contact with de Havilland, who had resumed his place in the armchair.

"Gaveston, this is all highly compelling—snowy footprints that may or may not have been smudged, my gammy leg, not to mention my highly suspicious can-do attitude and willingness to assist those clearly floundering in a crisis. I can see why you've deduced that I'm a murderer—the evidence is inarguable."

Stephen turned to his sister. "I think there might be pistols at dawn, Lyds. Bagsy not being Hugh's second."

"Quite, Mr. de Havilland—as you call yourself. None of that adds up to much more than a nagging doubt prodding away at one. So permit me to return everyone's attention to the victim— for that is what he was. As mentioned, David was—and it brings me no happiness to say this—a man whose conduct was, at times, dubious. His behavior toward Rosalind, of course, but further than that—this 'Mayfair business.'"

Edward abruptly appeared more alert than before, while Lord Westbury slumped into his seat and said, somewhat impatiently, "Must we, Hugh? Really? That old claptrap? It was stuff and nonsense—a bad bunch trying to tar David."

"I put no more credence in rumor than you do, Lord W. And I rarely invoke cliché but, well, there's no smoke without fire and, in this case, there was a helluva lot of smoke."

"Hugh, I don't see what this has to do with…" Lydia began, before trailing off. Her tone was one of confusion, rather than irritation—Hugh took that as a sign that his retelling of events was less outlandish than he had feared.

"I mention it by way of…pertinent background information," he continued. "It became pertinent the more I puzzled over this." He produced from his pocket the letter fragments he had retrieved from David's room. Outlining how and where he had come upon them (Lady Westbury was less than pleased to hear that he'd been rummaging in another guest's bedroom), he explained that the letter had remained a stumbling block.

"I couldn't pin down who had sent it to him, and why. He most assuredly still had some skeletons in his wardrobe, and when I couldn't confidently match anybody's handwriting to the letter, I thought it might be a shadowy figure from his past, come to—"

He was interrupted by Lydia. "Wait, wait, wait. You couldn't 'confidently match anybody's handwriting to the letter'? What exactly does that mean, Hugh? How could you have matched *any*body's handwriting to it—unless you had gone about secreting bits of our scrawlings…" A pause while the penny dropped. "Oh Hugh, you didn't? All of us? Even *mine*? Even…*Mother's*?"

"Thorough and methodical, Lyds. It'll be in my epitaph."

"Might need to get that engraved sharpish if you keep throwing murder accusations at people," Stephen gaily quipped.

"As I was saying—the handwriting didn't match anybody's, so it might have been sent by a person unknown. David might have brought it with him from Malaya. Any number of possibilities. Except that when I heard about the Mayfair business—David allegedly blackmailing those associates into silence—something clicked. What if David hadn't *received* the letter—what if David had *written* the letter?"

Something evidently clicked in Lydia's mind too.

"And *that's* why you wanted those postcards that David had sent me!" she exclaimed.

"Exactly, Lyds! And Bob's your uncle—it was as darned near

a certain match as one could hope for." Hugh reached into his other pocket and produced a postcard from Paris.

"Regular box of tricks you have there, Hugh. What's next? A white rabbit?" Stephen commented.

"If you inspect the loops of the l, you'll notice a distinct similarity, as well as in the—"

"Hugh, it's exactly the same handwriting. Any fool can see that," Lydia admitted.

"Now that I could confidently conclude that the letter was *from* David, my next question was—"

"Who had he written the letter *to*—who was he blackmailing?" Lydia was catching up, fast.

"Precisely. Now, this was a tricky one, I'll grant you. The letter sheds no light, gives nothing away. I had to employ logic. Which of the people in this house could David have wanted to blackmail? Following logic, it seemed improbable that it would be someone he had known for any length of time. Why would he choose *now* to do it? If, for the sake of argument, he was blackmailing you, Lord Westbury—he could have chosen to do that at any point over the last however many years, yes? Why would he wait until now? I'll admit that it would be possible—some new information may have come to light in the preceding twenty-four hours, some undesirable nugget that David had discovered and decided to use. Certainly, that would be possible. But the avenue that seemed more likely was that he was blackmailing somebody who had not been a permanent fixture in his life heretofore."

Hugh paused, allowing the implications of this to dawn on his audience.

"There were only two people who had not featured in David's life up until Christmas Eve—William Ashwell and the gentleman calling himself Anthony de Havilland."

Glances were cast toward both men. Hugh noticed that de Havilland's nonchalance was looking more strained.

"So far, so far-fetched," the politician muttered. "But do please proceed—I haven't been to the pictures in quite some time, and this is far more imaginative than any of the drivel that's on at the Regency."

"I must say that it was all rather neck and neck between you two chaps," Hugh said, eliciting a grunt of disdain from the one and a look of supercilious amusement from the other. "It was Lady W who nudged me in the correct direction."

She blanched slightly.

"Mother? What on *earth* have you been bleating about?" Edward demanded.

"I simply shared some…information with Hugh," she said.

Hugh relayed Lady Westbury's encounter with David in the library that she had told him about.

"The phrase 'bigger fish to fry' was telling. Exceedingly telling. For, and please know that I intend no offense by this, William—I would hardly describe you as a big fish," Hugh explained as tactfully as he could. "So who—or what—was David referring to?"

Despite—or perhaps because of—the tension of the situation, Rosalind couldn't quite suppress a giggle.

"But once again—it was a mere hunch, a feeling, nothing more than that," he went on.

"I'm glad you admit as much, Mr. Gaveston," de Havilland

snorted. "Tell me, is there any meat on the bones of this increasingly ludicrous story you're spinning?"

"Oh, I think you'll find that we're getting to that, Mr. de Havilland—do excuse my continuing to use that name. Force of habit," Hugh continued. "Lady W thought that David had been speaking with someone in the library—presumably the aforementioned big fish—but he didn't care to tell her. It was when I made my visit to the Crown and Cat that it was plain to me that it couldn't have been William Ashwell—because late on Christmas Eve he had been nursing a vendetta and a scotch at the bar there, acquiring a gun from Mr. Harding."

"Presumptions and speculations have never been so well argued, Mr. Gaveston. You ought to come and work in Westminster—I'm sure your talents for unfounded claims and empty words would see you go far," de Havilland said.

Frowning, Lydia once more prompted Hugh to the next juncture of his theory. "But—supposing for one mad second that you're right, that David was blackmailing Mr. de Havilland… what could it have been? I mean, it could have been anything."

"Yes, it could have been. It's not uncommon for men in power—as this gentleman, regardless of his name, is—to have certain indiscretions that they would prefer not enter the public domain. I was stumped, I'll grant you, as to how I would get to the bottom of that—for, undoubtedly, it had to be something awfully serious, something terribly compromising, for anyone to be murdered over. And something of that nature would be tricky to sniff out."

De Havilland held his hands up. "Please allow me to confess here and now, with you all as my witnesses, that, yes, I did once take a gobstopper without paying for it. That, however, is the extent of my so-called indiscretions. I have no secret lover—or lovers—no unseemly debts, no questionable associations with criminal overlords. Do, though, feel free to engage in extensive investigation of my skeleton-free wardrobe, Mr. Gaveston." Here he strode to the sherry decanter and replenished his glass. Was that a faint tremor in his hand Hugh noticed?

"Ah, now, here's the devilishly handy thing about it, Mr. de Havilland. I didn't need to engage in any investigations to get the scent of a secret—you led me directly to it." There was an irrepressible edge of satisfaction to Hugh's voice. He was getting closer to cornering the man, he could tell.

De Havilland returned to his armchair. "Oh goody, a twist. Do tell. How exactly did I lead you to anything of the sort, Gaveston?"

Hugh reminded them all of the unfortunate episode last night, his tumble and subsequent brief loss of consciousness.

"Now, being, as I am, a dabbler in the world of taxidermy—"

"Oh, here we go. Was it a squirrel that done it after all, guv?" Stephen cut in, to multiple shhhs from the others.

"I am also a dabbler in the world of chemistry. Various notions and potions are essential in any taxidermist's workshop, and I have more than a passing interest in the make-up of the solutions I use—like to know exactly what it is I'm dipping my nib into, as it were. All of which is to say, I am more than slightly acquainted with chemicals and miscellaneous facts relating to them."

"Go on." Lydia was gripped.

"Now, when I came round last night, and was concerned about having cut my head—you, Mr. de Havilland, assured me that there was no blood drawn, no need for Dakin's solution, the antiseptic that you used in Ypres, correct?"

De Havilland merely nodded at this.

"A statement that leaped out at me even then, stupefied though I was. You see, Mr. de Havilland, it's the queerest thing. You fought in Ypres in 1914, yes?"

Another silent nod.

"It's just that Dakin's solution wasn't in common use on the field until two years after that—in 1916. So I was perplexed as to how you could have been familiar with it from Ypres."

A pause.

"I'm sorry…I'm sorry, *this* is why you think I murdered David Campbell-Scott? My misremembrance of medical treatments during a battle I fought in over *twenty years* ago?" de Havilland burst out. "For a moment there, I was giving you credit, Gaveston—but this, oh dear me. A rather lamentable clutching at straws!"

Hugh smiled patiently.

"That's just the thing, though, isn't it, Mr. de Havilland? You didn't fight in that battle—you didn't fight in *any* battle during the war."

De Havilland appeared to have lost his tongue at this.

"You see, Mr. de Havilland, the mention of Dakin's solution, though not in itself a fatal clanger, was enough to send me barking up the entirely correct tree. Middlesex Regiment, wasn't it?" Hugh didn't need to wait for a response before pressing on. "My dear old friend Rufus, he was medical corps during the war, and he confirmed that yes, Dakin's would have been nowhere near

Ypres in 1914. Rufus is an awfully useful chum to have; his circle of acquaintances is one of enviable dimensions and impressive eclecticism. And he's always terribly keen to help a friend when they're in a jam. I spoke to him this morning, and he was kind enough to put in a few enquiries over his breakfast, while I was on the train from Little Bourton."

The mood in the room had shifted considerably, as had de Havilland's entire demeanor. The casual air of entitlement had vanished entirely, his posture now bespeaking one ill at ease.

"Rufus was only too happy to help out, you see, as were his own veteran pals. One of whom, a"—consulted his notebook—"a Charles Dunbar, was a lieutenant—in the Middlesex Regiment. And he has neither knowledge nor memory of any Anthony de Havilland in the regiment, at Ypres or at any point after that. Which begs the question—who exactly *are* you, Mr. de Havilland?"

43

No snide remarks, no condescending comments, no self-assured denials emanated from de Havilland's armchair.

All eyes were fixed on him. Hugh could almost see the cogitations occurring within the man's mind.

An unsettlingly hollow laugh was de Havilland's first response, followed swiftly by a plainly unconvincing, "Well, I've never heard anything so preposterous in my life! The absurdity of this house knows no bounds. Rubbish, all of it."

"David knew it, didn't he? Christmas Eve, at the dinner table, he knew he recognized you, but you brushed it off." Lady Westbury's meditative contribution astonished everyone—not least Hugh.

"This must be a prank—an exceptionally ill-judged prank. I will take my leave of you all, and you have my word that I shan't darken these doors ever again. The insults and effrontery…" De

Havilland's composure was fast disintegrating, and this unraveling was not lost on Lady Westbury. Watching him begin to squirm and lash out in a most unseemly manner, she couldn't help but feel both disappointment and embarrassment: he had been her prized guest, after all.

"You can take your leave by all means, Mr. de Havilland, return to your home—where the police will collect you. Which might make for a scandalous front page tomorrow morning. Or you could stay here and the Little Bourton constabulary can escort you to the station—at least that way you won't encounter any tabloid photographers," Hugh reasoned.

De Havilland slumped back into his chair.

"This is rubbish, isn't it, Anthony? Complete rubbish?" Eddy insisted plaintively.

A momentary pause, during which the glint of determination in the MP's eyes appeared to be extinguished, his composure bridling under the weight of his current predicament. A weary sigh of resignation.

"It would appear that the game is up. Finally," he uttered. "It was, of course, I suppose, inevitable. But I've always contended against the inevitable. My entire life—my entire career—has been one in the eye for inevitability."

Lord Westbury appeared flummoxed in the extreme.

"Will somebody please explain, in plain English, just what the blazes is going on?"

"Your young Mr. Gaveston here…he has outdone me. Unraveled me," de Havilland exhaustedly answered.

"I said, plain English, man. What is happening?"

"He is, regrettably, entirely accurate. In all of his suppositions. All of them. I did kill Mr. Campbell-Scott."

Gasps ricocheted around the room.

"You killed David? But you're an *MP*…a war hero…the future Prime Minister…" Lord Westbury struggled to construct his reaction to this admission.

De Havilland looked an entirely different man: his calm, reassuring solidity had dissolved. He had been vanquished—whether by Hugh or by greater powers, he could not deduce.

"On Christmas Eve, as soon as I laid eyes on Campbell-Scott, I knew precisely where I had encountered him before. It was two decades ago but, as well you know, his is a face difficult to forget. He was full of charm, full of confidence, swaggering around the office. It must have been spring of 1915. He was a strapping captain, about to be shipped out to the front. I was a pen-pushing desk-jockey in the barracks at Deal. Your old muckers from the Middlesex Regiment were right—I was never in their troop. Never at Ypres. I never made it across the Channel. Not for want of trying—it was this bloody leg that swung it. Officially, an invalid. Invalid. So much in one word. Don't mind if I have another sherry, do you?"

Lady Westbury shook her head as he sloshed a liberal quantity into his glass.

"Campbell-Scott was there for something or other—I forget what—but we had quite the chinwag, I recall. Nothing out of the ordinary—just two chaps chewing the fat, one about to stride forth to glory, one shackled to administrative ignominy."

He sighed.

"Everything I had planned for, dashed in one fell swoop. I'd had it all mapped out—make a name for myself on the front, return swathed in medals and bathed in glory, straight to Whitehall, then to Westminster, then to Downing Street. Except fate, of course, had contrary ideas."

"Hang fire. Let me make sure I'm keeping up with this. You *never* fought? Not even a little bit?" Stephen was unusually keen to be in possession of all the facts.

"Stephen, don't be so dense—that is quite literally what he just said." Lydia rolled her eyes. "So what exactly did you do during the war?"

"I sat at my desk, I filed my paperwork…I did my job," was de Havilland's dejected reply.

"I don't understand—where's the shame in that?" Lydia asked.

"There's no shame, no shame at all. If you're content to sit out the war in a cushy post and then return to a civilian life lacking in ambition and worth," de Havilland countered. "I was resentful, I'll admit it. Envious, jealous of all those fellows who were over there making their country *proud*. That's the stuff of leaders. Not alphabetizing filing cabinets by the seaside. When the war ended, men were coming pouring back into the country—it was chaos, the office chaps could hardly keep track of which soldiers had returned from which regiment, who had died, who was wounded, who had shown valor, who had shown dishonor… From my gilded cage, I could see just how impossible it would be to account for everyone—or to verify everyone. It was my opportunity, you see, to exploit the mess and to reinvent myself. No longer Anthony Harper, admin fodder, but Anthony de Havilland, hero of Ypres, leader of men."

"What, that was it? You just…made up a new name, pretended you'd fought…and done deal? Easy as that?" Stephen asked incredulously.

"Easy as that. The country was broken, the men coming back were broken—everyone was desperate to rebuild what had been destroyed. The more war heroes people had, the better—boosted morale, being able to listen to tales of derring-do rather than hear about shell shock and mustard gas and trench foot. People believed what they wanted to—and soon enough, Anthony de Havilland was exactly who I had wanted to be. Who I *should* have been—who I could have been."

De Havilland was staring at a fixed point somewhere in the distance ahead of him, his eyes taking on a glazed quality. Hugh stirred him.

"And David knew who you really were, though? Anthony Harper. He knew that you'd built your career on falsehoods and deception. He threatened you with exposure."

De Havilland glanced at him, swilled his sherry.

"After dinner, I went to my room to find that—that *letter*," he spat, "on my bed. Threatening to go to the newspapers if I didn't pay him…a substantial sum of money. Of course, I was incensed. But foolishly, naively, I thought I could reason with the man. The letter had told me to meet him in the library, so I did as instructed, gave him his dirty letter back. Told him that yes, I would pay him the money, but that I would need time to amass it. He was enjoying having me on the rack, it was obvious. I told him to meet me on Christmas Day morning, so that I could propose…a payment plan, as it were. He loved knowing that I couldn't hand it over in one go—nasty piece of work, through and through."

Lord Westbury was shaking his head in sadness.

"After I returned to my room, however, I knew I couldn't be beholden unto him. I couldn't trust him. I had to have a contingency plan—and that's where Edward came into things."

Edward's gaze had not been diverted from de Havilland for some minutes now; he was transfixed as the confession came tumbling forth.

"Edward clearly had a grudge against the man—if I could find out what Campbell-Scott had done, perhaps I could use it against him. Leverage of sorts. So Edward and I conspired to expose Campbell-Scott's Mayfair swindle. With my connections, it would be easy to bring the whole house of cards crashing down."

"'The time for talking is over'…" Lydia murmured. "It was de Havilland you were whispering with that night, Eddy? Cooking up a plot against David?"

"Yes. But how did you know that?" Eddy asked.

"I heard you. I…I thought…I was worried you'd been talking to David. *Threatening* David. I thought that it might have been you…"

"What might have been me? Wait…you thought that it was *me* who killed David?" Eddy exclaimed. "For a start, where would that have gotten me? If he was *dead*, there'd be no justice!"

Lydia murmured something and returned her attention to de Havilland. Hugh looked at the guests, all of them rendered speechless by the admissions of this once-promising pillar of society.

"So if you agreed to pay him, and you knew you could reveal

the truth about what he had done…why did you kill him?" Lydia asked. It was something that had been troubling Hugh as well, and de Havilland's explanation tallied with the hypothesis he had eventually formed.

"Pay him the money, put him in jail…neither of those eventualities would remove him from my life. He would be a perpetual blot, ghoulishly haunting me. I couldn't live with the fear of David Campbell-Scott nipping back from Malaya every year or so to demand more money. He would have taken pleasure in ripping apart everything that I had worked so hard to create—not just my reputation, but all the good I was going to do, all the change I was going to catalyze."

Eddy asked the question that had been on his mind since de Havilland had begun his confession. "Were you really going to give me that job? Or was it just…I don't know…buttering me up, keeping me on side should you need a gullible fool in your back pocket at some later point?"

"Eddy, I'm not a monster…" de Havilland began, then seemed to upbraid himself for forgetting the current situation. "Allow me to clarify. I still believe in change and a better future, and I meant every word of that. Our conversations were so refreshing. They made me believe I could put this nasty business behind me. That David Campbell-Scott wouldn't succeed. It appears that he has, however—he has ruined me."

Hugh was mindful of keeping deviations to a minimum.

"Christmas morning, then—what happened?"

"I had told Campbell-Scott to meet me down at those damnably spooky stables—told him to meet me there at six."

"But you had no intention of meeting him or his demands... you'd already decided to kill him," Hugh said.

"Yes. I had," de Havilland replied simply. "It seemed the only way out of the net he'd thrown upon me. He left the house, I followed—with the smallest gun I could find in the cabinet. Nothing too unwieldy, you see. He began sauntering—even from behind, even in the early-morning dark, I could tell that he was sauntering, brimming with smugness—and I followed in his footsteps, quite literally. Then, when he paused, I seized my moment—I shot him. That was that. As easy as taking a new name all those years ago. He was dead. My problem was gone. I deposited the gun beside him, retraced the steps—though, as you so perceptively deduced, Gaveston, my leg seized up, compromising my fastidiousness—and went back to my bedroom, waiting for the discovery to be made."

He gulped down the last of his sherry.

"Bloody hell," Stephen murmured.

Lady Westbury sat motionless, but said, "Mr. de Havilland—or whatever your name is—whatever you had or had not done during the war...we believed you to be a good man. For lying about that, you could have been forgiven—the good you were doing spoke for itself, your career would have survived. But you have killed a man. There can be no return from that. David Campbell-Scott hasn't ruined you. You have ruined yourself."

De Havilland looked shaken by Lady Westbury's pronouncements, as though the enormity of his actions had previously been in doubt.

"Mr. Gaveston. I take my hat off to you—your tenacity has been admirable," the MP commented. "What now?"

"Now, Mr. de Havilland," Hugh said, "we wait for Constable Jones. Who should"—he checked his watch—"be here any moment, as I arranged with him this morning."

"One question, Gaveston. How did you know that I hadn't called him yesterday?"

"The font of all knowledge in Little Bourton—Rita Ludgate, formidable proprietress of the Crown and Cat—told me that there had been no brawls there on Christmas night—contrary to your report after your phantom phone call yesterday."

Lydia smiled at her friend: thorough and methodical to the end.

Jim arrived at the drawing-room door, doing his utmost to maintain an air of professionalism in the face of the dramatic events. Announcing a Constable Jones, he departed, not without a backward glance—who were the police here for? he wondered. *A shilling says it's for that bald grumpy old fellow*, he inwardly wagered with himself.

Hair neatly slicked down today, Constable Jones nodded a greeting as everyone rose from their seats.

"Constable, thank you for your punctuality," Hugh began and, gesturing toward de Havilland, he said, "I think you'll find him cooperative and forthcoming in this matter."

Jones cast a look dripping in disappointment at de Havilland. "Sir de Havisham, it is to my immense and commensurate displeasure that I should be here on this most inauspicious and inconspicuous of occasionings. You, my lord, are a wrong'un."

"Constable, while I admire your alacrity in this matter, hadn't you ought to…well, ask the gentleman some questions, ascertain the veracity of my account? Call me a stickler, but I—" Hugh asked.

"Sir, I offer you my deepest thanks for your assistance, but it is of paramount importance that I, an officer of the law, conclude this business at the police station. This glorious abode is no place for the intricate machinations of the law," the constable explained.

At that, Jones—with a conciseness previously unimaginable—recited the formal declaration appropriate at instances such as this, and led de Havilland out to his waiting vehicle. Despite the MP's assurances that handcuffs were not necessary, Jones was yet to have call to use his restraints, and if an officer of the law couldn't use handcuffs when arresting a murderer, then he didn't know when he would.

Lydia put her arm around Hugh. "Well, you did it—you found the truth. I don't think I can quite believe it all, though."

Lady Westbury sighed. "This has all stretched credulity, really it has. That man, a murderer, in our house. And it was I who invited him," she pointed out. A faraway look settled in her eyes, as though she were revisiting her part in the proceedings. If only she hadn't been quite so taken by the idea of housing such an illustrious guest; if only the pride she took in her good name hadn't run away with her…perhaps David would still be here. Perhaps, perhaps.

"You weren't to know, Lady W," said Hugh. "How could you have known?"

"Too true. If anyone was going to turn out to be a murderer, my money was on you, Lydia," Stephen remarked. "All that pent-up frustration of yours."

"Shut *up*," Lydia retorted.

Hugh smiled at the reliability of the Westbury siblings and their fractious exchanges. His smile faded as he looked around the room at the bewildered faces that surrounded him. Frayed, exhausted, and decidedly shaken by the proceedings, they shared an obvious uncertainty about what to say, or how to say it. The world of Westbury Manor had been irrevocably altered, it seemed to Hugh.

"Is there any more sherry, or was that the lot?" came Freddie's voice.

Most reassuring, Hugh reflected. Evidently, some aspects of normal life could never be banished.

44

The hour had come for departures. Freddie had been collected by his footman—he promised Lady Westbury that he would return on New Year's Day, that he would turn over a new leaf, and that she should have Mrs. Smithson stock up on soda water in anticipation.

William Ashwell took his suitcase and strode off to catch his train home—Rosalind told him that she would engage a solicitor to be in touch about the divorce. Accepting Lady Westbury's invitation to stay a little longer, she fancied that she might convey herself to Edinburgh for a spell: William had always said that Edinburgh was full of nothing but whisky and capers, and only a fool would go there.

Lord and Lady Westbury had retired upstairs—it really had taken the wind out of Lord Westbury, all this nonsense—and, no doubt equally fatigued by the weekend's happenings, our perspicacious observer would now marvel at the scene unfolding in the drawing room: that of Hugh, Lydia, Stephen, and Edward availing themselves of gin. Harmoniously and willingly at that, with not a heckle or a barb to be heard—at least for a moment.

"I'll hear no more of it, Eddy," Lydia was exclaiming. "I don't want it, not a penny of it—how could I, with all good conscience, live off money that had been made from swindling goodness knows how many people? No—it will go to much better use with the Impoverished Boys' and Girls' League of East London—or whatever that place is called."

Lydia, upon hearing the various revelations about her god-father, had come to the realization that she had been burying her head in the sand regarding his conduct—and that she could do so no longer. No, the inheritance he had left—which he had accrued through any number of disreputable means—would go to those far more in need than her.

"Well, that's inordinately good of you, Lyds. They'll be speech-less with gratitude when I tell them," Edward said, touching her hand lightly.

Stephen emitted a sound not unlike a donkey being stran-gled. "Fabulous, just fabulous. Now she's going to be even more insufferable. Brilliant. Campbell-Scott's parting gift to us all—unparalleled levels of sanctimony into perpetuity."

One might forgive our trusted spectator for indulging in a moment's reflection upon Christmas at Westbury Manor: murder, a jilted lover, fraud, blackmail, divorce. And yet, and yet…the Byronic clock ticks on, Bruno's tail never fails to wag, Angela struggles onward in her battle against crockery-laden trays, and

Mrs. Slabley, unseen and all-seeing, continues to be vigilant to any nastiness yonder.

And so it was that, in the drawing room, our few remaining players consumed their gins and once again exchanged their insults. The siblings suggested that Hugh defer his departure and stay until tomorrow. It had been a trying day, and Mrs. Smithson was making his favorite dinner.

But no amount of shepherd's pie could detain him. For Hugh Gaveston was already looking to the future—a future in which his enviable expertise would be called upon to navigate a matter of both delicacy and urgency.

"Sorry, chaps, no rest for the wicked. I've a recently expired alpaca arriving tomorrow morning, and there'll be hell to pay if I miss the delivery. Next time, though, eh?"

ACKNOWLEDGMENTS

Special thanks to Victoria Murray-Browne, because without her this book wouldn't exist, and to Rachel Cugnoni, for trusting me from the get-go.

My thanks to the rest of the team at Vintage for all their care and expertise, especially Alex Russell, Sara Adams, Polly Dorner, Tom Atkins, Beth Coates, and Etta Voorsanger-Brill.

I'm indebted to my parents—Fiona and Brian—for their support and encouragement, and to my friends for the help and inspiration they've given in all sorts of ways.

And a final thank you to Rachel Cranshaw, who has been there to listen, to read, and to tell me to keep writing.

ABOUT THE AUTHOR

Ada Moncrieff lives in London. *Murder Most Festive* is her first novel.